Lucifer's Sketchbook

Ofer Mazar

Strategic Book Publishing and Rights Co.

Copyright © 2013

All rights reserved—Ofer Mazar

No part of this book may be reproduced or transmitted in any form or by
any means, graphic, electronic, or mechanical, including photocopying,
recording, taping, or by any information storage retrieval system, without the
permission, in writing, from the publisher.

Strategic Book Publishing and Rights Co.
12620 FM 1960, Suite A4-507
Houston, TX 77065
www.sbpra.com

ISBN: 978-1-62516-834-4

Design: Dedicated Book Services (www.netdbs.com)

Dear Shelly Kamara,
With best wishes,
Ofer Mazar
Dec. 2013

Dedication

To my brother Benjamin (Boni) Mazar

With love and appreciation

For believing in me and for being my friend

Contents

Prologue

Documenting My Shame

It's funny how life sometimes grabs you by the balls, squeezes hard and neglects to let go. This is how I would generally characterize my life—one long, hard and painful squeeze of the most delicate human organ.

I think it was Mark Twain who once said that we should not go around saying the world owes us a living because it owes us nothing. The world was here first. Indeed, the world owed me nothing and it made the extra effort to prove it. Equally enough, I owed *it* nothing, or anybody else for that matter. For much of my life I also made the extra effort to prove it.

This clash I had with the world, lasted long enough, and took a toll greater than anything I could ever describe. It is for the sake of all those hurt by this unyielding clash that I have decided to document its main features in an autobiographical account.

I also do this for the sake of Thor, my 14-year-old son. He thought my life story was worth documenting. I remember thinking, "*who gives a shit about my pathetic life?*" I mean . . . even *I* did not give a shit until that sweet boy of mine was conceived. Yet, the child stuck stubbornly to his guns and I ended up with a manuscript outlining my excruciating journey in this maze called 'living'.

I think an apology is in order before we proceed. This testimony is not sophisticated, classy, or stylish. I decided right from the start to be an unworldly and unrefined *me*, outlining my no-nonsense, to-the-face, uncensored and sometimes uncivilized story.

You see . . . I had no choice. Otherwise, it would be impossible for me to explain the kind of life I lived—a life of someone who is the living example of folly, of wickedness and of a colossal set of mistakes.

The regrets I have are eternal. Nothing can erase them or wipe them off the walls of my soul. I accumulated them as I traveled along life's different pits and obstacles, and they are a well-deserved punishment for all the pain I inflicted on others throughout my life.

Oddly enough, in writing my life's story, I found comfort and relief. I re-lived it through the construction of each and every paragraph. In some twisted manner, it helped me make peace with myself after years of internal turmoil and self-loathing.

It is as if by acknowledging and documenting the guilt, the blame and the shame, I was forgiven.

Better yet—I forgave myself.

Chapter 1

Vikings

A dark and cold night in the snow-covered Norwegian city of Bergen marked my coming into this world, the unplanned and undesired daughter of a famous supermodel and a mediocre musician. I am the dismal result of their one-night-stand.

Angus Svensen, the keyboard player of a rock band called 'The Ugly Vikings' and the stunningly beautiful Mariana Mortensen quickly tied the knot to save face.

Mariana's pregnancy temporarily halted her very successful modeling career—home and abroad. She was, at the time, Norway's hottest and most successful international model. Five foot nine of pure beauty and sheer elegance, blue eyes, blond, slim with never ending long and silky legs—my mother was by far the greatest Norwegian export of her time. Blessed with smooth and faultless skin and fully equipped with perfect measurements, she ruled the catwalks in the world's most prestigious fashion capitals; and being an international brand name, Mariana Mortensen's photos were published in every respectable fashion magazine of the era since she had turned 17, advertising anything from make-up to bathing suites. In six years of activity, she not only became an international figure—she became a source of national pride.

She was only 23 when she gave birth to me, and from the very first breath of air I ever took, she considered me the biggest mistake of her thus far wonderful life. Born in the winter of 1966, at the peak of her career, I was the last thing she ever wanted or needed. I spent years hating her for hating me. I couldn't stop imagining how she must have looked at the infant me and how she must have felt toward the object of her blunder.

She should have known better, when she stepped into a bar in Bergen one evening to have a drink with a friend. She should have known better, when a breath-taking, six foot two inch hunk with ocean blue eyes and charcoal black hair made a pass at her. Instead, they rented a small room in a nearby hotel and spent the night screwing each other's brains out. They should have known better because it was I who had to pay the long-term price of their short-term pleasure. Everyone else could have lived a better life if Mariana had kept her legs crossed, or at least made Angus use some kind of precautionary measures. But no . . . my parents instead made the mistake and then blamed me.

Lucky for Mariana, she remembered the ridiculous name of her one-night-stand's band, because eight weeks down the time-line, when she found out she was pregnant, there was no doubt in her mind that the child growing in her womb was its keyboard player. Contrary to later years, at *that* period of her young life, Mariana did not sleep around. Apart from being Catholic, she had a reputation to protect. Norway in the nineteen fifties was a conservative land, and her parents belonged to the strict and traditional Roman-Catholic minority. They believed in God and feared his wrath. Tormented by pangs of guilt for her awful sin, my mother was eager to minimize the damage. She went searching for my father until she finally found him playing in a small bar in Stavanger. Shocked and confused, 26 year old Angus demanded proof the child was his but got a noisy slap across the face instead.

"Now you listen to me, loser," Mariana barked at him with blistering eyes. "I don't fuck around! You are going to marry me and be the father of my child, or I'll crush you like a bug!"

It took a few good seconds for the guy to burst into laughter, and Mariana soon joined him.

"Let me buy you a drink, you beautiful creature," he said when they got a grip on themselves. "You can tell me all about it later."

In a way, I guess it should be a consolation to know your father was not a prick, and when the going got tough . . . well . . .

you know. Angus assumed responsibility for his mistake. *Thank you frigging very much dummy. You should have had me aborted!*

My parents got married in a modest ceremony in a small church in Bergen. They thought they could appease the raging self-righteous Mortensens by tying the knot; but it did not take long for them to realize that nothing they could ever do would appease the elders.

When my mother's belly started showing and the country realized Mariana was conceived before she was legally wed, the local papers slashed at her ruthlessly. Consequently, job offers diminished to a bare zero. The blow to Mariana's career was so devastating that she confined herself to her bedroom for weeks to come, hating herself for being so immorally sinful and sexually careless. She stopped eating and cried herself to exhaustion for days. In fact, if not for my father shoving water down her throat, she may have died, and you—dear reader—would have been doing something productive right now.

If my father had any doubts about the infant being the outcome of the eruption of sperm from his loin, it vanished in a swift second once he glanced at his newborn baby for the first time. Being the son of a Norwegian mother and a Spanish father, Angus had inherited his mother's blue eyes and his father's complexion. I took my colors from his side of the family. I had his blue eyes and his black hair. My grandmother, Charlotte, testified that I was the spitting image of her son when he was a baby, and she had the photos to prove it.

Although my complexion was much brighter than that of Angus, it was still somewhat darker than the anemic-white of my mother's side of the family. Being all pure white skinned, yellow haired, blue eyed, typical Nordic Scandinavians, my mother's family did not appreciate the colors bestowed upon me. They looked down at me from day one . . . as if having dark hair and a slightly darker complexion marked my inferiority.

Worse, these sorry excuses for human beings saw it as God's punishment for my mother's terrible sin. Even today, more than four decades later, I still get angry just thinking about it.

I was named Jennifer, after the beautiful wife of Louis, the poor, dying artist from George Bernard Shaw's 1906 play 'The Doctor's Dilemma'. In that play, the character Jennifer tries to convince a doctor, who only had sufficient medicine to cure one person, that her husband was the one worth saving. I mean . . . come on! Who in his right mind names his newborn baby girl for a fictional figure from an old play dealing with such black circumstances? Well, I have a theory about that but let's not jump ahead.

My father's line of defense was so moving I almost puked on his shoes. The girl in Shaw's play was smart and beautiful, and she had a good heart. She was loyal to her husband and she did her outmost to save his life. Even the doctor himself fell in love with her, eventually. For Angus Svensen, Shaw's Jennifer was all he ever dreamed for in a wife, or a daughter.

Well . . . tough luck, dad, you sure missed out big time there.

It was not long before my father realized that both women in his life were as far from Shaw's Jennifer as Norway's fjords are from Jules Vern's Center of the Earth.

Two months after I was born, we escaped to America. The local media's cruel ongoing abuse of my mother's immoral behavior and her family's vicious stance on the matter convinced my father to pack up and follow a third of our nation, which had immigrated there back in the 19th and early 20th century. But unlike most of *those* immigrants my parents did it in the middle of the night, without saying goodbye—bearing with them a painful grievance to last a lifetime in the land of opportunity.

Angus and Mariana promised never to return and they never did.

We first settled in Boston, where my father found a job in the diamond trade. Not long after, my mother started picking up the pieces of her bruised modeling career; and gradually, gorgeous and sexy Mariana Mortensen managed to connect with the American fashion world—especially the one active in New York.

Having a little child to take care of, my parents took upon themselves a responsibility to maintain no more than the semblance of a normal family. Tying their destinies together with the flimsy thread of a mutual mistake, they soon agreed upon an open marriage, one in which they remained free to engage in separate love lives.

Still stunningly beautiful, my mother never missed an opportunity to jump into bed with anyone she deemed important enough for the reconstruction of her career; and job offers were soon pouring down upon her like an Asian Monsoon.

Parallel to my mother's reconstruction of her modeling career, my father quickly mastered the secrets of the diamond trade business and, with the help of the money generated by my mother's modeling contracts, he soon established his own diamond import company. It was not long before this savvy and intelligent businessman started making tons of money. We became rich—very rich.

The open marriage, the modeling career, and my father's financial success had a price; and, like the pattern evolving in my future life, I was the one to exclusively pay it. I hardly saw my parents, and when I finally did, they were always too busy to waste their valuable time on unimportant Jennifer. I was four months old when my career-driven parents recruited my first nanny. I would be brought up and surrounded by strangers from that moment on.

I remember vividly how, as a small child, I longed for my parents' attention but got none of it. Sadness and gloom still seems to be the guiding emotion I remember from back then.

"The hell with them!" I concluded at a very early age.

A nagging flashback throws me back to being three, waking up at night from a terrible nightmare. I'm running out of my room into the dark corridor, terrified, crying hysterically, looking for my mother to save me but pretty quickly realizing I was all alone on the huge floor. I'm crying myself to exhaustion, losing my voice, sitting on the floor at my mother's room doorstep, covering my eyes with my arms, afraid to look over my shoulder. I'm screaming when a hand touches me. It is the hand of Silvia, my Nanny. She was the one who saved me, calmed me down, tucked me in and sang a lullaby in Spanish, waiting by my side until I fell asleep again.

My mother soon began bringing her lovers home. Hearing her moaning and groaning from the other side of the wall and picturing those filthy strange men rubbing their bodies against her clear and gentle skin would have me out of bed in an instant, rushing for the toilet to vomit.

At six, I had already lost the naivety and innocence that characterizes normal children my age. At seven, I started bringing the harsh images in my mind to life, documenting, with the help of charcoal, my everyday reality in a sketchbook. Throughout the different periods of my life, I have filled up many sketchbooks— all that I still keep in my possession, about six hundred at last count . . . When I look back at my first sketches, all I can see is a lonely, sad and frightened little girl facing a harsh world. Some of my early sketches describe fat and ugly naked man with disgusting sausage-like penises—sharp and nasty sword, stabbing a helpless woman.

A helpless woman . . . Jesus . . . how could I, being so young back then, have deciphered that about my mother?

Being a celebrity Mariana Mortensen's naughty behavior was smeared all over the tabloids. She made no effort whatsoever to conceal it. Giving the papers something to write about, I overheard her explaining one evening to someone over the phone, kept her always in the public eye. Being incredibly beautiful was not enough anymore. Her life had to generate something more, something outrageous, and something shocking and scandalous for the journalists to inform their gossip-frenzy readers about. This was how she managed to stay on top for so long. It was how the game was played.

My father also maintained a lively love life. The man was never home. His business took him around the world and I hardly saw him. Endlessly eavesdropping, I was exposed to information provided generously by my mother to her friends. It seemed my daddy loved young women in their early twenties and they loved him back. He was strikingly good looking, rich and free as a bird. He would bring them expensive presents and sweet-talk them into spending the night with him. He never kept a steady lover. I overheard her explaining to one of her model friends, visiting our house one evening, that her husband loved the thrill of conquering young women. Once he completed the mission successfully, he moved on to the next. I despised Angus for that no less than I despised his wife; although I *did* give him credit for keeping his sex life discrete from the world—discrete from me.

I remember praying to Jesus every night, asking him for a normal family. I wished for my parents to love each other—I wished for my parents to love their daughter. But no, Jesus was too busy with the other billions of hopeless cases. He had no time to grant some pathetic Norwegian child one small wish.

One night, I thought Jesus had finally granted me my wish.

Overhearing my mother's footsteps, I opened my door and followed her quietly along the corridor leading to my father's bedroom. She knocked on his door, emotional, breathing heavily. He opened it, half asleep.

"I need to be with you tonight!" she moaned and stormed into his room without waiting for his reply. The door was left slightly ajar and I peeked in.

I never knew my parents spent nights together. It was an exciting new revelation that gave a small and desperate girl hope. Hypnotized, I watched my parents make love, kissing, hugging, touching and caressing one another—so gentle and loving—I felt joy like never before. The image of my parents in each other's arms, having sex—barely fit for a child my age—were exhilarating to capture with my own set of eyes and record in my own mind's image bank for eternity. For me, those wonderful moments were in no way frightening, repulsive or bizarre; for little loveless Jenny, they were genuinely beautiful. They meant compassion. They meant normalcy.

When they were done, my mother placed her head on my father's shoulder. "Angus," she said to him in Norwegian as he gently caressed her long hair, "it's getting harder to get jobs now. They look for fresh meat."

"You're still young and pretty," he assured her.

"I love you endlessly," she whispered. "You know that, don't you?"

"I know," he replied.

"We came from the same pit-hole, you and I. Nothing can match that!" she said and started sobbing softly. I found myself crying too. "We are Vikings! We can survive this rough place if we only stick to each other. Will you stick by my side? Will you do that?"

"Always Mariana, always," he promised. "Just be more discrete about your love-life . . . for Jenny's sake."

Some frigging hope . . .

Chapter 2

Seeds Planted

By the time my mother's modeling career had faded away, my father was one of the biggest diamond importers in the country. I was not aware of how rich we had become until we moved to sunny California. My father purchased a spacious estate on Beverly Hills' prestigious Alpine Drive. We had about a dozen people in our household staff and my father's hobby packed our huge garage with some very expensive cars—new and classic. I now had a driver driving me around in a brand new Rolls Royse. Can you believe it? These parents of mine . . . what the hell were they thinking?

Growing up, I often felt like a female Richie Rich. Obviously, my family was richer than most of the other very rich families whose children were attending Beverly Vista, my new elementary school. I had my own cash box filled with 50 and 100 dollar bills that my father would stuff every time he wanted to clear his conscience for being away most of the time. I used to empty it from time to time, stashing thousands of dollars in shoe boxes hidden away in my closet, neatly arranging them in bundles—as if this was a game of Monopoly. I never used the money to buy anything. I got whatever I asked for anyway. Later on in life, all that accumulated cash would come in very handy.

Diamond tycoon Angus Svensen purchased an office floor in an impressive building on Wilshire Boulevard and set up his company's offices there with about fifty employees. Being a successful businessman, good looking and married to an ex-Norwegian supermodel, my father soon got his share of media attention, too. Every few months we would read articles about him—mostly positive and related to his business success.

While engaging in her New York based modeling career, my mother was smart enough to think of the day after. She studied fashion management, so when that day inevitably arrived, she quickly hooked up with some of the industry's movers and shakers and started learning the industry from a different angle.

Soon enough, Fred Reeves, a famous LA fashion house owner and CEO, offered her a lucrative job as his personal assistant. The papers celebrated the famous ex-supermodel's choice; but the tabloids would soon inform their readers of the hot and exciting love affair between Mariana and her new boss.

How shockingly surprising . . .

By then I was eight years old. Students in my school were hearing about Jenny's mother extramarital affairs and, kids being kids, I got my share of teasing and mocking. I was ashamed of my mother and hated my father for not doing anything to stop her. In fact, at that stage of my young life, I loathed them both infinitely. Even then, I was already mature enough to ask myself why my parents never thought about the repercussions of their lifestyles on me. But then again—why should they?

I'm in third grade. I'm eating my lunch alone, seated on a bench in the playground. The bell rings as a group of girls approaches me. They mock me for being my slut mother's daughter. Tears form in my eyes but I remain courageously seated, looking away, biting on my sandwich time and again, chewing silently— waiting for it to end. I get up, look at them defiantly, and without a word, walk away.

"Fine," I thought to myself. *"I'm a descendent of the mighty Vikings and I'm strong enough to deal with whatever comes my way."*

That was the first turning point in my life. It was also a point of no return.

Years of neglect and lack of parental attention started blooming in the form of anger and disillusion. The sketches I made during that period leave no room for misinterpretation. The main theme was always a small girl, an outcast ridiculed by her peers, drifting away from the shores of her home, fighting a rough ocean, floating helplessly on a small raft.

One sketch in particular moved me to the bones when I came across it. It was a sketch of that same little girl setting fire to her home and, while the flames consume the first floor of the house, her parents cry for help from the second floor windows. Yet, she is walking away.

The teenage inclination to rebel, which in most cases emerge in adolescents two or three years my senior, conquered me sooner than anticipated. At the age of ten, hatred and resentment toward the two people responsible for my birth were the only emotions I knew. I was old enough to understand that I had been mistreated, mishandled, mismanaged . . . *mis*-everything!

I remember looking around, seeing happy kids with loving parents and tons of friends, while I was lonely, not a parent in sight, never knowing what it was like to have a best friend— never enjoying the company of others. Ironically, this made me excel at my studies. I had nothing better to do but use my free time to read and do homework.

Increasingly, our staff—the only people around me who really cared—started noticing the changes. From a good and polite girl, I became impatient and nasty. Female hormones were slashing at me mercilessly, and the combination led to some very harsh outbursts and rebellious behavior.

One evening, my father came into my room while I was reading a book. He sat on my bed, looking at me with loving eyes. He caressed my hair and smiled compassionately. "You are turning into a very beautiful young woman," he said softly.

"What do you want?" I threw at him angrily, placing the book aside.

"Huhh . . .?" he reacted with astonishment written all over his face.

"What's this sudden interest in me? Don't you have better things to do?" I asked. He looked at me with a sad face. "So . . . what do you want?"

"I know I'm a lousy father . . ." he whispered. "I wish I could spend some more time with you, but I'm very busy. I want to ensure that you and your mother enjoy a good and prosperous life. . ."

"Spare me the bullshit!" I barked at him. "I don't need you or your make-believe-wife. I'll handle life on my own. I'm a Viking!"

Stunned, my father got to his feet. I had never spoken to him the way I did that evening. "Jenny, please. . ." he tried to calm me down.

"Don't Jenny me . . .," I screamed, eyeballing him with hatred. "Don't you come into my room expecting to ease your conscious with a pep-talk. I hate you!" Strong, rich and influential Angus Svensen was clearly in a state of shock. The high decibels brought my mother rushing into my room.

"What's going on?" she asked concerned. My father just looked at her, still overwhelmed at my outburst.

"Oh . . . both of you home . . .how wonderful—a real family reunion," I commented sarcastically with a fake smile. "What's wrong, mother? Is Fred too busy with his other whores to spend the night with you?" My mother's mouth opened wide in bewilderment at my sudden full-fledged attack. I got to my feet and approached her. "Kids at school refer to me as the daughter of the greatest slut in US history." I said. "Mother, you're a whore, plain and simple, nothing more, nothing less . . ." she slapped my face. The pain was intense but I remained composed. The last thing I wanted was to give her the satisfaction of seeing me cry. I just looked at her and smiled. "You know, for years I used to pray to Jesus Christ to make us a normal family and all along I was missing the point. I should have prayed for your death. I hate both of you." I screamed and left the room running, locking myself in my bathroom. It took them four hours to get me out of there.

I was only 11.

The following day, my father brought home a therapist, one who specialized in children. She was a woman in her forties who had a kind face and a pleasant smile. He introduced her to me as "someone who would help you understand your emotions better at your confusing age." I shook my head in disbelief as he had said that. *Don't you get it?* I thought to myself; *it's not me—it's you!*

'Brenda the shrink' spent a few hours a week with me, and I must admit that I found our sessions rather comforting. Finally, I had someone listening to what *I* had to say, focusing all the attention on *me*—even if she was paid handsomely to do it. It made me feel better, although it did not change my attitude toward my parents. In fact, the hours I spent with Brenda were counterproductive where my parents were concerned. Our conversations only highlighted the magnitude of their neglect. There were moments during our conversations when I detected the moisture building up in Brenda's eyes. Although I was very young, I could interpret my shrink's body language. She found my stories hard to swallow.

After about ten sessions with me, Brenda asked to speak to both my parents. She came over one evening, not long after my father returned home from one of his many business trips abroad. I could hear the entire conversation. By then I was an expert in the art of eavesdropping.

Brenda slashed at my parents mercilessly for almost half an hour, although she did it politely and very professionally. "A child is not a pet," she concluded harshly. "Forgive me for being so direct and maybe out of line here, but you two must have done something very wrong to have your child antagonized to this extent. Your little girl testifies to nothing but heartache, shame and grief all through her young life. I spoke to her for 15 hours. . . . 15 long hours. . ." She chocked on her own lump, "and I could not get her to describe one happy moment with you two. Not even one!" My parents accepted the scolding quietly.

"I was not prepared emotionally for Jenny. I was young and immature when she was born. Later I was too concerned with my career to notice what was going on." My mother said emotionally. "Oh, Angus, what have we done?"

"How can we correct things now?" my businesslike father asked, characteristically assuming immediately that everything broken can be fixed.

"You have a lot of hard work to do!" Brenda exclaimed. "You need to give her enough of your time and attention and to be there for her. Try to get close, show her compassion. Let her know how much she means to you. Let her know you love her." My mother's sobbing got louder. Brenda waited for her to calm down a bit before she proceeded. "Now, I'm not going to lie to you. It is a long process. You will have to find a way to win her over and it is not going to be easy . . . I hope she'll let you into her heart again. She is bitter and she carries a lot of animosity towards both of you." My mother took a large quantity of air into her lungs and released it slowly. "Jenny is a special case." Brenda continued, "I have never seen a girl so young and yet so mature, so experienced with life's hardships. You know what bothers me the most?" she asked rhetorically. "Your daughter is certain that she doesn't need you two anymore. She is convinced she can make it on her own."

The next few weeks were the most I had ever seen of my parents up until that point in time. They were all over me, trying to correct things, trying to make me feel better. My mother took me twice to the movies. She even took me shopping and asked for my opinion choosing clothes for us both—something she had never done. We traveled to Orlando and visited Disney World, the three of us, like a real and normal family. We actually had a wonderful time.

One sketch I found in a sketchbook from that period describes a rare and hopeful scene of three figures, two adults and one small child, holding hands, standing in front of the ocean, looking to the horizon. Never again throughout my childhood would I sketch such a hopeful scene.

I decided to give my parents a break but it did not take me too long to figure out that, while physically near, their minds had traveled elsewhere. The whole 'being together' thing felt insincere. They did not really want to spend that time with me; they merely felt they *had* to.

As expected, a few weeks later, things returned to their usual state of affairs. My parents were too busy to spend time with me and I hardly saw either of them. The only good thing coming out of all the fuss Brenda the shrink created around me was my mother's realization that her public love life was causing me pain and shame. Although still very much engaged in a love affair with her boss, from here on she did her best to keep it out of the public eye.

Chapter 3

The Ills of Friendships

Go figure life. It hits you repeatedly in the head with the heaviest hammer and then, unexpectedly, bestows on you a gift beyond your wildest dreams.

By the seventh grade, it was obvious I was turning out to be one of the hottest chicks around. I did not make much of it at first, but when boys started approaching me, seeking my proximity, I realized I had to change my whole approach to social interactions. It was awkward at first; I had never been too friendly or fun to be with. It seemed to me shallow and insincere to want to be with someone just for his looks. Yet, this was a fact of life and it was working now to boost my social status in school.

I was never lonely again. With all the attention I got from the most popular boys—the girls wished to be closer too. Suddenly I had many friends. I knew better than to believe it was for my charming personality, but who cared . . . I was finally getting a break. Blessed with my mother's bodily characteristics, I was considered an exotic beauty. My ex-super-model mom saw the potential and soon enough had me participating in an advertising campaign her fashion label was launching for a children's underwear line. Suddenly my photos were all over town, starring on the company's brochures and posters, displaying a lot of white, smooth and silky girlish skin.

I'm walking alongside my mother at a mall. We bump into a huge poster of me in panties. We enter the store and a crowd gathers around. I'm used to people gathering around us in public places, lining up to get my supermodel mother's autograph, but not this time. This time they lined up to get mine. Girls of all ages ask to take their photo with unimportant me, and the feeling is awesome.

I never saw my father as infuriated as he was when my mother proudly presented the company's brochure to him. She clearly had not considered consulting him before the shoots and thought it would make him proud. He had just come back from a weeklong business trip to Hong Kong. The man simply exploded at her with a nuclear blast of a rage. He sent me to my room and yelled at her with ferocity I had never thought him capable of.

"Are you out of your mind?" He yelled in Norwegian. "Do you want her to live the kind of life you had? Creeps all over, touching her . . . wanting to get into her pants . . . having booze and drugs all over the place—no way! Not my only child! One model in the family is more than enough!"

"Angus, you're overreacting," she tried to explain, astonished at this sudden outburst. "If you calm down and look at her you'll see that this girl of yours has phenomenal potential. She is the most beautiful thing and she can make it big. I've gotten dozens of job offers for her thanks to this campaign . . ."

"Now, listen to me Mariana Mortensen and listen to me good because I'll only say it once," he said to her with the meanest tone of voice.

"Angus, let go of my arm. You're hurting me," I heard my mother begging, realizing for the first time in my life that my gentle father could become physically dangerous.

"If I ever catch you promoting Jenny to one of your fashion campaigns again, I swear to God, I will break every bone in your body and throw you out of this house with nothing but your underwear. Don't you *dare* mess around with me on this one! Do you hear me?" he yelled at her.

"Let go of me," she cried from pain.

"Do you fucking hear me?" he screamed at her in English.

"Yes . . ." she cried. "I hear you."

He slammed the door as he left the room, leaving my confounded mother behind whimpering.

It was the first time my father had gone out of his way to protect me—even though I could not understand what the fuss was all about. Actually, I was quite pleased with all the attention and I truly enjoyed seeing my photos published. I felt like a young celebrity, contently detecting the envy and admiration in the eyes of my peers.

That night, my mother went to my father's room again. With time I realized that this was the mechanism that had kept their open marriage functional all these years. In some twisted way, my parents really loved each other and based their union on their mutual upbringing.

Other than discovering my exotic beauty, the seventh grade had me dealing with another tantalizing and confusing revelation about myself. It had to do with a girl. Her name was Lisa Anne Epstein and she was by far the most beautiful thing I had ever set my eyes on. Taller than me, eyes as blue, blond hair with a face sculptured in heaven, a body curved by Michelangelo himself, legs shaped in an artist's class in Florence, and skin clearer and smoother than a newborn baby's behind, Lisa was the personification of divine beauty.

We shared a homeroom class so I got the chance to observe her from up close. I even took a shower with her once after physical education class. I stared at her 13-year-old body, my heart pounding against my chest faster and harder than ever, when she got soap over her eyes, thrilled from the beautiful images my eyes caught and were sending to my brains for interpretation. The shiver my body experienced and the electricity that ran across my most private bodily organs were unimaginable. I was left breathless. I have many sketches capturing that wonderful moment of exhilaration. I drew Lisa from every possible angle. I just could not stop thinking and fanaticizing about her.

Not only were Lisa's external looks exceptionally magnificent, but she was also blessed with a phenomenal intelligence and a warm heart. She was, by far, the most intelligent student in school, winning all sorts of competitions—our school's pride and joy. The girl was just too perfect to grasp. You would think someone like that would feel and act superior to all of us shallow, normal kids, but not Lisa Anne Epstein. This wonderful creature treated everyone with respect and was adored by one and all.

Well . . . I had fallen in love. The realization that I could love humans of my own gender was surprising and excruciating, but it had little influence over the course of my life. What did have lasting impact was my love specifically for *Lisa*. I did not fully understand it back then. I was 13 years old and these kinds of emotions at that particular and confusing age were brand new to me.

All I wanted was to be close to her.

One day, I gathered enough courage to sit beside her during lunch break. She was reading, but when she realized I was staring at her, she placed the book aside and smiled at me. "Hi, beautiful Jenny," she said. I was moved by the gesture.

"Do you want an orange? I have an extra one." I offered, nervously.

"No. Thanks." There was a moment of silence.

"Lisa, I'm really embarrassed to ask you for a favor," I said.

"Don't be."

"I'm having trouble with math. Can you come over one afternoon and help me understand it better?"

"Sure. I'll be glad to," she said smiling. I looked at her beautiful face and trembled. A wave of emotions crashed at the shores of my being. I shifted my gaze so she would not suspect.

"Are you all right?" she asked concerned and placed her hand on my shoulder. I don't even pretend to know how to start explaining the type of bodily reaction I experienced when she touched me. It was so scary that I jumped up to my feet, startled and baffled.

"Yeah, I'm fine. Thanks," I said and fled the place. *Holly crap. What was that all about?*

We became friends.

Lisa came over from time to time to help me with math and soon we found ourselves going out occasionally to catch a movie, or to eat something in Westwood Village. We even spent several Sundays together. I felt a happiness I had never thought I could.

Fate made sure that Lisa and her mother, Dr. Myra Epstein, were there for me when I got my first period. I was feeling humiliated and miserable, my panties soaked with blood, sitting on the toilet bowl in school, hating everything and everyone around me, at a loss for action. Knowing we were friends, someone had called Lisa. She rushed in, cleared the bathroom and saw me through it all. She gave me my first tampon and showed me how to use it. She washed my panties and gave me clean ones of her own. She even had Alex, my driver, drive us to her mother's clinic, where Dr. Epstein dedicated more than an hour of her valuable time calming me down and explaining to me how a woman should deal with her period and what to expect when this catastrophic phenomenon occurs. Dr. Epstein even tracked my mother down in New York and informed her of my entrance to womanhood.

Mariana called me that evening. "I'm so sorry for not being there for you, sweetheart," she said emotional.

"Well, I'm not!" I barked at her as I slammed the phone, disconnecting the call.

But there had to be a party breaker in every one of my life's periods, and this time it was Lisa's long-time best friend, Amanda Willis. The two had known each other since their kindergarten days and loved each other deeply. Amanda hated my guts, fearing I was about to steal her best friend away. She acted cool about it at first, but as my relationship with Lisa evolved, Amanda started demonstrating a profound hostility towards me. I knew I was sitting on a powder keg. I suspected that Amanda would not sit idly by. Something had to be done!

Thinking about it, my thoughts led me to some extreme solutions—I contemplated ways of ending her life. Six of my sketches display me as a hangman tying the rope around Amanda's neck. Luckily for mean little me, it remained a childish thought, but one that showed I was willing to kill for Lisa.

If I enjoyed the fact that my looks helped me enhance my social circle, Lisa could not have cared less. Every human male in school, teachers and parents included, fantasized about her. You could see it in their eyes when they looked at her. Some of the older boys in school tried their luck and asked her out. She always turned them down politely. "I'm too young for that now," she once answered my query, "and they'll be a distraction from my studies."

One afternoon, studying together in her room at her parents' estate in Beverly Hills, we paused for some orange juice and cookies. Then, we lay down on our bellies, reclining side by side on her queen size bed, watching television. John Ritter was making a fool of himself as Jack Tripper. We laughed. I stared at her perfect face for a while. She turned her gaze. Our faces were closer than they ever were. I could not help it. My lips were drawn to hers uncontrollably. I closed my eyes and kissed her lips. She did not refuse my kiss. My body trembled with pure teenage passion. When I opened my eyes, I could see surprise hanging on Lisa's face—not the reaction I had hoped for. She gave both of us a moment to recover. Then she placed her hand on my cheek, smiled and said: "that felt nice, Jenny. It really did. But I think that in the future we should show compassion to each other in a less physical manner." Then she acted cool, as if nothing really happened.

I was devastated for days to come. The hammer . . .

And as if this blow was not enough to break my spirit, Amanda saw us sitting together during one of the breaks and sat beside us. "Lisa," she addressed her best friend emotionally. "You have to choose between us. You can't have two best friends. I can't carry on like this. It's either me or her. You must decide now!" Lisa was shocked. She tried to change Amanda's mind, but the girl stood firm like a rock. Finally, seeing that Amanda was close to tears, Lisa chose her.

"Don't be mad at me," she said to me the next day, "I had no choice. She was serious and it would be like breaking her heart."

"It's okay," I lied. Did she notice I was far from sincere? I believe so.

"Please, Jenny, give her some time, I'm sure we can be friends again in a short while."

The fact that Lisa had given up on me so easily again raised some familiar emotions. I was shattered by her obvious choice. I ached all over. I thought she could have managed the crisis better.

I thought she could have left me a portion of her time and attention. I would have settled for less, much less. Only, she decided instead to abide utterly by Amanda's preconditions and overlook my huge love for her.

Jenny, being Jenny, was left out in the cold again.

Chapter 4

Blossoming

Fast forward to some scenes from the next three years, during which Jennifer Svensen turned into the hottest chick around. This fact did not escape some important people from my mother's line of work. There was something about the combination of my looks and the way I moved, as my mother believed, that kept them coming back. I was considered not only beautiful but also very sensual.

Those three years also turned me from an angry adolescent into a cynical and bitter teenager. I hated everyone and everything around me... oh... yes... and I still hated everything that had to do with my parents!

My love for Lisa, on the other hand, had become an obsession. After she made her choice, I went through an excruciating period of bulimia followed by a long period of depression. In between, I experienced frustration and anger. I promised myself revenge. I would find the opportunity to have Lisa experience some of the heartache and pain her choice had caused me.

Consequently, I had to learn all on my own how to cope with urges of verbal and physical abuse. Now, a freshman in Beverly Hills High School, I was sent twice to the Principal office for using the 'F' word while engaging in 'discussions' with my teachers. Then, I was suspended for a whole week for slapping a girl who accidently stepped on my backpack. I even launched a mighty kick to the balls of a boy who had caressed my ass on the football field, trying to prove his manhood to a cheering crowd of horny teenage males. He was rushed to the hospital; I was rushed to the principal's office . . . again.

Eventually, my mother was summoned to school. We were told I was the school's leading candidate for expulsion. The principal insisted that the only way they would consider keeping me was if I got professional help. "Either she learns to tunnel her negative energies toward positive channels, or she has to find some other educational facility!" he concluded.

So, I found myself, unwillingly and most reluctantly, seeing a shrink again.

The first one my parents hired was a woman in her fifties. She got on my shaky nerves right from the start with her invasive questions and condescending attitude. During our third session, I deliberately spilled a glass of coke on her blouse. Although she found me 'challenging,' as she put it, I was not willing to see her ever again and gave my parents hell about it.

Understanding the gravity of the situation, my father hired a new therapist who was considered one of the best in the business. His name was Dr. Richard Ward and he soon won a special place in my life story.

Ward was a mid-fortyish, tall, very handsome and very impressive professional. Among his other very appealing characteristics, he was also charismatic, straightforward and smart. The author of four best sellers in the field of psychology and nationally recognized for his skills, Ward charged accordingly. Each hour-long session cost my rich father $350.

He was also a man with a lively libido. I grasped that the first time we met. The man scanned my body, head to toe, pausing for a long second on my boobs. His grin gave him away—all I saw transmitted from his eyes was pure and eager lust. By now, at 15, I was an expert on the looks men gave me. Ward gave me the 'I want to fuck you so bad I could die' look. I knew I could use him for something I had been thinking a lot of lately: sex.

It was time for my first sexual experience with a man, and I wanted it to be with someone experienced. Ward, judging by his looks, had lots of it. Besides, truth be told—I was genuinely physically attracted to him. For a short while after kissing Lisa, I had suspected that I was only into girls. It very soon turned out that I was also attracted to certain boys—preferably the more athletic type. I wasn't relieved.

In order to fully grasp what made a 15-year-old girl, even if reckless and impossible to handle as I was back then, plan such plans, one must understand that my new adolescent character seemed to thrive on the edge. It had started with driving other people's cars at high speed along LA freeways, or sneaking into other people's yards to swim naked in their private swimming pools—often while they were sleeping behind the window above, or even stealing gum or lip-gloss from a 7-eleven . . . just for the excitement of it. It was intoxicating.

I had been making some friends who I'd met once at a punk-rock party. I got to play the crazy rich kid with money to finance everything they desired. This and some leadership qualities (today I understand) gave me the power to control the group's agenda. They were all punk freaks, anti-mainstream music types, anti-establishment, anti-family, anti-people—anti-everything. They strapped themselves with bracelets, chains and rings wherever they could, on their bodies and clothes. They wore black leather clothes and black boots, and they covered their bodies with colorful tattoos. I found most of their pretentions superfluous but the quest for adrenaline bursts glued us together like a horse and its skin.

I guess I could have died several times over.

We are standing on the tracks facing a speeding train, wasted and testing each other's courage. This time we are trying to determine who would jump away from the tracks last. The train comes at full speed. One by one, they jump away. I win—I am still there. My shoe tangles underneath the metal bar. I get it loose at the very last second. As I jump away, I feel the train whistling inches from my flesh. My heart is beating faster than the train's speed ever could. I burst into hysterical, demented laughter. Too bad about the shoe, I think as I limp shoelessly away, my panties soaked with my own urine. The sensation is awesome. My friends look at me with dread.

Ward happened as puberty and adrenaline coincided. I would be having sex; it would be with a looker; and it would be totally unethical (me seducing my therapist, of course). The repercussions were unimportant. What mattered now was meeting the challenge.

At first, our sessions were proper and interesting. Gradually, I began dressing with shorter skirts and transparent shirts, losing my bra at the ladies' room just before coming into his office. Inside, lying sensuously on Ward's sofa, I enjoyed watching him fight the urge to jump me, trying unsuccessfully to hide the lump in his pants. To complete the task, I began wearing white lace panties that left no room for the imagination. I saw him staring at the crack beneath my skirt—and I gave him plenty of chances to do just that. I was testing Ward's basic instincts.

One day, I became impatient and began fondling his hair, telling him there was nothing in this world I wanted more than to have sex with him. In his defense, I will say that he tried fighting the urge. He explained why he could never have sex with me. I simply smiled and shifted my hand smoothly down his belly and into his pants. My ethical, professional and value-driven shrink did nothing to remove it; and following some less-equivocal objections, he soon started moaning to the rhythm of my hand traveling up and down his muscularity.

Dr. Ward finally gave me the sexual experience one remembers for life.

"So, Richard, how does it feel to deflower a virgin patient?" I spat at him, as I got dressed, "Aren't you worried about the psychological life-long repercussions on my delicate and fragile mind?" I taunted him. He looked at me astonished. "From now on, Dr. Ward," I said before leaving, "I think I would prefer we dedicate our meetings to sex. I'm not so sure I like people like you peering into my psyche. You'll even get paid for it the ridicules amount of money you charge my father for seeing me; and if you refuse, I'll tell him."

I had just found out how far men were willing to go for sex. I also realized that my powers over men were limitless . . . if I use sex. My sketchbook from that period is packed with embarrassing erotic images. My first sex experience on Ward's sofa is documented so vividly that it constitutes sheer porn. If while writing my story I have often played with the notion of publishing some of my sketches, those ones convinced me otherwise.

While I was maturing awfully, Lisa seemed to be maturing wonderfully. Beautiful and sexy, now a freshman student at Beverly High, she was still very much single. She kept to herself and to Amanda Willis. She studied hard and contributed trophies to our new school's trophy cabinet. She also wrote some very interesting articles in our school's paper. I used to watch her jealously from a safe distance, hoping to someday find a way back into her heart.

Although Richard fulfilled my sexual needs for a short while, I saw the agony in his eyes each and every time we were done. He begged me to free him but I would not. One day, as I took off my clothes, he just stood there gloomily and said he would no longer play the game. "Give me a chance to rehabilitate myself," he begged. "Keep us a secrete you take to your grave."

"And if I disagree?" I asked.

"Then I'll have to tell my wife and give up the profession, Jennifer. It's not your fault . . . it's completely mine."

"No shit . . ."

I took his hand and placed it on my breast. "Richard, don't be so bleak. I just love fooling around with you. You men are so predictable and pathetic . . ." He looked at me with a somber face. "Don't worry. I won't ruin your life." He smiled with relief. "Now . . .," I said and placed his other hand on my other boob, "take off your clothes and fulfill my needs for the last time."

Richard Ward did not get off that easily. The deal was he would write a false evaluation stating I was doing fine and had the tools needed to control my anger. This was submitted to my school and filed.

Now, after sex with my therapist there was one mind-blowing experience left I had to try—getting high. In an environment as rich as Beverly High drugs were all around us. I got to try dope at one of the parties. I loved it so much that I decided to buy enough to share with my young gang.

I got the name of a supplier and the address of a bar on Sunset Boulevard. The supplier was an attractive college student named

Ralph. After paying him, we went to a nearby motel. He was far below Richard in *that* department but the stuff he sold me was top quality.

A bold idea popped into my head as we smoked it together.

"Say, Ralph, or whatever your real name is. How would you like to make $5,000 in a rather short period of time?"

"Go on," he replied. I looked at him satisfied, loving the idea that was going through a refining process in my head.

"I'll pay you 2,000 bucks now, in cash and another 3,000 at completion if you break a girl's heart."

"You're kidding me right?"

"No. You should let her experience the wild side. Have her smoke pot and drink booze. I'll pay for the stuff. Have her fall in love with you. Then dump her."

"It's a piece of cake!" he exclaimed.

"No it's not. It's a challenge. She's a good girl." I turned somewhat somber.

"Is she pretty?" he asked.

"Pretty?" I chuckled, "this girl is the most beautiful thing you ever saw."

"Sounds interesting," he said.

"But you'll have to promise me you'll keep it clean. You have to promise me you keep your dick in your pants." He nodded. "And you'll never use violence! Never! Otherwise our deal is off."

He nodded. "Whatever you say . . ."

I got closer to him. "Ralphy boy," I said, looking into his eyes, "if you as much as leave a scratch on this girl, I will hunt you down like a boar and kill you. Do you understand?"

He looked at me somewhat amused and smiled. "Yeah . . . whatever . . . what's her name?"

Chapter 5

The Bitter Taste of Revenge

Being still so juvenile and immature, I regarded the Lisa project as something I could control. I had initiated it, set up the rules of the game and controlled the proceedings. I tried to steer the course using the power of my green bills; what I failed to comprehend was the kind of game I had gotten myself into and the people I had chosen to play with.

It all started fine.

Ralph tailed Lisa for a while, studied her habits and found out her schedule. He decided to make his move at the Beverly Hills Public Library. He 'accidentally' bumped into her, carrying some books about space and nature under his arm. They started a conversation, which ended in a café on Beverly Drive. Romantically, she wasn't interested at first, but Ralph intrigued her and she agreed to meet him again. They caught a movie together and ate at a fast food restaurant. I guess Ralph was charming and interesting because that date led to another that led to another. A couple of weeks down the line, Ralph started taking Lisa to some wild parties where they were seen drinking together.

I should have stopped the whole thing the first time the guy used the phrase: 'the finest piece of ass he ever saw'. He was deviating from the plan without seeking permission. This college-student-slash-drug-dealer was primarily an ordinary guy and far from stupid. He well understood what had fallen into his hands. Lisa's profound beauty and unique personality captured him too.

Ralph was using drug-money to pay for college and keep himself living fancy. He was not the usual criminal. He was a young man from a good home who had gone sour. He was the smiling handsome son of the polite couple from across the street.

Lisa was in danger because he had what it took to win her heart without raising suspicion. Not realizing it, I was losing control. My wish to see the girl I loved get a share of the pain she had inflicted on me, blinded my eyes to the extent that I overlooked the Frankenstein I had created.

With the weeks passing, Lisa was spotted with Ralph at Terranova's notorious annual party. This was a $100-a-ticket event, 2000 participants, drugs and booze . . . run by a goon who managed to trick the LAPD each time by never getting to his party on time. Everything surrounding that party was a secret. The participants were informed of its whereabouts only an hour before it began, by telephone. When buying the tickets from Terranova's hoodlums, they had to supply their home address and telephone numbers. This maintained a balance of fear between Terranova and the participants. No one dared inform the police about the party, knowing Terranova's hoodlums could get to them and their families rather easily.

This was the first indication for me that Ralph had taken the assignment much too far; but at that point in time, I had no idea as to what was going on between Ralph and Lisa. I still thought he hadn't made his move, yet.

The next day I followed Ralph around with my driver until I found out where he lived. That night we ambushed Lisa's boyfriend, hiding behind the wide pillars in the underground parking lot of his apartment building.

We jumped him as he exited his car.

"I need more time," he justified what was going on while held by Buzz, Jerry and Doug—three of my gang punk-friends. "You wanted her falling for me, didn't you? That hasn't happen yet. You have to be patient. I'm no fucking Casanova."

"It's been three months," I said to him, "it's taking you too long."

"I need more time. I've got her doing the booze and the dope, but it will take me a few more weeks to have her fall for me."

I bought his excuses and let him go.

Meanwhile, at school, Lisa was going through a rough change—her lovely smile was gone, she stopped being nice to everyone and retreated to an inside world, always moody and melancholic.

I must admit that at first, not fully grasping what was going on, I enjoyed the fruits of my plan. I wanted Lisa's perfect life to experience some pain and misery. But the biggest triumph of it all was seeing my arch-foe, Amanda Willis, losing her best friend. Five months into my plan and the two were no longer being spotted together. I found Amanda one day sitting all alone on a bench in the school's back yard. She was writing something in her notebook when I approached her.

"Hi," I greeted her as I moved her backpack and sat beside her.

"Hi," she replied unenthusiastically. It was obvious she was not in the mood for a conversation. I proceeded nonetheless.

"I'm looking for Lisa. Have you seen her today?"

"No. I have no idea where she is," she said without even looking at me.

"How come?" I persisted.

"It's none of your business!" she said.

"Listen, Amanda," I said placing my hand on her arm, trying to act as someone who really cared. "I care about Lisa. Something is wrong with her lately and I want to help. Please, let me help."

"You can't help!" she exclaimed, looking at me with a harsh facial expression.

"What do you mean?"

"Do you really want to help?" she asked undecided.

"Off course . . ."

She took a big gulp of air into her lungs and let it all out slowly. "Then talk to her. Help me convince her to tell her parents about the drugs."

"What drugs?" I asked petrified.

"Heroin," she said with a somber face. I started sweating all over, feeling the blood in my body streaming down to the palms of my hands. My heart was beating fast. *What have I done? That son of a bitch . . .!*

"How awful," I whispered. I guess the girl noticed my feelings were authentic.

"I wish that was all of it," she whispered.

"What do you mean?"

"I can't tell you," she replied.

"What can we do?" I asked shattered.

"I don't know . . . I've threatened to tell her parents, but she stated she'll never speak to me."

I looked for Lisa everywhere in school and found her sitting alone in her math class, staring at the blackboard. I sat beside her. She didn't react to my presence. "Lisa, honey, how's stuff?" I whispered.

She moved her gaze and looked at me with a weary look. "I'm fine."

"No. You're not!" I exclaimed. "You're hanging out with creeps." She looked away. I noticed her eyes getting moist.

"Thanks for your concern, Jenny, but I'm just fine," she said, got to her feet and left.

The guilt slashed at me ruthlessly. I didn't sleep that night, tossing and turning, hating myself, thinking of ways to free Lisa from Ralph's grip.

The next evening we followed Ralph around in Buzz's Chevy. Buzz was 21, the oldest member in my gang and the only one with a driver's license. We saw Lisa park her Porsche on Doheny drive. She got into Ralph's car and they drove away. We followed them. They parked the car near a house in Crescent Heights. Judging by the noise, we assumed it was a party. I asked the gang to wait for me as I went into the house, looking for Ralph. I did my best to keep away from Lisa's eyesight. About five minutes later, I spotted him. He was making his way to the kitchen. I followed him.

"Follow me outside!" I ordered, pulling his arm forcefully. He demonstrated no resistance and followed me out willingly. There were people sitting on the patio so I led him to a dark and secluded part of the back yard.

"Let go of her!" I ordered.

"Or else what?" he said with a belittling look. "You'll kill me?"

"Damn right I will!" I yelled. His fist was in my face so fast I didn't have the chance to see it coming. The powerful blow sent me to the ground, stunned and disoriented. He started kicking me in the stomach mercilessly as I started coughing, unable to catch my breath. He then bent over, held my head by my hair and slapped my face repeatedly. My face burned with soreness. Then he picked me up with his strong arms and threw my body aggressively on a small wooden table.

"Now, you listen to me, slut," he said holding my neck with both his powerful hands, squeezing it to the point I could not breathe or scream. "The next time you get near me I won't be as gentle. This is the real world. In this world *I* rule. Our deal is off." He let go of my neck and I fell from the table to the ground, banging my head and losing consciousness.

When I woke up, I was aching all over. Blood was running from my nose. I dragged myself out to the street. My friends were nowhere to be found. Some merciful soul of a teenager who saw the shape I was in, took me home.

It turned out my friends had been beaten up by Ralph's goons. Buzz got his nose broken, Doug lost a tooth and Jerry suffered a severe concussion. We swore to find the opportunity and have our vengeance. But this was secondary to the calamity my plan had inflicted on Lisa's life. The guilt would haunt me for the rest of my life.

About three weeks later, in an attempt to minimize the damages to Lisa's life, I took $3,000 out of one of my shoeboxes and headed to the Northridge University campus. I found Ralph sitting in one of the cafeterias, eating lunch.

"Guys, clear the table please!" he said when he saw me. They followed his command. "I've got to hand it to you," he said, "you sure have big balls coming here."

"I beg you. Ralph. Let her go," I pleaded.

"Forget it! I dig her," he said and continued eating as if I was thin air.

I took the envelope out of my pocket and offered it to him. "There's $3,000 inside. Our deal is off. Now, let her go!" He grabbed the envelope, tore it open and peeked inside. Then, he placed it in his Jean's rear pocket.

"Life is a game to you, isn't it?" he asked, placing the fork and knife on his plate, drinking from his Seven-Up and reclining on his seat. "Well, guess what? It isn't. You can't just mess around with people's life."

"Please," I begged him.

"I'll tell you what I'll do," he said. "I'll take this money off your hands and consider us even. You hooked me up with her and she is costing me a fortune to maintain. You're off the hook. Now scram!"

I'm sitting in one of my father's cars that same night in front of Lisa's place, the one I just took without permission from the garage and drove without a license. As much as I want to, I don't have the courage to go inside and tell her everything. I'm feeling helpless, imploding inside, frustrated and feeling like shit. Eventually, I close the car windows and scream like a wounded animal. Then I put the stick in drive and drive the 30 year classic Jaguar like someone with a death wish. I slalom the I10 with the hope of crushing and meeting my creator. I hate myself so much when I realize I'm back home safe and sound. I have failed miserably even at that easy task. It seems I can't do anything right.

Time was moving on and Lisa was absent from school for days. I tried to convince her to tell her parents about her addiction. She just looked at me sadly, thanked me for my concern and asked me not to interfere. I burst into tears. Her reaction made me feel worse. She just embraced me warmly and helped me calm down. "It is my own doing and I will find the way out of it." She whispered in my ear.

Then, one morning, our school principal summoned an assembly.

"Very early this morning," he said, "a student of ours was found unconscious in the school parking lot due to drug overdose." I started breathing heavily. Students around me started whispering, speculating. "She is in critical condition, hanging between life and death. I pray for her wellbeing. I wish you'd do so too. This is a painful reminder to all of us of the devastating consequences of drug abuse. May God save the innocent life of Lisa Anne Epstein."

Chapter 6

Intoxication

You should see my sketches from that period. Lucifer is staring out of all of them. I drew myself holding his trident; standing on Lisa's bleeding body. Another sketch shows me with horns spitting fire, burning Amanda. Another sketch describes a room full of men, and Ralph and his friends taking turns, raping helpless Lisa. And then there's me, holding hands with the devil, satisfaction written all over our twisted faces.

I found myself reporting to Richard's office one day without fixing an appointed. I was exhausted after days of self-inflicted injuries, drained of the vitality of being alive. I needed someone to listen, someone to comfort me, someone to relieve my aching conscious—someone to hold me. As usual, my parents were nowhere to be found, and my former therapist—seeing my emotional condition—asked his secretary to cancel his sessions for the rest of the day.

We spent four hours talking. I spent most of them crying. Even the experienced and renowned Dr. Richard Ward, who had seen and heard almost everything in his 20 year career, was shocked to hear about the travesty. His harsh guise couldn't hide his revulsion.

I begged him to help me get better, to help me stop hurting those around me, to help me feel better about myself. I told him I was tired of years of hating life and despising myself. I wanted to be loved but had always been deprived of that basic emotion. I asked him to hug me and he did . . . in a fatherly way. He subscribed some anti-depressants, which worked instantly and made me feel physically better, but could not help me get over the agony.

I called Lisa's home one night and spoke to her father. I said I was a friend from school who wanted to know how she was doing. Her father was polite, thanking me for the interest, promising she was being cared for by professionals and that she would soon stand back on her own two feet.

It relieved my pain to a certain extent, knowing she was getting better. I promised myself to find a way to do good where Lisa was concerned. I was yet to fully grasp, though, the magnitude of damage my actions had imposed on the person I loved the most. Not only did Lisa suffer emotionally and physically, but she was expelled from school for a whole year, suffered humiliation and social degradation, lost most, if not all of her friends and was now forced to start over in a new high school.

I decided to let time take its course. I would find the time to reconnect with Lisa in the future and compensate her for the turmoil inflicted on her life by my actions.

At this point in time, my parents started showing a renewed interest in my life. At sixteen, it was a bit too late. I would not hear of it. I suspected it had something to do with Richard, so I stormed his office one day, again uninvited, interrupting a session he had with a patient. He grabbed me by the arm and pulled me forcefully all the way to another empty room. "You have to stop showing here uninvited!" he scolded me. I looked at him with fire in my eyes. "Yes. It was I. I just asked them to act like real parents for a change," he confessed.

"Richard, don't you ever mess with my life again!" I ordered.

"Listen, Jennifer," he said softly now. "You were deprived of some very basic emotional needs in your childhood. Nothing can change that. Still, your parents love you very much and they can be the source of the love you are looking for. Give them a chance. They want to be there for you now."

"Oh . . . I gave them plenty of chances to be there for me; they blew it," I said angrily. "My father is never home and my mother prefers spending nights screwing her boss; so don't give me this 'your parents love you' shit."

"Give them a break, will you? We are all humans and we make mistakes," he said. "Hell . . . you witnessed firsthand the greatest mistake of my life, didn't you?"

I got a new Corvette for my sweet sixteen. My parents thought I would be thrilled and maybe cut them some slack, letting them into my life. I took the keys and said thank you nicely. Not a kiss or a hug! They did not deserve it, and material things never meant anything to me to begin with. The next day they asked to speak to me, so we sat around the dining-room table and they gave me two very emotional five-minute speeches about their joint assumption of responsibility for the situation. I had every reason to be angry and disappointed in them, they admitted—they were not good parents. *No shit . . . !*

"So?" I said when they were done, "what do you want from me now?"

"We want you to give us another chance to be your parents," my father said.

"Sorry . . . No can do . . ." I replied.

"Why, honey?" my mother asked with sincere pain in her beautiful blue eyes.

"I'll tell you why, mother," I said calmly. "Because you're late. Your train left the station for the last time when I got my first period. And as for you, daddy; well . . . your train never reached the station to begin with."

I gradually went back to being wild and reckless Jennifer, trying to satisfy my constant need for adrenaline. I was now sleeping with Buzz, just for the sex and the warmth. It was during that period that I started appreciating the embraces of someone who cared. I would dive into his big body and cuddle up in his arms, feeling safe and secure.

My driver's license and my new sports car made the quest for adrenaline easier. Now my gang and I got to more faraway places and did far riskier things, discovering new boundaries—testing our new limitations.

We are at a gas station. We are holding it up at gunpoint, stealing $75 in cash and being shot at by the owner as we escape.

I have about $500 of my own sitting in the Corvette's glove compartment . . .

We challenged life and law. We found ourselves trying some pretty dangerous stuff, like giving the finger to some Mexicans in a pick-up truck, who chased us all though the streets of LA for more than 40 minutes, shooting at us with a shotgun, smashing both of Buzz's rear and front windshields. Heather screamed as she realized the bullets were whistling about an inch away from her ear. We finally managed to shake them off, thanks to Buzz's driving skills. The adrenaline in our bodies skyrocketed . . .

One night we tried getting into the Los Angeles Zoo and Botanical Gardens, aiming to free the gorillas but found ourselves face to face with two very frightened and trigger-nervous young guards. We fled the scene as fast as we could, two gunshots going off behind us.

I was terrified one of my friends was hurt. Fortunately, they were not. We met at our regular rendezvous, and discovered that Buzz and Doug had fought one of the guards and managed to steal his gun away. Now it was sitting in Buzz's glove compartment.

We thought we could outsmart everyone, we thought we were invincible, but something was bound to happen. It was my idea and the flashback is vivid today as if it happened only yesterday.

We are sitting in Buzz's car. We stop near a police car. Jerry puts his arm out of the window, holding a bottle of Jack Daniels, acting drunk. He asks the cops for direction to the nearest whorehouse. That starts a 10-minute car chase. The cops chasing us calls for backup and soon two police cars are chasing us. At the last minute, we realize the cops have lured us into roads leading to a roadblock. Buzz tries to escape by taking the dark parallel gravel route. It is exhilarating. I am too high with adrenaline to notice Buzz missing the turn. The car is thrown into the air, hitting the ground 15 feet below us and flipping over repeatedly. I manage to notice one of the car's back doors flying away with Jerry's following it before the car bounces up into the air again and hits the ground. I lose consciousness.

I woke up in a private room with a concussion, some bruises and a broken finger. Doug, Buzz and Heather all had minor injuries, broken bones and open flesh wounds.

Jerry Montgomery Tucker, 17 years of age, died.

I had outdone myself this time and my sketchbook attained more images of the devil and my dark and evil soul . . .

We were all tested clean for alcohol and drugs. The case was reported in the national media and the police were kicked around for chasing some innocent kids for no reason and for causing the death of a 17 year old. Someone high in the LAPD even lost his job. Heather, Doug and I were released; Buzz was charged with reckless driving causing the loss of human life and was sent to four months in prison. At that point, my parents finally took charge over my life. "No more the nice guy approach with you Jennifer Svensen!" my mother scolded me when I returned home. "You are grounded until further notice!"

I was stuck at home, confined to my room for one whole month. The closet in my room with all my shoeboxes was locked and my car keys confiscated. Hanging over my head was my father's threat to send me to a boarding school in Switzerland if I dared act rebelliously or refuse my mother's instructions even once. If there was one thing I knew too well, it is that you don't mess around with my father when he gets angry; and let me tell you—Angus was pissed off to an extent unimaginable.

For the first time in her entire life, Mariana took time off from work and spent it with her only daughter. She tried to understand what had happened. Realizing I was not about to sing, she concluded the following: "Your life has taken the wrong turn, and I will steer it back in the right direction, so help me God!"

Overwhelmed with sadness and feeling responsible for the loss of a precious human life, I spent days lying in bed, bashing myself relentlessly for being born—for being what life had turned me into.

Chapter 7

The Suppressor

The 1982-1983 school year found me under strict supervision. Even busy diamond tycoon Angus Svensen was seen more at home now, spending time with me at the poolside, coming to visit me often in my room, taking us out to dinner—always trying to make conversation. I must admit that some of those conversations were quite moving. Having my father tell me he loved me more than anything led me to discover some hidden emotions I thought were nonexistent. On the outside, though, I kept projecting the indifferent brat image, believing he did not deserve to be treated better. Yet, the truth must be told: he *did* succeed in opening a small crack of the very tiny window leading to my heart.

The accident may have been a wake-up call for both my parents, but I was turning 17 and the interest they suddenly showed was a bit too late. Keeping them constantly aware of the grievance, so I believed, kept me always at an advantage so I continued behaving accordingly.

Jerry's death influenced our overall attitude towards life. We were now more reserved and cautious, but we did not give up on our basic right to have fun. Waiting for Buzz's release from prison, Doug, Heather and I explored the Punk scene in LA, still the only mental and musical environment I felt most comfortable with. This was also the point in time at which Heather introduced me to some socialist-communist literature like Marx and Engels' 'Communist Manifesto' or Vladimir Lenin's 'What is to be Done?' I found their theories fascinating and, as such, worth exploring. I watched documentary films and movies about the Communist Revolution. It fascinated me.

My parents were appalled by my choice of friends and their outrageous costumes. My mother, the ex-supermodel turned fashion executive, thanked God I had settled for the more reserved approach. She attributed this inclination to what I had absorbed at home—fashion-wise. I used to wear black, and in that sense I was Punk-compatible; but it was always the expensive designer skirts and shirts my mom used to buy or order especially for me. In fact, none of it had anything to do with what I had or hadn't absorbed at home; I simply did not find sense in the whole chains, bracelets and tattoos set-up. I simply didn't feel like making any kind of statement.

In light of my parents' new involvement in my life and my own acknowledgment of my personal faults, that year was the calmest I had ever experienced.

Life continued outside the narrow boundaries of my unimportant life. Lisa was serving her one-year expulsion from Beverly High, attending Fairfax and completing her rehabilitation program. I longed for her but time had diminished the intensity of the emotion to a bearable level. I truly believed I was becoming less of a fanatic. But, just as I thought things were going in the right direction, I bumped into someone who unintentionally set my life on a collision course with the world again . . . well, to be more exact—on a collision course with the whole universe . . . and for the rest of my life.

It was May 1983. Heather and I were attending a Punk party in the San Fernando Valley. The A-Holes, one of the most appreciated local Punk-Rock youth bands in LA, was playing Sex Pistols covers and we were all jumping around frantically and drunk.

I was making my way to the ladies' room unsteadily when a clean-cut, tall and painfully handsome teenager, wearing our school's athletic blue jacket, crossed the hall. I lost my breath. His face had an expression I saw often in men—a deep appreciation for my beauty. Yet, I detected something else, as well. I thought it was sheer surprise. Surprise at finding someone dressed down amongst those lunatics who were jumping up and down all around him to an appalling noise they had mistaken for music.

Suddenly, out of nowhere inside me, a profound anger erupted. I approached him as he passed by me. "Capitalists will vanish, you miserable pig!" I yelled at him. He was taken aback.

"Excuse me?" he replied with what I thought was a patronizing tone of voice.

"Don't you condescend to me, you arrogant, chauvinist asshole," I assaulted him on all fronts, feeling the booze controlling what came out of my mouth. "The world is filled with worthless capitalists like you. What the fuck are you doing at this party anyway? This is not a zoo. Did you come here to watch how the freaks have fun?" I said and got nearer and nearer to him, breathing in the wonderful scent of his cologne.

He took a step back. "My presence disturbs you?" He asked calmly, staring at me unflinchingly. I lost my capacity to speak for a moment. This guy had charisma in quantities unfamiliar to me, and the look of his remarkable eyes melted my heart.

"You're damn right it does," I managed to say breathless. "People like you exploit the poor; you suck the blood of the world's workers and run over the weak. You are human garbage. Punk will win!"

"You're drunk," he established. "I suggest you find someone to drive you home."

"And I suggest you take your friends and your capitalist blue jacket and get the hell out of here," I yelled at him. The condescending look he gave me before he turned and walked away made me explode with rage. Without comprehending what I was doing, I jumped on his back, wrapped both my legs around his waist, and locked my arms around his neck. "Death to the exploiters!" I screamed, "Punk will win!"

Everybody was looking at me now, clapping hands and cheering. Seconds later, two people disentangled us, leaving me sitting on the floor breathing heavily; failing to understand what had just happened.

Everything blurred.

I woke up in Heather's car. I had passed out. My friends rushed me away. I puked my guts out beside a nearby tree and then they took me home. Waking up in my bed the day after, suffering the worst hangover ever, I forgot all about the incident.

About a week later, circumstances brought me together again with the mystery boy of the week before. He showed up during a mandatory assembly in our school auditorium, choosing to sit in the row in front of mine.

"Who is this guy?" I asked the student sitting next to me.

"His name is Roy Cohen. I think he's a sophomore."

"How come I never saw him at school?"

He looked at me surprised. "The guy is a soccer genius. Don't you read the school paper? He scored the varsity's winning goal last Saturday against Santa Monica."

The fact left me indifferent and unimpressed. "Is there a girl in his life?" I asked impatiently and he gave me an answer that took me completely by surprise.

"I think he's connected to Lisa Epstein, although I'm not sure it's romantic."

'Not sure it's romantic' my sexy behind . . .!

My emotions flooded me, rising from the inside and suffocating me—proof that I was still very much in love with Lisa. This hunk was about to steal the object of my eternal love. *No fucking way!*

I'm walking to my car, day dreaming. My mind is running wild on the verge of short-circuiting. I'm hot for this guy all right and at the same time he is connected to my Lisa. I wonder how the hell I find myself tangled in these kinds of situations. A car horn startles me. I'm in the middle of road. I almost run over. A teenager in a black Datsun 280Z yells at me. I give him the finger and kick his front bumper, "Screw you, asshole . . ."

From this moment on everything happened fast.

I checked up on the hunk. His family had emigrated from Israel a few months earlier. Apart from playing for our school's varsity soccer team, he was also a gifted musician, and he was about to perform at the upcoming senior prom as the singer and rhythm guitarist of 'Expel,' an upcoming youth rock band.

But the fact I found most disturbing was that he was in love with Lisa. The only thing still working for me at this stage was that she had him on hold, claiming she was not ready for a romantic relationship during that complex period of her drug rehabilitation process.

I went to see him play soccer the following Saturday morning as part of my research. He was awesome, and he looked even hotter in shorts than in Levi's. It was there and then that I realized the gravity of the situation. This was obviously no ordinary guy. He was Mr. Perfect. The risk of letting him hang around Lisa was too great.

I had to do something fast. I had to come up with a plan to steer him away from her while it was still possible . . . But how?

Rudy, the team's goalie, had tried his luck with me a while ago. I thought he was a good place to start, so I started sending him some very inviting smiles. It was easier than I thought. One ridiculously quick blowjob in the back seat of his car opened the magical door of information. He told me everything I needed to know about Roy.

Apparently, his immigrant family didn't have the means to live in Beverly Hills and he was attending school thanks to his uncle's legal guardianship privileges. The most valuable piece of information I got was that Roy was looking for a summer job. He had just turned 16 and wanted to buy a car. I had a bold idea. My father was looking for a substitute driver for the summer period. Thomas, his faithful driver for 12 years, was about to leave for his homeland Italy with his family for two whole months. I could make this happen for Roy and draw him close, locking him in with the only good thing bestowed on me by nature—my looks. He was a teenager and, like all other teenage boys his age, had probably only one thing on his mind. I could give him enough to draw him away from the Queen of Sheba, Helen of Troy, certainly Lisa Epstein.

Now I had to convince my father.

Angus listened attentively without saying anything, but his face gave him away. He hated the idea. Nonetheless I continued. "You would insist that he'll live in our guest house all summer and be available 24/7."

"Jenny, honey, I can't have a 16 year old kid drive me around and run errands for me. I'm not even sure there's an insurance policy covering a minor working as a driver."

"Nothing is impossible!" I turned impatient. "You taught me that yourself."

"I don't like it!" he exclaimed. "And I hate the guest house idea. Why do you want him living in our guest house?"

"For once in your life, walk the extra mile for me . . . I think I'm falling in love with him and I have fierce competition. Am I not entitled to enjoy a normal life? Don't deny me the opportunity to have a decent boyfriend . . . I'm 17 years old . . ." he looked at me for a long while and then looked away. I knew him, he was about to surrender. "Daddy . . ."

He heaved a heavy sigh. "Okay . . . okay . . . but I want to interview him first. I've seen the types you bring home and if he is one of these punk freaks of yours, you can forget it."

I smiled with satisfaction, "Thanks Dad . . . I have a feeling you'll like this guy . . ."

I published the job details in the school paper and got Rudy to direct Roy's attention to the opportunity. Nina, my father's secretary, waited for Roy's telephone call while informing all the other appliers that the position was already taken. Roy eventually called and Nina set him up for the interview.

Things were going according to plan.

Now I had to look for someone to take me to the prom. Roy was about to perform there and I wanted to find the right opportunity to correct the horrible impression I had made. I got the name of a boy who had never been seen with a girl before. His name was Ashton and he almost fainted when I offered to be his date. He had won the lottery.

Prom night and we are moving around to greet some of Ashton's friends when I suddenly see Lisa. My heart is pounding painfully. She is so beautiful in her blue dress as she smiles her perfect smile to everyone. It moves me to the bones. I go over to greet her and we embrace. I stare at her most of the evening.

Although Lisa had come with Eric McLaughlin and rumor was that Roy had given up on her, she watched his awesome performance with so much love and admiration that I realized I had to act fast.

Roy performed incredibly. He played a wonderful rhythm guitar and he knew how to sing. There were moments I forgot about Lisa. I watched him hypnotized as he rocked the night away. He was so attractive and charismatic—it drove me crazy with desire. Regardless of my plan, I wanted him in my pants tonight.

When the band took a break, I followed Roy to the soft drinks counter. He grabbed a can of Coke and rushed out of the gym. I followed him quickly outside. I found him sitting on a bench by himself, sipping from the can, catching his breath, cooling his body.

"Hi," I said as I approached him.

"Hi," he replied and got to his feet. He looked at me carefully and I could clearly detect physical attraction in his body language. I was dressed in a short black and white dress, showing a lot of skin.

"Jenny," I said smiling. We shook hands.

"Roy," he replied.

"Actually, we know each other already," I said smiling.

"We do?" He asked, looking at me curiously.

"You are a capitalist pig, suppressor of the weak," I recited.

He laughed. "Yeah, I thought you were familiar. What's a socialist like you doing in this capitalist prom?"

"I'm the date of one of the suppressors," I replied and he smiled. "I go to this school too, you know. I'll be a senior myself next year."

He looked surprised. "I never saw you in school."

"Well . . . it's a huge place and I often skip classes," I explained. He looked at me with a look I knew too well and I smiled to myself with satisfaction. "Forgive me for the other night. I was a bit drunk."

"It was a memorable experience, I must admit."

"You gave quite a show tonight," I said, changing the subject.

"Thanks. I enjoyed every minute of it."

I sat on the bench. He sat beside me. I came right to the point. "Can I take you out to dinner or to a movie sometime?"

"Sure," he stammered perplexed by the bluntness. "It would be my pleasure," he replied smiling, pleased with himself for putting aside any preconceptions he may have had about women who are too forward.

"There will be no alcohol, I promise," I said, placing my hand on my heart.

He laughed. "Well, Jenny, I'm glad I met you sober," he said and got to his feet. "You're even more surprising when you're not drunk." The sudden and simple complement took me by complete surprise, but before I had time to react, he was getting up. "I have to get back on stage now."

And he was gone.

Chapter 8

Infatuation

I gave Ashton a long kiss on the lips in front of his friends as a show of gratitude for taking me to the prom. Then I escaped.

Excitement overwhelmed me. I did not fully understand the reason for such spiritual uplifting; but later on, as I analyzed the events, I realized that my body was sending me a message that was not entirely sexual and which I could not fully comprehend.

I rushed home, changed my dress into something more *comfortable* and drove my car back to school. I waited for about an hour until I spotted Roy walking out of the gym with a guitar case in his hand. I switched on the engine and drove ahead, stopping the car close to him. He stared at the Corvette with glowing eyes. I turned off the engine and stepped out of the car, barefoot. "I thought it was you," I said, walking closer to him.

"Wow, what a car!" he exclaimed. "You want to drive it?"

He looked at me with disbelief. "I would love to."

"Then pop right in," I said and threw the car keys up in the air. He caught them just in time, looking at me with disbelief. He shoved the guitar case into the small space behind the front seat and took the driver's seat. I opened up the T-top and threw its parts back over the guitar.

"Here, take this," I said and handed him a small pill he probably mistook for a mint. He threw it into his mouth. It was speed. I took one too. He turned on the engine. "So let's rock!" I stated joyfully and boosted the volume. Cheap Trick's 'I Want You to Want Me' from their Budokan Theatre concert exploded from the speakers. "Let's go," I said. He placed his hand on the shift and I placed mine on his, pulling it to drive.

The car jumped edgily ahead.

We drove through LA's streets fast. I was becoming ecstatic as the pill took effect. I completely forgot my plan. The long-lost adrenalin-inspired satisfaction and the unfamiliar feelings that were erupting inside of me were about to beat everything I had ever experienced. I urged Roy to drive faster and faster. He willingly carried out my request, turning into the Hollywood Freeway, increasing speed to levels I had never dared reach, slaloming his way through the Harbor Freeway. I lost touch with what was going on around me. I started reciting the Sex Pistols' 'I Wanna Be Me': *"And I'll take you down on the underground. . . . Down in the dark and down in the crypt. . . . Down in the dark where the typewriter fit . . . Down with your pen and pad ready to kill . . . To make me ill. . . ."*

I stood up on my seat, the upper part of my body outside the speeding car, stretching my hands in the air, screaming and laughing while Oingo Boingo's 'I'm on the Outside Looking In', blasts through the car's stereo loudspeakers . . .

I wake up to the sound of the car door slamming. The sun is shining and a beautiful view of the ocean is awaiting my appreciation.

Where the hell am I?

I am wearing the Beverly High blue athlete's jacket. Shit . . . Roy. I look out and see him gazing at the ocean, stretching his muscles. I take the car keys out of the switch and throw them into the glove compartment. I step out of the car and walk in his direction. I embrace him from behind.

"Good morning," I said, laying my head on his back, closing my eyes. "What a beautiful day."

"How did we get here?" he asked.

"We drove all night until you picked this spot opposite the ocean. You said you were beat. You fell asleep instantly."

"It's scary; I can't remember anything since we took the exit to the Harbor Freeway." I inserted my hand underneath his shirt and let it climb, rubbing his chest gently with my fingers.

"Excuse me," he said disengaging from my grip, walking to the water edge to relieve his bladder. As he sat back in the driver's seat, Roy realized the car keys were not where he had left them. He looked at my smiling face, figuring out the ambush I had prepared for him. He had landed right in it.

"We have to finish what we started," I said, taking off my panties.

"Jenny . . ." he said with a surprised look on his face.

"It's your turn now," I said as I took off my shirt. He smiled with approval, reclining his seat to a horizontal position and taking off his pants.

What happened next was the greatest fireworks show ever on the face of our planet. I have a sketch drawn on that same day trying to capture in chalk that groundbreaking event. A car is parked in front of the ocean—stars, explosions and fireworks bursting out of it.

It was the oldest trick in the book and it was obvious he would be coming back for more. I had no other choice. Lisa was about to return to Beverly High and Roy posed the greatest obstacle to my reunion. Being physically attracted to him was simply nature. What I found a bit scary, though, was the sudden longing, which started burrowing inside of me. It is one thing longing for the sex side of the equation, but the longing I felt for his proximity or company was beyond my capacity to understand. I found myself waiting impatiently for him to occupy the guesthouse.

When he finally did move in, he drove my father around for the day and then left the guesthouse before I could get to him. I waited impatiently for him to return. It was about 2:45 am when the guy finally returned to his new place. I put on my bikini and went straight to the pool. Chad, our German shepherd, barked happily when he saw me, wagging his tail. "Good boy," I told him, caressing his fur, "keep on barking." I jumped into the pool. I floated in the water, noticing that the curtains in the guesthouse were moving.

Roy was watching me.

It was far and dark enough for him not to recognize who was swimming in the pool. I smiled to myself with satisfaction. It was a matter of time until he would join me, so I believed. I fooled around in the pool for about five minutes, trying to be sexy, waiting for him to come out. But he didn't.

I emerged from the pool. The curtain was still open. I took off the top of my bikini and squeezed it dry. "Now, let's see him stay indifferent," I said to the dog sitting beside me.

The minutes passed and . . . nothing happened. "Okay . . . have it your way . . ."

Early the next morning, Roy had to drive my father to the airport. He reported for duty at about 8:30. My mom invited him to join us for breakfast. He was sitting at the table as I came down from my room, still in my very revealing nightgown.

"Roy Cohen. What a lovely surprise," I said and wrapped my hands around his shoulders, kissing his neck. The guy was astounded. He removed my hands and jumped up bewildered, connecting the dots, realizing who I was.

Dressed in a blue suite and a red tie, Lisa's guy looked good enough to eat.

"God . . . Jenny . . . what the hell . . ." I wrapped my arms around his neck and he took them off again. "No! Your parents can't know. Please. I need this job!" he said still very much staggered. It was hilarious seeing him so flabbergasted.

My mother came in. "I see you two have already met," she said, playing along. "Jennifer, honey; go up and put something more respectable on! We have a guest for breakfast," she said and walked into the kitchen, leaving us behind.

"We'll have the guesthouse all to ourselves this summer," I notified him with ever-growing excitement.

"They can't know . . . Please, Jenny, don't screw this job for me," he begged.

"Don't be silly. I want you around here more than anything."

"Go up and change before your mother returns!" he ordered.

"She is used to me . . ."

"Please, she will suspect," he said, looking tense, uncomfortable with the fact my gown was so transparent.

I laughed again. "Fine, but you owe me one," I said, kissing my finger, placing it on his lips.

Our new driver drove us to a café on Canon drive. We tried to convince him to join us, but he unequivocally refused, insisting he should act like a driver should.

"I've got to hand it to you, sweetheart," my mother said as we sat around the table. "You've chosen well this time—handsome, clean-cut, polite . . ."

"I know."

"How come?" She asked, curious to know the reason for my uncharacteristic choice.

"Because he is a great lay," I said.

"For God sake . . . Jennifer . . . I'm your mother . . ."

"Well, you know more about it than I do."

"Stop it!" She ordered with an offended look. I sipped my Pepsi, and looked out the window. Roy was standing by the Benz, tall and impressive. There was a moment of silence. "Be careful," she advised. I nodded. "Look," she said after another minute of silence, "I know I'm not the best role-model, but you're my daughter and you're still very young. I don't want you to make the kind of mistakes I've made when I was not much older than you are today."

"You mean having me?" I threw at her.

"Of course not!" she said defensively, "I meant having sex at your age."

I looked at her with piercing eyes, smiling a vicious smile. "Mom, I lost my virginity when I was 15." She looked away angrily, confused, utterly dumbfounded and lost for words. I was enjoying every second. "Look at me!" I ordered and she did. "I was five fucking years old when you started bringing all those stinking men home, mom." I said to her. I took a big gulp of air to calm my rising emotions. "If anything, I'd say you initiated my sex education a bit too *early*, rather than too *late*, don't you think?"

"You hate me, don't you?" she whispered conclusively.

"No." I said. "I don't." she looked at me with sadness. "I just can't forgive you for stealing my childhood away." She said nothing for a while, sipping from her coffee—sad and gloomy. "You see this guy?" I said to her. She followed my gaze with hers.

"Roy?"

I nodded. "This guy is my chance to start over, to have, for the first time in my pathetic life, something normal to cling to." She nodded in agreement. I looked at her again. "I need you to help me make it work."

Chapter 9

Eruption

Later that day we dropped Roy at the guesthouse and drove to my mom's gynecologist. I was now 'on the pill.'

When we returned home, it was late afternoon. I put on my bikini and rushed to the guesthouse. I climbed up the stairs to Roy's room and saw him sleeping like a baby. I thought of surprising him with something nice to eat when he woke up. While cooking the soup, I began to grasp how his presence was affecting me. Looking at the boiling soup, I suddenly realized that outrageous, reckless and sometimes violent Jennifer Svensen was actually preparing a romantic dinner. "Lord, help me . . ." I whispered to myself with a smile.

"What's cooking?" I heard Roy's voice over my shoulder.

"We're having Italian minestrone," I said, hanging my hands around his neck.

He stared at me. "You knew all along, didn't you?"

"Uh huh . . ." I admitted and started moving him to the sound of the beat of the song playing on the stereo.

"What are we going to do about it?" he asked.

"About what?"

"About the fact that I work for your father and that I live in this guesthouse, only two hundred feet from where your parents sleep at night."

"We are young and we are allowed to make foolish mistakes. Our parents will always forgive us," I said with a naughty smile.

"Jenny, we need to keep this discrete. I need this job. I am not a rich kid like you. I'm saving to buy a car."

I placed my head on his shoulder. "Don't worry. I won't tell."

"Where do you want this to go?" he asked.

"Nowhere special, let's take it one step at a time."

"I am in love with someone else. I don't want to mislead you," he informed me candidly.

"I know. Lisa Epstein. You'll get over her," I said matter-of-factly. At that moment, the soup boiled over and the sound of burning liquid cut short our dance. I rushed back to the kitchen.

He sat at the table as I served. I sat opposite to him.

"I've been in love with Lisa forever and I can't get over her. You should be aware of that!"

"And yet, here you are, with me and she goes to the prom with Eric," I viciously reminded him. He reclined in his seat, chewing the bread, looking at me undecided. "Reality sucks, doesn't it?" I stuck the knife deeper and twisted it further.

He got closer, hypnotizing me with his dark, magnetic green eyes. "What do you want from me, Jennifer Svensen?"

"I don't know. It feels good being around you." I confessed truthfully. "That's all."

"I can't promise anything."

"I know. I can't either."

"So is it just physical?"

"Let's explore this for a while. Why establish that now?" I suggested.

"Okay . . . but we have to set some ground rules," he said, "I need this job and I like your parents. I don't want them to know about us. We can go out together, but we can't have sex here."

"You are overreacting. Knowing me, my parents probably assume I will hunt you down."

"It's too risky!" he concluded. I looked at him with only one thing on my mind. He mentioned sex and I was burning with desire. "Thanks for the soup." He said. "I'm going to Ben's café; would you like to join me?"

"Yeah, sure," I said, loving the idea that he had offered me to tag along.

"Go change! I'll take a shower and meet you outside in fifteen minutes," he said and went up the stairs.

I cleared the table, placed the dishes in the sink. Then, I took off my cloths as I walked up the stairs. I got into the shower with him, smiling with excitement.

"You are unbelievable," he laughed, looking at my body with longing.

"I can see my presence makes you very happy," I said observing his uprising bodily change.

"Well, I'm going to lose this job anyway, so I might as well enjoy it while I can," he said and pulled my body closer to his.

We met his friends at Ben's place. I saw disapproval in their eyes as we walked in hand in hand. They smiled fake smiles and were nice to me for Roy's sake. Frankly, I couldn't care less: I was on a mission and that was all that mattered.

The trouble was that, as the days passed and we spent more time together in bed and out, my sense of direction blurred to something unfocused and unclear. Having a sweet, kind and very hot teenager hold me in his arms whenever I wanted, show me compassion whenever I needed, caress my hair, hold my hand, embrace me warmly and whisper kind words, steered me completely off course. I was amazed to discover how much I wanted this guy near me. It thrilled me as much as it frightened me, because instantly and without doing anything special to achieve it, Roy was having a huge influence over me.

It got worse. This incredible young man, who by his second week of employment earned both my parents trust and affection, now held my heart in the palm of his hand. One morning, I burst into a painful cry. I couldn't understand the reason for such an outburst of emotions. It was like a volcano erupting inside of me. It happened when Roy left for work that morning, leaving me lying in bed, yearning for him. I found myself crying, hugging his pillow.

What the hell is happening to me?

The emotions left no room for misinterpretation. I had fallen in love. All I wanted was to be a tiny blood-drop traveling inside his veins, making my way inside his blood-cycle, going in and out of his heart. It seemed that I had fallen in love with both a girl and a boy who loved each other more than they loved me. Tell me if there is anything more bizarre and pathetic.

I waited for him to fall for me. I thought it would happen sooner or later because we were spending a lot of time together, and it was obvious he truly enjoyed being with me.

Roy was also the first human being I found it easy to talk to. We talked for hours about all kinds of things. He said he found my somewhat dark worldview intriguing and that he had never met anyone my age with such animosity and spite. *You should see my sketches*, I thought to myself. He offered me a different angle—a positive and moving one, one lacking the cynicism I was so used to. He spoke of values and moral standing that rested on principals and high ethical standards. No one had ever talked to me about anything using this kind of terminology, let alone truly believed in it.

"I'm no goody two shoes," he said to me one night, after I commended him for being a man of values. "I slept with my best friends' girl."

"That's pretty low . . ." I said.

"Yeah . . . it is. She caught him cheating on her and seduced me to get back at him. My whole set of principals collapsed when she took off her clothes. After we were done she claimed men were all the same—facing a beautiful woman, we think with our pricks."

"I like this girl," I said laughing. "I don't know about other men, but she sure was right about you." He wasn't smiling when I said that and he turned to the other side of the bed in a show of resentment. "Oh, come on, Roy. Give yourself a break; we're only human."

Eventually, he turned back to face me, looking offended and apprehensive. "There was no excuse for what I did . . . no excuse!"

Well, disgraceful as it was, at least I had found something in Roy's past that made him human; up until that moment, the guy seemed to be too perfect.

One of the things Roy was not able to understand was my animosity towards my parents. I never told him about my childhood or about their many faults; I just treated them rudely, and whenever we got to talk about one or both of them, I had the same facial expression—one of anger and disrespect. One night he pushed me too hard on the matter. I could not understand why, but he insisted on knowing why I was so mean and disrespectful to 'such wonderful people.'

"Such wonderful people, my ass . . ." I barked at him emotionally, "You know nothing whatsoever about us."

"Then tell me," he said. I could not control my emotions. He looked at me as if I was just an ungrateful brat.

"It's none of your business!" I said harshly. "Stay out of it!"

"I'll tell you what," he said. "How about me staying out of your life?" I burst into tears. All the pain and frustration of years of neglect exploded at once. He embraced me. "Shh, baby, I'm sorry, I didn't mean to hurt you."

It took him some time to calm me down. I hugged him tightly, wrapping my legs around his waist, securing his physical attachment to me.

There was a long silence, which I broke first. "Don't be fooled by what you see in this house. Everything here is a fake. In this house, we all go around in masks. It's all one big and ugly fiasco. Everybody cheats on everybody. Everybody is only thinking of number one." I disconnected myself from him and sat on the bed. "I took drugs, drowned myself in alcohol, slept around, saw a shrink. I used to be bulimic; you name it—I had it." He sat beside me. I rested my arm around his shoulders, looking at him helplessly. "Will you be my friend?"

"I *am* your friend," he whispered and kissed my forehead.

The next morning, I wake up with a painful longing that burns me from inside. I call my dad's secretary and get the number of the company in Pomona, where my father has a meeting. Emotional, I call and ask for my father. I beg him to give Roy a day off. He hears the distress in my voice and sympathizes but his day is packed with meetings. They can't drive back home for another six hours. I put the phone down; and suddenly I'm short of breath and in a complete panic. I believe that something is very wrong with me. I'm becoming a nervous wreck and it is obvious to me that the only remedy is Roy's proximity. I call Angus again, crying, asking him to cancel the rest of the day and bring Roy to me as soon as possible. He promises to do so. I wait with a beating heart for two hours until they rush into the guesthouse. I glue myself to Roy for a very long time, embracing him tight, not willing to let go. They are concerned. I am too.

On Sundays, we hiked. We climbed huge trees and jumped rocks into lakes. We made love in all sorts of places. It was obvious he found me exciting. He had never done these kinds of adrenaline-enhancing activities. For him, riding the Colossus at Six Flags was an uppermost superior form of excitement. It struck me as odd that I, of all people, found this kind of juvenile humility and modesty so appealing. Or was it the fact that at this point of our relationship, I was simply so much in love with the guy that I just found everything about him appealing?

The sense of normalcy he managed to insert into my life was also a complete first. I was into a boy now, not a girl; and I craved his proximity, not only the sex. Nor did normalcy stop there. Roy was smart, talented and handsome; but the pre-Roy Jennifer would never have considered him exciting or fun. The little adventures we had together were always initiated by me. If it were up to Roy, we would sit by the pool, swim a little and listen to some music, or catch a movie. At best, he would pull out his acoustic guitar and sing some love song to me.

Boring right? Well, wrong! Dead wrong! With him around, acting like any other normal creature on earth was wonderful. I guess the state of mind known as 'Love' had conquered my world and changed it to the extent that I found everything about my new lover amazing.

The fact that my parents were utterly in love with Roy was a mind-blowing first for everybody. They knew we were fucking like crazy in their guesthouse and did nothing about it. By now, they probably realized that the alternative would have been much worse. In jolly retribution, Roy's respect and appreciation for my parents—especially my father—moved them. He was only 16, and he managed to completely conquer our hearts and minds in a matter of weeks . . . easily, by simply being himself! They had never seen him play soccer or perform on stage to capture his exceptional talents; they simply loved the modesty, the hard-working nature, the honesty and the politeness of this young Israeli kid. Above all, so I believe, they appreciated the fact he was around their reckless, troublemaker, rude and problematic daughter.

They were right—more than they would ever know.

They would have loved him even more if they had known about an incident that almost cost me our relationship. It revealed a hidden side of Roy—one that would burst out only in extreme situations.

It was during his fourth week working for us. Roy had left for work very early in the morning. I woke up at about 9 am, made myself a cup of coffee and read a magazine for about an hour. A sudden craving for marijuana started nagging me. I felt like getting high. I took the bunch of grass I hid behind the video cassettes in the guesthouse' living room cabinet, rolled myself a joint and smoked it at leisure. I closed my eyes for about a minute or so, enjoying the sensation. When I opened them, I saw Roy staring at me with astonishment. I placed the joint on the ashtray.

"What the hell are you doing?"

"I . . . I . . . I don't do this often . . . Roy . . . I just wanted to cool myself a bit." His face was turning all red now. It was scary. He grabbed my hand and held it so forcefully I screamed with pain. "*Cool* yourself a bit," he yelled at me and started pulling me up the stairs. "I'll give you something to cool yourself a bit." The pain in my wrist was so overwhelming that I could not react. I just followed him up the stairs in hope he would ease his ruthless grip if I would not resist. He opened the bathroom's door and pushed aside the shower' curtain, shoving me aggressively inside, pulling my wrist down, sitting me on the floor. He pulled the showerhead, turned the cold-water handle until a strong stream of water flowed out at my body, hair, face, arms and legs. I was too shocked to respond.

"Here, I'll cool you down a bit," he yelled at me furiously. I placed both my hands over my head and looked down while he kept directing the water at me. "Are you cool enough now?" he yelled. "Are you?" I trembled all over. It was freezing cold.

After a long minute, he stopped the flow of water, positioned the showerhead back in its place and stood there looking at me with disappointment written all over his face. I looked up and saw a young man dressed in a suit, looking at me with a sad and disillusioned face, and I loved him more that second than I ever did. That teenager boy, the one I had fallen in love with, cared for me. Nobody, not even my parents, had ever cared for me that much.

He took a long breath of air and looked away while I remained on the floor, bent, trembling, embracing my legs with my hands, looking at him with anticipation. He pulled a clean towel out of the closet and offered me his hand. I used it to stand up. He helped me take off my soaking wet shirt and panties and then covered me with the long towel. He lifted me up and carried me inside. I looked into his eyes all the way to bed apologetically. He sat on the bed and placed me gently on his laps. I wrapped my arms around his shoulders, still shivering. We kissed a long and meaningful kiss, after which I placed my head on his shoulder.

"Roy . . .," I whispered after a long silence. "Please don't be mad at me."

He looked at me calmly but wearing a very serious facial expression. "If you ever touch this stuff again, I'm out of your life for good. Am I clear enough?" he said. I nodded. He got up, took his jacket off, revealing a stained shirt, probably the reason he had returned home. He changed it, tied a new tie and left without saying another word.

The experience made me look up to him. Not only did he care but he showed me his tough, uncompromising, assertive side— the first human being in my entire life who had successfully exerted authority upon me. I was ready to submit to whatever he wished, wherever, whenever.

And talk about my adrenaline rush during his outburst!

I have dedicated no less than thirty-three sketches to that incident throughout the years. In most, Roy is portrayed as a divine figure and I as a profound sinner.

That night, after making passionate love, he got up from bed and put his shirt and shorts on. "Put your clothes on and come down!" He commanded. I did as he asked and rushed downstairs.

It was about 2:15 am. He was holding a glass of water in his hands. "I hope you're not about to splash it on me," I said smiling, trying to make a joke, hoping to ease up the tension. He didn't smile.

"Where do you keep it?" he asked.

"Keep what?"

"Do you think I'm playing games with you?" he asked harshly. I shook my head. "Where do you keep the stuff?" I opened the cabinet door and pulled out the nylon bag. He took it from me. "Stay here! I'll be right back," he ordered as he opened the door and walked out. I saw him walk to the alley. I rushed up the stairs to the second floor and looked out the window as Roy dropped $400 worth of grass stuffed in a nylon bag, into a trashcan.

A few nights later, I had my supplier drop off a small shipment in that same alley. It was around 3:30 am and Roy was sound asleep. *"Sorry, Roy,"* I said to him silently as I embraced his warm naked, sleeping, body. *"With the overwhelming emotions I experience around you—I just have to cool myself off every so often."*

Chapter 10

My Place Under the Sun

A brief account of my life thus far would bring one to the unmistakable conclusion that my plans never work. Now, the stakes were high and I had to be super-careful. I was terrified of losing this once-in-a-lifetime opportunity of being connected to a person like Roy. Therefore, I decided not to plan anything. I would go along with whatever he wanted until I felt our relationship was stable and secure enough.

On the last day of July 1983, my father handed his temporary driver an envelope containing his first salary . . . in cash! Angus Svensen was very generous, even compensating Roy for the twice-a-week gig at Ben's place he had to give up in order to be available 24 hours a day. Roy's eyes shined with joy. He smiled blissfully as he glanced at the envelope's contents. It was evident my father was moved by Roy's somewhat childlike response.

Being so filthy rich, I never had to think twice about money. I had almost four times the amount Roy received that day for working a whole month sitting in my drawer, not to mention the thousands of dollars sitting in my shoe boxes or the fortune my father held in my trust fund.

"Hold on to him," Angus said as we walked back to the house, leaving Roy behind in the guesthouse. "You don't see boys like him around often."

This was one time I agreed with my father wholeheartedly, "I guess I finally did something right," I said.

"Yes, Jenny. You sure did . . ." he said. "If I had a son, Roy would be the kind I would want him to resemble." I stopped walking. My father did the same. My heart was beating fast. "Are you okay?" he asked. I just nodded, fighting my emotions.

Jesus . . . what has become of me?

Yet, in the final summation, what drove me crazy about my boyfriend was his goddamn honesty. Roy insisted on constantly reminding me of his never fading love for Lisa. *I mean . . . come on . . . give me a fucking break.* By now, he knew I was head over heels in love with him and he was coming in and out of my body whenever he felt like it. Wasn't this enough to get over a woman who would not consider having a serious relationship with him? I remember agonizing over it and wanting to scream at him, *I want you! She doesn't! Can't you get it into your seemingly intelligent head?*

But I never did.

One day my father asked me to join him and my mother for a family weekend at Palm Springs. I rejected the idea. I would not miss a minute away from Roy and weekends were his days off. Being wise, he offered to bring Roy along but Roy turned me politely down when I suggested the possibility. He said his parents would never approve, and anyway, it would be too awkward and too obvious. He would spend the whole weekend wondering what my parents thought we were doing in his room.

I made the stupid mistake of laughing. "It won't make any difference to them, you silly child," I said, "You don't really believe they think we're playing checkers in your bed every night." This just pushed him further into the corner, and I had to spend about an hour to convince him to let me spend the night with him.

But not a man like my father, who never let an opportunity slip by, would give up that easily. He asked Roy to join him for an evening swim and succeeded in convincing him to join our family vacation. He went further than that. When he heard Roy's parents were not so happy about him also spending his weekend away from home, he bought them flowers, drove to their house and managed to convince them Roy was doing him a great personal favor by joining.

We got to Palm Springs on Thursday evening. After checking into our hotel rooms, my father took us to a seafood restaurant. Roy told us some funny stories from behind the scenes at the Beverly High soccer team. My parents were enjoying themselves, laughing, relaxing and having a good time. My mother adored Roy. She would look at him in a certain way that at one point embarrassed me. She was probably thinking, 'if he was ten years older . . .' but he wasn't and he was mine and I resented the looks . . . or maybe I was just imagining . . . jealousy—another emotion I was getting used to with regards to Roy and Lisa.

I could tell that my father's exceptionally good mood actually came from loving the fact that I was on cloud number nine. He looked at me smiling from time to time, and I allowed myself to smile back, letting him know that inviting Roy for our family vacation was a great idea and he deserved the credit.

We dropped my parents off at the hotel that evening and drove to a bar Roy knew from previous visits with his friends. They played live music, and that specific night was a special classical Rock night. A group named The Devil's Advocates was playing covers of the finest rock groups ever. Afterwards, we kissed good night at my doorstep and he went to his room. I took a shower, got my white shower robe on and walked back to his room. The guy actually tried to block my way in, for God's sake.

"Jenny, you promised," he said when he opened the door, blocking the entrance to his room with his body.

"Come on," I said smiling, "you knew I was not going to keep that promise. Let me in!"

"You're unbelievable . . ." he whispered in disbelief, "what if your parents decide to look for you?"

"They won't. They'll assume I'll be spending the night in your bed," I said and pushed the door open. He closed the door behind us and locked it.

I took off my robe and got into bed. He sat on the bed beside me, looking at me with disbelief, shaking his head. I took his hand and placed it on my boob. He fondled it. I closed my eyes as the wonderful sensations of pleasure rose up from inside my body. He suddenly stopped. I opened my eyes and looked at him disappointed. "You know what . . . you're unbelievable . . . really . . . Roy . . . who in his right mind would turn out a beautiful, ripe, sexy woman and refuse to have sex with her?" I asked with frustration. He just looked at me somberly. I heaved a sigh and sat beside him. "Okay, spit it out."

"Nothing," he replied, gazing forward.

"It's Lisa Epstein, isn't it?" He nodded his head in confirmation. "So, what are you going to do about it?"

"I don't know. It's over between us but I can't get her out of my mind."

"Jesus, Roy. Your honesty is killing me. Would you please stop being so candid? Can't you lie a little? For *my* sake," I said with growing annoyance. He smiled and embraced me.

"I feel like I'm misleading you and I hate it," he said.

"No, you are not. I enjoy our time together. Anyway, in a few weeks, you'll fall madly in love with me and forget all about her." He nodded. That was enough for me. "Now, I am as hot as an oven; what are you going to do about it?"

On Saturday morning, we drove to a shopping mall. I had to get some cosmetics and asked my mother to help me find them. We decided to split and meet again at the same spot in an hour. Later, we met my father. Roy didn't show up. My father said he saw him enter a musical instruments shop nearby, so we all made our way there. Walking into the shop, we saw Roy sitting down with an electric guitar on his lap, jamming with some other musicians. He sounded awesome, so we just stood there enjoying the music until he got up all startled, looking at his watch. My mother placed her hand on his shoulder and asked him to play some more.

Watching Roy play the guitar, my father's eyes sparkled with excitement. The mediocre musician of Bergen's Ugly Vikings came to life. He stood there hypnotized, watching the musicians jam together. Later, he told Roy he thought he was incredibly talented.

"Wait until you hear him sing," I bragged.

"This is the best guitar I have ever played on," Roy told the shop assistant when he handed it back to him. He looked at the instrument with admiration as we left. It was a black American Standard Fender Stratocaster and as you will find out later on, it has a special place in our family's History.

When we returned to LA, my father showed me that same guitar lying on his bed. He had secretly purchased it for Roy. It was the first time in years I hugged him voluntarily and unreservedly. "It will be our present for his loyal service," he said, surprised by my show of compassion and rather emotional himself.

My friendship with Roy became tighter the following weeks. We spent all of his free time together. I eased up on the adventures, and his friends began getting used to the idea that I was Roy's girl. They started giving me a break.

I recollect an enjoyable evening with Roy's friends at a party. Roy and I are in a swimming pool. I'm in my panties and bra and Roy is in there with me in his underwear shorts. We are the only people in the pool and we're dancing tight to the sound of the beat and kissing. It's the Doobie Brothers 'Long Train Running' and all eyes are upon us.

I was calm and happy and in love. I was seeing reality through a new and exciting set of lenses. The future was looking in a different, brighter light. Being so much in love released all the demons, hatred and resentment I had cultivated for years. My soul had found a perfect alternative for my once dark and hopeless existence.

The month of August rushed by us like a rocket ship on its way to Mars. I was getting grouchy by the day, realizing Roy had to relocate back to his parents' apartment. "I'll ask my dad to speak to your parents," I said to him. "They only live twenty minutes away . . ."

He smiled lovingly and caressed my hair. "My mom regrets letting me stay here all summer, as it is. Even your father's magical persuasive skills won't work this time." I looked at him disappointed. "I'm just moving a few blocks away. You're not getting rid of me that easily."

"I want you near," I said annoyed.

"Come on . . . it's not the end of the world."

I looked at his face with dread—the paralyzing fear of losing him. "It is for me."

On Roy's very last evening as my father's driver, my parents took us out to dinner. I felt so bad I hardly touched my food. My father saw I was a nervous wreck. He understood the reason. It was the end of something wonderful and nobody could guarantee it would continue.

"You're keeping the keys to the guesthouse!" he said to Roy decisively. "Come and go as you wish."

Roy smiled gratefully. "Thanks . . . your trust means a lot to me."

"Oh. I completely forgot," my father said and lifted something neatly wrapped. "This is for you."

Roy opened his present. It was a book about Leo Fender, the founder of the Fender musical instruments company. Roy was ecstatic as he turned the pages, taking in the photos of the legendary guitars the company had produced over the years.

"Wow. I don't know how to thank you. What a wonderful gift." Roy said.

"Imagine how he's going to react when we give him the guitar," my father whispered as our courses arrived.

Later that night, Roy was packing his things when my parents came up the stairs to our bedroom. My father handed Roy the envelope containing his final salary. I was very excited and emotional, waiting impatiently for him to give Roy the guitar. I could not believe what these past two months had turned me in to.

"We'll all miss you. You are a part of our family, and you are welcome in our house whenever you choose to come," my father said.

"I'll come and visit. Your daughter will make sure of that," Roy replied, and my father smiled, looking at me, realizing how nervous I was.

"Okay, we'll leave you two alone now, but before we do," Angus said, rubbing his hands with glee, "please open the closet." Roy looked baffled. He turned his gaze towards me for a sign or explanation. I just smiled with shivering lips, urging him with a head gesture to do what my father had asked him. He got up and opened the closet's door.

His open mouth and shining eyes were the reaction we were all hoping for. Roy was bewildered. "You didn't . . ." he said excited, touching the black Fender guitar case.

He took the case out and placed it gently on the bed, looking at my parents with disbelief. They were enjoying every second. He opened the case. The black Stratocaster he'd played in the mall in Palm Springs, was lying there, new, shining—all his. It was obvious he was struggling with his emotions. My mother embraced him.

"I don't know what to say," he said when my mother freed him. "This is a dream come true. I can't thank you enough. Please take this out of my salary."

My father laughed. "You don't pay for presents. Enjoy it," he said and gave him a fatherly hug.

"We'll leave you two alone now," my mother said and they left, leaving Roy staring at the guitar in disbelief.

I rubbed his neck. "I love you," I confessed for the first time ever. He looked at me with compassion but said nothing. "You don't have to reciprocate. I know you are still confused. But I have fallen in love with you, and you need to know that."

He looked at me overwhelmed with emotions, pulled me into his arms and embraced me tightly.

Chapter 11

Stinging Reality

The first few weeks of the 1983-1984 school-year found me displaying my new boyfriend to all those stuck-up, arrogant rich sluts in school who had always looked at my punk friends with condescending eyes. What a great feeling: reckless, aggressive, ill-mannered Jennifer Svensen had won the heart of one of the most admired students in school. It was obvious from the envious looks I got that I had struck oil. To twist the knife in their chests even deeper, I glued myself to Roy like a leach. I was all over him every single second during every single break for everyone to see—embracing, sitting on his laps, kissing him, caressing his hair. Luckily, Roy played along. He seemed to enjoy the attention.

Lisa was back at school after serving her one-year expulsion from Beverly High. Seeing that beautiful creature for the first time in ages brought back some old feelings I thought were dead and gone. It frightened me to realize I had no control whatsoever on those deep and burning emotions.

I sometimes think I should have gotten a whole page in the Guinness Book of Records for the category of 'the only fool who was (1) in love with two people at the same time, (2) in love with two people from two different sexes, (3) in love with two people who love each other instead of loving her.

Funny isn't it?

Hell no! It was torture.

Lisa was a constant reminder of Roy's feelings for her. To his credit, he stopped mentioning it for the time being and, although he never told me he loved me, I was hopeful our intense relationship had eased up his deep emotional attachment to that perfect girl.

Dead fucking wrong!

We were walking through the school's parking lot to Roy's new Sirocco when Lisa drove by in her Porsche. She didn't see us; but, seeing her, Roy's mood changed abruptly. His happy, smiling face turned instantly dark and despondent. I felt a sharp and poisoned arrow shoot straight through my heart. I said nothing; but it was the biggest warning sign thus far that the situation was explosive.

I was out of ideas. What else could I do? I was hoping he would use his common sense. A bird in the hand . . . As I contemplated it back then, I concluded that I was safe for the time being. On the one hand, he had beautiful, smart and loving Jennifer granting him everything a teenager dreams about; on the other, there was Lisa Ann-Epstein, who not long ago had refused his quest for intimacy and rewarded his friendship by going to the prom with Eric.

The trouble was that I miscalculated the magnitude of the emotions involved.

A few weeks down the line, still hoping Roy was on the right track falling deeply in love with me, we made passionate love. It was about midnight. Roy seemed preoccupied with something.

"What's wrong?" I asked, lying on my side of the bed. "You're not yourself tonight."

"I saw Lisa today," he replied. I stopped fondling his belly and moved away from him so he wouldn't catch me fighting the urge to break down and cry. I wanted to hit him with my fists and scream at him until we both lost consciousness.

"I thought you were over her," I managed to whisper.

He embraced me, placing his head on my shoulder. "You're the best thing that happened to me since I moved to America," he whispered in my ear, trying as always to make me feel better.

"Yeah . . . sure I am," I answered, feeling my eyes getting moister by the second.

"You're kind, and loving. I'm hurting you and it's killing me."

"You're not over her?"

"I'm sure I'll get over her someday."

I turned toward him and embraced him forcefully, knowing he was making a promise he couldn't keep, realizing I had lost this game to someone who wasn't even playing.

I made love to him aggressively, crying all through until I climaxed. Then, I got up, took a shower and left without saying another word. It was over. I was shattered. The pain was so immense I couldn't breathe. I had to relieve it somehow, but even pot didn't help this time. I had to find a way to escape.

And escape I did—in the worst possible manner. The next day I called my supplier and asked for something heavier. I picked it up near a deserted factory in the San Fernando Valley at about 9 pm, getting some user instruction on turning powder into liquid, the right quantity to use and where exactly in my body to inject it. "Stick it behind the knee," he suggested, "that way it would be unnoticeable."

An hour later, in my bedroom, I was turning the hydrochloride salt into liquid, mixing the powder with some water on a spoon and heating it with a cigarette lighter. Then I took the syringe out of its sterile nylon bag and sucked in the liquid. I tied a scarf just above my knee and search for a vein behind it. It took a few tries during which I started bleeding both outside my skin and underneath it; but eventually I found the right vein and injected the syringe's content into it. The stuff kicked-in in about 20 seconds. I lay my body upon my bed, lost all understanding of where I was or what I was doing and drifted off. When I opened a sleeping eye I found myself tucked into the safest place in the world—Roy's arms. When I opened them again he was gone. I figured it was part of the wonderful world of heroin.

I stayed home that day, telling my mother I was sick and felt weak. The truth was I couldn't face Roy. I did not answer phone calls, knowing it was probably him concerned about my absence from school. I tried to read a book but couldn't concentrate. The unbearable longing for my boyfriend was painful and impossible to handle, so I threw my body back to bed.

Roy came into my room that afternoon while I was trying unsuccessfully to read again. I did not greet him or move my gaze.

He sat on a chair in front of me, looking at me silently for some time. I fought the urge to lift my eyes from the open book.

"Let's go out for a ride," he finally suggested.

"I don't feel like it."

"Look, I didn't come here to fight," he said softly.

"Then why did you come?"

"You're my girlfriend . . ."

"Am I?"

"I never misled you. You knew all along I was having a difficult time getting over her," he said. That took me off balance. Anger and frustration attacked from all over. I stood on my feet, threw the book away and looked at him with tears in my eyes. I was in rage, confused, at a loss for action, at a loss for words.

I took off my clothes and stood in front of the man I loved, naked. "Come on. Fuck me. It's all I'm good for. What are you waiting for, Mr. 'I'm not fucking over Lisa.'"

Roy was shocked. He started collecting my clothes from the ground and approached me slowly. "It was never just the sex; you know it wasn't. Please don't do this," he said quietly. I took a step back. "You know you mean a lot to me."

"Do you love me?" I cried like a little girl, dying to hear a positive reply. He just stood there, speechless. "Do you fucking love me?" he remained standing silently, looking at me with pity. "Say something," I cried. He remained silent. "Please, Roy, say something." The guy remained speechless. I collected myself, took a deep breath of air. "Get the fuck out of here. I don't want to see you ever again," I said with the nastiest look I had ever mustered.

"But, I . . ."

"Get out of here," I screamed at him. He left my clothes on the chair and took a few steps backward. He looked at me with sadness for a long minute and then left.

I entered a complete deadlock, overwhelmed with grief; I couldn't function. I remained at home for about a week. I wouldn't talk to anyone. Roy called a few times but I refused to take his calls. I just could not face him anymore, knowing he was not capable of loving me.

A family dinner. I'm staring at my plate with an empty look, trying to figure out what the hell made me leave my room to sit with my parents for dinner in the first place. My father is talking to me. Much as I try, I can't make anything of what comes out of his mouth. I cannot speak or eat. I can hardly breathe. The next thing—a doctor is checking me while I lie in my bed. It's scary. I realize that about an hour of my life has been erased from my memory and can never be salvaged.

I dragged myself to school the following week, knowing life had to go on, promising myself to stay hopeful and open-minded. I took Heather to Ben's place to watch Roy perform. We entered as he started performing and left before he was done. I just couldn't face him. Heather also accompanied me to one of his soccer games. I had to see him, even if from a distance.

I sat there at the end of the match enjoying my last seconds of proximity to the boy I loved so much when he spotted me. He rushed up to the gallery and asked Heather to excuse us while we talked in private. I nodded, so she did.

"I'm sorry," he said, sitting by my side.

"What are you sorry about?" I asked, still gazing forward, avoiding eye contact.

"I'm sorry for being such an asshole."

"Well. You can't help it," I replied.

I caught him smiling with the corner of my eye. "Yeah, I guess I can't," he said and I couldn't keep a straight face anymore . . . so I smiled.

"That's my girl," he said, assuming he had broken the ice. "Can I see you again?"

I turned at him with a straight face. "Are you over her?"

"I don't know," he replied.

"Do you love me?"

"God . . . Jenny . . . why do you have to make things so complicated?" He asked with frustration.

"Do you love me?" I insisted. The guy remained speechless. "Then fuck you, Roy Cohen," I said calmly as I got to my feet, rushing home for a fix.

Chapter 12

The Grand Design

Everybody makes mistakes but only idiots make the kind of mistake I made back in the fall of 1983. What the hell was I thinking, pushing Roy away like that? Why on earth did I let my emotions influence my judgment to that extent?

By the time I was ready to do something about it, Roy was holding Wendy Rubin in his arms—a pretty, blond cheerleader who cornered him at the end of soccer practice. After a sleepless night, I concluded that things could have been much worse. At least this girl derailed him from the track leading back to Lisa. It gave me time to plan.

Wendy was a good girl from a good home, the kind who keeps her innocence for her future husband; and, although Roy Cohen was special, when it came to sex, he was just like any other teenager: hungry, demanding and uncompromising. I just had to sit quietly in the background and wait for him to bounce back.

By now, Buzz was out of prison and the four of us soon reconnected. It felt good being around my old friends again. It gave me a sense of a security, because I was able to share a place that was far from the world with the people I trusted the most. Apart from Heather, the others knew nothing about my summer with Roy. I thought they would not understand, so why bother. I dragged them to Ben's place for Roy's first performance as the new lead singer and rhythm guitarist of Expel. My friends were reluctant to waste time on what Doug called 'a band going kitsch' playing covers, but I insisted. The place was packed and the band gave a hell of a show. Even my skeptic punk-music-freak friends were impressed. Heather thought Roy was hot and Doug, a wannabe musician himself, declared that this version of the band 'kicked-ass.' I took a few steps away from the bunch as Roy sang a ballad. I did not want them to see what Roy had turned me into—an emotional crybaby. Our looks met at a certain point in the song. Roy locked eyes with me from across the stage. He smiled and I reacted like a jerk, escaping to the ladies' room, catching my breath, trying to get a hold of the storm raging inside of me.

Lisa was also in attendance. She too looked at Roy with profound love and admiration.

I had to act fast but, as always, I was beaten to the chase. Amanda had arranged for the perfect couple to spend a perfect weekend together with her and *her* perfect boyfriend John in Catalina, and that was enough for the inevitable to happen.

Calamity. I had finally lost them both—to each other.

The sight of the two of them, walking hand in hand at school sent my spirit to a new all-time low. I found consolation in the heroin—by then I was very much into it—and in Buzz's arms. I think he fell in love with me; otherwise why would a bright and talented 22-year-old man waste so much time with a bunch of teenagers?

Buzz had a day-job working for his rich uncle, making a nice enough salary to keep him going and saving. He had started working in the warehouse of one of the chain's hardware store and gradually climbed the ladder to manage inventory for the whole chain. His uncle depended on his skills now and rewarded him well. He was my rock at a time when I found no positive aspect in being alive. I never loved Buzz, but with time, I learned to appreciate his loyalty and good heart. By now, Doug and Heather were a couple, so it was only natural to spend time together as two couples. Jerry's death had left a huge mark on us all, and our time together was no longer characterized by the quest for adrenaline.

All this was the background for the 'Grand Design'—my long-term plan premeditated to split Lisa and Roy. It was based on my intention to find the crack that would lead me back to their lives by reconnecting with Lisa or by using external forces to do the job.

I now had a sense of mission and no emotions attached.

"Why isn't Roy a part of your life anymore, sweetheart?" my father inquired over dinner.

"I don't want to talk about it." I replied impatiently.

"Can I help?" He insisted.

"How?"

"I can talk to him. He values my opinion. "

"Do as you wish."

"I need to know where you two stand before doing that."

"He's into blond."

"What happened?"

"I dumped him."

"So why are you so miserable?" I bit my lips with pain. "Why are you sad honey?" He persisted.

"Because I feel just like you and mom felt back in 1965, when you dealt with the awful news you were having me," I said with annoyance. "I now know what it feels like to make the worst mistake ever."

My father held a barbeque for some friends and family and used the opportunity to invite Roy. I greeted my ex with a disrespectful "hi" when he showed up at our doorstep. Then, I disregarded his presence for the duration of his stay. About an hour later, I saw my father talking to him. Both faces were grim. I followed Roy as he made his way out the main door.

"Can we talk?" I asked a second before he stepped out. He nodded and followed me up the stairs to my room.

I sat on my bed. "You are endlessly in my thoughts," I confessed sadly.

He took a big breath of air and released it slowly into the atmosphere, keeping his silence, looking away. "I didn't mean to hurt you. You know that, right?" He asked. I nodded. "Can't we just be good friends?"

"No!" I whispered decisively, "we can't!"

"So, this is it for us?" he asked. "No!" I said, "I can't give you up just yet!"

"Jenny . . . you are unbelievable. The circumstances are different now," he said with frustration.

"You can't stop me from trying to win you back," I said as I got to my feet and walked to the window. I looked outside at the people in and around our pool. I didn't really see them.

"I don't understand," he said. "What are you saying?"

"I'm saying that I will do everything in my power to win you over, regardless of your current circumstances."

"And if you fail?" he asked in disbelief as he moved closer to me. I turned around to face him.

"If I fail my love," I said heartbroken, "then nobody else, I mean *nobody* else . . . will ever have you."

He left angrily. I, on the other hand, felt somewhat relieved. I had stated my mission and it was now official.

The weeks passed and the relationship between Lisa and Roy seemed to be tightening. Both of them were doing very well. Lisa went back to being the best and the brightest. She even got her own column in the school's paper—a relatively pompous set of pieces on science and philosophy, I think. Expel became un-believably popular and Roy was admired by one-and-all for his many talents.

I kept waiting in the corner for a crack to open.

With college just around the corner and hearing about Lisa's acceptance to Harvard, I thought the fracture was finally reveal-ing itself. Lisa would have to move to Boston and Roy, being a year younger, would have to stay behind for his senior year. I applied and were accepted to UCLA. My parents were thrilled. They had long ago given up on college prayers for their untam-able offspring.

Buzz escorted me to my senior prom. Expel performed and Lisa was breathtakingly beautiful. She approached me and we embraced. "You are so beautiful," she whispered in my ear. I was overwhelmed and remained speechless as she returned to Roy. Of course, she was elected Prom Queen and Roy sang their song to her—Journey's 'Open Arms'. How I wished I was her at that particular moment. It was beyond envy. It was a sense of mixed emotions—jealousy of both of them, anger for my stupidity and a burning resentment of my cruel set of circumstance.

After the performance ended, I followed Roy to the punch table. A quick look around confirmed that Lisa wasn't around.

"You sure know how to be romantic when you want to," I said to him. He turned and smiled.

"Hi, beautiful," he said, leaving his punch glass on the table, moving near, hugging me. "You look gorgeous."

"Thanks," I whispered as he disengaged.

"Are you still mad at me?" He asked.

"I was never mad at you. I got accepted to UCLA." I informed him.

"Good for you!"

I waited for something to say, something I thought he might say, but the silence turned encumbering amidst the general noise. I turned and left, looking for Buzz to take me as fast and as far away from there as possible.

Chapter 13

Renewed Friendship

And then, the unpredictable unfolded.

Expel's leader, John, was leaving for Canada with his girl-friend Amanda, and Roy was going to visit Israel for two whole weeks with his family. It occurred to me that these two factors posed an opportunity for me to get back into Lisa's life. So, on July 5th, I tailed Lisa's Porsche across the streets of Beverly Hills. I followed her into the underground parking lot of a small shopping center on 3rd street. She was peering into a book as I entered the bookstore. I feigned surprise at bumping into her. She seemed authentically happy to see me, so I offered to buy her a cup of coffee. Her body language signaled hesitation; the fact I was Roy's ex may have crossed her mind. She agreed. After all, we did have a mutual past long before either of us knew Roy.

"Seeing you always reminds me of the day I got my first period," I said with shivering lips. I think she was moved because she smiled compassionately and placed her hand on mine. "I will never forget how you and your mother came through for me."

Defenses slowly came down, warning signs shoved aside. We spoke for over two hours and found each other's company more than pleasant. At a certain point, I told Lisa I would be attending UCLA.

"So will I . . ." she said matter of fact.

"I thought you were going to Harvard," I said, puzzled at this new revelation, not knowing if it was a positive or a negative development.

"Yeah, I contemplated moving to Boston for a while, but leaving Roy behind was out of the question." The mention of

Roy for the first time in our conversation silenced both of us for an uncomfortable moment.

We spent time together every single day over the next two weeks. I quickly found out that being outrageous Jennifer worked amazingly well on her. She was intrigued so I used it to strengthen our bond. We sunbathed in the beaches of Santa Monica and Venice or by our pools. We watched movies together, dined at fancy restaurants, strolled through Westwood's Village and talked a lot.

Making Lisa laugh gave me the greatest satisfaction and I would go out of my way to try and squeeze another giggle out of her. I would flirt with men who would behave pathetically and then send them cruelly away, just to prove a point. My approach excited her. But most of all, I admired her exceptional mind, the way she presented things, the way she used language to make things interesting. After all she has been through; the woman maintained an optimistic attitude. She testified that Roy was the reason behind the reconstruction of her life. What made her eyes moist was realizing that Roy had made it possible for her to erase the junky label. I tried not to ruin her euphoric mood, so I said that everything was just peachy with me, too, now that college was around the corner but it was far from the truth.

The truth of the matter was that the angst I hid was excruciating.

On top of it all, there was the desire, and it was killing me. Lisa was physically near and we were usually in our bikinis. She was so hot and I could hardly keep my hands to myself. I think she noticed that but did nothing to turn down the sexual tension that was ever mounting. I didn't know what to make of that. I'm embarrassed to remember that I found myself pathetically envious of Roy, having her all to himself. *Jesus Christ, how pitiful . . .*

We spent the last weekend before Roy's return in a private house my father had rented in Palm Springs. We went sightseeing and then came back to the pool. It took me an hour to convince Lisa to sunbathe in the nude. It was amusing to realize that the woman was shy about her perfect body. I claimed we were all alone and that there was no risk of anyone seeing us but us. I took off my bikini. Eventually she took off her top.

I wanted Lisa that afternoon by the pool like there was no tomorrow. She could not have missed it. My body gave all the signs, and one thing we girls know is how to read these kinds of *signs*. Still, she kept her cool and it drove me crazy. I followed her into the house when she went to refill her water bottle. I took her hand in mine and led her to bed. She looked at me with a look I could not interpret, but other than that she did nothing to stop me. I saw that as permission to proceed. Once in the bedroom, I helped her take off the lower part of her bikini. I caressed her gently as I got closer and kissed her lips. She reciprocated and soon our tongues were fighting over dominance in our mouths. Our hands were all over our bodies moving slowly around curves, touching, caressing and squeezing gently.

Afterwards, we lay there in each other's arms, sweating, still breathing heavily. She caressed my hair and smiled. I smiled back. "I love you," I said to her. "I've always loved you." She looked at me compassionately but did not reciprocate.

"Sweetie," she said to me later, as she got dressed. "This will always be a memorable experience for both of us . . ." She came closer and sat beside me, ". . . but it will never happen again." I looked away, feeling as if the Empire State Building had collapsed on my head. I nodded but remained hopeful nonetheless.

We spent our last evening together in a beautiful restaurant set beside an ancient Indian burial ground. I felt it was a good opportunity to try to relieve what I thought was Lisa's greatest concern about our relationship.

"I won't lie to you," I told her when I thought the time was right. "I still have feelings for Roy." She looked at me wearily while gulping from her water glass; "but I want you to know that I understand it's over and done with."

"Look, Jenny," she said looking into my eyes. "Roy is my soul-mate. I'm in love with him beyond comprehension. I would rather die than lose him. Do you understand?" I nodded. "I need you to say it."

"I understand," I whispered.

"Good . . . now . . . if you can live with that and still be my friend, then I don't see why this relationship cannot continue. But if you have the slightest problem with it . . . and I mean the slightest . . . then there is no point in ever seeing each other." I nodded again, looking sadly into my coffee cup. "Can you?" she insisted.

"Yes, Lisa," I said quietly. "I can."

Back in LA, I dropped Lisa off at her parents' house and continued home, still excited. Unloading the Benz, I heard a familiar voice. "Let me help you with the baggage." I turned around surprised, smiling when I realized who it was.

"I don't believe it." I said and hanged my arms around his neck. "Weren't you supposed to return tomorrow?"

"Yeah," he said, taking my arms off his neck. "I miscalculated the date of arrival."

"So, Roy Cohen, what are you doing here? Don't you have a girlfriend to say hello to?"

"Let's go in. We need to talk!" he said, carrying the bags to my room.

"So, what's on your mind, ex?" I asked when we entered my room. He placed the bags on the floor and sat on my bed. I quickly sat beside him.

"Please don't do this," he asked, looking tired and weary.

"Do what?"

"You know what?" he insisted.

"No . . . I don't."

"Don't spoil it for me and Lisa. I know what you're up to."

I took a deep breath and got up. I walked to the window and stared outside.

"Jenny, you can have anyone you want. You don't need me in your life anymore."

That condescending asshole! I turned with anger in my eyes. "Who the hell do you think you are?" I threw at him. He was taken aback. "You have no right to ask me to end my friendship with Lisa. We are friends and it's innocent. You can't deny us our friendship." I was still eyeballing him as his composure changed slowly . . . but drastically. He suddenly looked very threatening—a look I could not easily associate with him.

"Fine, but don't expect me to sit idly by. I'll be watching you," he said, pointing his finger at my face. "If you hurt her, I'll be there."

"Have I hit a nerve?" I asked, looking at him with a cynical smile hanging on my lips.

"What are you talking about? Why are you smiling?" he inquired with an angry look.

"Oh . . . my love . . . you're so naïve. You'll never beat me at this game because I'm better than you. I've had years of practice, and I learned it from the best—I learned it from my parents." He heaved a sigh and turned around, walking toward the door. I quickly followed him and wrapped my arms around his waist, placing my head on his right shoulder. "I'll do anything for you," I said quietly, letting the love I felt for him flood me.

"Then leave her alone!" he demanded.

"You leave me no choice."

He turned to face me. "Jenny . . . please . . ."

"Stay with me tonight," I begged him, "for old times' sake. Lisa doesn't even know you're back in town."

"No! It's over! Accept it!" He said resolutely and left.

I picked up the phone with a sense of urgency. I knew this guy well enough to foresee his actions. I had to be the first to warn Lisa; otherwise, she might get the wrong idea.

"Roy's in town," I informed her as she answered. "He just left my house on his way to yours." There was silence on the other side of the line. Lisa was probably surprised and I suspect even a bit offended. "He came over to ask me to leave you alone," I continued. "Lisa, he thinks I'm trying to hurt you."

"What did you tell him?" she asked harshly.

"That it's innocent and that he has no right to tell me who to associate with."

"Okay, thanks."

"Please tell me you know I'm just trying to be a friend. We have been there before. Don't let anyone spoil our relationship again, not even Roy. Lisa, tell me you know that all I want is to be your friend . . . please," I found myself begging.

"I do," she said quietly, hopefully recollecting the previous time she had spurned me so unkindly. "We'll talk later."

Chapter 14

Opportunity

I knew being Lisa's friend under that set of our particular circumstances was not going to be easy, but I did not anticipate the immense pressure Roy was about to exert on her. She called me twice that week concerned and at a loss for action. Roy was very edgy and Lisa was concerned the situation would lead to a crisis. He claimed that I was still in love with him and that I was seeking their separation. I kept reassuring her that this was not the case. She chose to back our friendship and tried her best to calm him down. When things got out of hands, Lisa used our friendship to cement a golden rule and was adamant to stick to it vehemently. It centered on her autonomy to choose her friends or, as she put it to him: "I love you more than life but that doesn't give you the right to choose my friends for me!"

Expel's gig at the Setting Sunshine, a popular bar on Sunset Blvd, was a blast. I danced with Lisa all through the show. I detected signs of concern, not only from Roy on stage but also from Amanda. I wasn't wrong. The next morning Lisa informed me of a conversation she had with Roy on the way home from the gig. He finally caved and promised to trust her better judgment. I—on the other hand—remembered the marihuana incident. Roy was not the compromising type and there was no talking him out of something he firmly believed in. I adored him for that. It made me look up to him: he had convictions and he exerted authority. This was working against me now.

I evaluated the situation and emerged from my reflections with only one conclusion—my presence in Lisa's life had the potential of splitting them up. I just had to be there as much as possible and have Roy's concerns do the rest.

It happened sooner than I thought—much sooner.

At the beginning of August, Roy accompanied Lisa to the UCLA campus. She was scheduled to meet her counselor and intended to buy some books. I planned to be there too. I tailed her that morning as she picked Roy up from his home. I followed her into a parking lot on Westwood Boulevard and waited at a safe distance for her to park the car. As I saw the couple take the university shuttle, I parked my car close enough to Lisa's for Roy to spot it. I counted on his love of cars. He would not miss my Corvette.

I turned off the engine, took the pad out of my handbag and wrote a note:

"Sweet Lisa,
Call me. We need to plan our first college year together.
Kisses to you and regards to Roy.
Jennifer."

"Now let's see how you manage *this* situation?" I said to myself.

What happened next far exceeded my expectations.

Lucky for me, Amanda and John were still on their coast-to-coast trip of the US, so Lisa had no one to turn to but me when the second greatest crisis of her life erupted. The next day, she called and asked me to come over. She said she needed me. I raced through the streets of Beverly Hills, excited and hopeful. I found her hurt and angry. It seemed my note had generated the worst and noisiest fight they had ever had, right there, in the parking lot. Roy forbade Lisa to see me ever again and Lisa stood firm on her right to do so. He was so angry that he just took off, leaving her there. She drove after him and begged him to get into the car. He disregarded her pleads ruthlessly.

"You should have seen him," she said emotionally, "his fists closed as if he was about to launch them into my face. My God, Jenny, I was afraid of him. I always knew he was short-tempered, but I never thought he would direct such rage at me."

"What do you want to do now?"

"I don't know . . ."

"Is it the end?" I asked hopeful.

She looked at me terrified, as if I had just broken some dreadfully upsetting news to her. "Of course not!" she trembled, sitting on her bed. "I can't live without him."

"So . . . call him and make up." I suggested, knowing she was not in any position emotionally to do that.

"No! It was his decision to escape the scene and abandon me there. He has to be the one to initiate reconciliation—not me!" She said decisively. *Good. That's not going to happen.* It occurred to me that I knew her boyfriend better than she did.

I felt sorry for Lisa. Seeing her so devastated and moody, again because of my actions, did not please me at all, but I could not give up on Roy. I found myself in a happy-sad kind of situation. It was awkward and sometimes painful, but I had to cope with it nonetheless. The problem was that the situation escalated so fast and to such an extreme that I was losing control over it—again.

Roy had simply vanished from the face of the earth and time passing drew Lisa deeper into depression. Her initial strong and assertive stance gave way to weakness and indecisiveness. Oblivion projected from her beautiful, empty, regretful eyes. Every day passing without Roy calling to apologize reaffirmed what she thought was happening and what I hoped would eventually happen: he had left her. At a certain point, she started calling him at home dozens of times a day but to no avail. She cried for hours until she lost her voice and dried out her tear ducts. She lay in bed for days without talking—a complete zombie. She ate nothing and refused to talk to anyone but to me.

It was cruel. There were moments when I embraced her and hated myself for creating this agonizing situation. There were moments during which I found myself hating Roy for not calling her. Yet, at the same time, I hoped he would never call her again. I wished he would call me.

When her sadness was too great to bear, I suggested she confront him face to face. It gave her hope. She even wrote him a letter urging him to call her—a letter to be left on the threshold of his apartment in case he was not present. She came back crushed. His car was parked outside in its usual parking place, so she presumed he was home. She knocked on the door, cried behind the closed door, pleaded and begged him to take her back, but Roy wouldn't cave.

"Are you sure he was inside the apartment?" I asked, sitting on her bed, watching her at her toughest hour. She nodded. "How can you be sure? This isn't like him. He might have acted like a jerk but the guy doesn't avoid confrontation."

"I just know," she cried. "I could feel his presence."

The days went by without any news from Roy. I tried to get some information as to his whereabouts, but his parents were still in Israel and all his friends were vacationing with their families out of town. Even Ben had disappeared and his brother was temporarily running his café.

By now, almost two weeks after their quarrel at the parking lot, Lisa was a shadow of herself and I moved around with a constantly nagging pain in my belly. Her parents were worried and did not know how to handle the situation. She would not leave her room anymore, would not eat or engage in conversation. All she wanted was to have Roy back in her life.

"Lisa, you've got to eat something," I begged her one night, placing a hot cup of her favorite tea with some cookies on the chest near her bed.

"I'm not hungry," she whispered. I sat on the bed beside her, staring at her pale face somberly, wishing I could get my way without inflicting so much pain on this wonderful person who had never done me wrong.

"What do you want to do now?" I asked, caressing her hair. "You can't go on like this. You need to proceed with your life."

She started crying silently. "What life?"

"You're so smart and beautiful. You have so much to live for."

"Roy is my only reason to live. I want to die!" she whispered painfully.

"Don't say that!" I said, horrified of the possibility that another human being I loved would lose his life because of me. "Jesus Christ, Lisa, don't even *think* in that direction . . ." There was silence in the room for a while. "Listen." I whispered compassionately. "It's not over. Try again. Go to him. Try to convince him he is wrong," I suggested, disregarding the consequences to my Grand Design. I just could not bear the thought of Lisa ending her life. I did my best that night to convince her that this was an idea worth exploring. Finally, after a long conversation, she concurred. She drove to his home again, armed with another letter in which, again, she begged him to take her back.

Roy's car was still parked in its usual place and Lisa again assumed he was home. She knocked on the door a few times, cried and begged again, assuming he was on the other side. She sat there, on the stairs leading to his apartment for almost an hour. The guy kept his stance like a rock; and even I, at this stage, loving him endlessly like I did, started resenting his cruelty. It did not add up. I thought I knew him better.

"Where would he go in this huge city without his car?" she cried to me when I came over the next day and questioned her conviction that Roy was present behind the door. "Even if he was out the first time around, what were the odds of him leaving his car there twice and exactly at the time of my visits?"

"But it's not typical of him." I claimed.

"Oh . . . he was there all right!" she said decisively, looking like she had spent another sleepless night. "I could sense his presence . . . we are connected . . . my heart can spot him from a distance."

"Nonsense!" I exclaimed. "For such an intelligent person you sometimes make no sense at all."

"Whatever . . .," she whispered; disregarding the voice of reason I tried to offer her. "Help me kill myself."

"What?" I said in horror, embracing her tightly, "Lisa, you have to be strong. I know how you feel. I felt the same."

"Please, Jenny, help me." She cried.

"No. I won't! Ask me anything but don't ask me to help you die."

"You have no idea how I feel inside."

"Oh yes I do," I said with suffocating emotions, remembering all the times in my young life this same thought had crossed my mind. "All my life I've been coping with heartache, with depression, betrayal, and loneliness." I threw at her.

"Never this much," she said to herself.

"Lisa—you have your family. I never even had *that*. I've lost friends, I lost a lover. I've been beaten up, insulted in every way imaginable. Everything I touch turns to shit—even our friendship, which I treasure more than anything I've ever had."

"How did you cope?"

"Did?" I asked harshly, "I still do!"

"How?" she asked. I looked at her for a long minute, wondering if it would be wise to tell her. "Please Jenny, tell me how?" she wailed. I felt numb. I could not say anything. I started breathing heavily. "If you consider yourself my friend, then by God tell me how!"

My eyes filled with tears. "This is how," I said as I took off my pants, turned around and placed my right leg on my bed. I pointed my finger at the back of my knee. Lisa moved closer, detecting the small, almost microscopic pinpricks. Suddenly she was very quiet, tracing the dots with her delicate finger. She took a deep breath of air and reclined on her pillows. I saw in her eyes the contemplation. "Oh . . . no . . . you don't want to go back there," I said as I sat on her bed.

"You just saved my pathetic life," she informed me flatly.

"Please think about this," I begged her.

"No! It's either that or death!" she exclaimed. "There is no third way. Do you have a steady supplier?" I nodded in confirmation. "So, from now on he'll supply you with double doses! It's the only way I can escape with my pitiable life unharmed." I nodded reluctantly, realizing I had no other choice.

She got up, went to her desk and drew an envelope from one of the drawers. She gave it to me. It contained $3,000. "How long will this carry me?" she asked.

"About three months . . ."

"Good. Now go and get me my fix. I can't stand this any longer."

Thinking about it later, I began to recognize the advantages in being Lisa's supplier. She would become dependent on me and I would be in a position to influence her life. I believed that the new situation could also be beneficial for my grand design.

The next day Lisa had the first of her second round of heroin fixes. This bigger-than-life human being wrote a beautiful and heart-moving farewell letter to Roy, in which she thanked him for the time they had spent together and stated she would love him forever. She went over to his apartment and pushed the letter underneath the door.

I felt like shit.

Chapter 15

Divided

A week later, Lisa showed up at my room in complete panic. She couldn't stop crying and I couldn't understand why. She didn't make sense. I embraced her and tried my best to convince her that everything was all right. It took me more than ten minutes to pull her back to reality and calm her down.

"He went on a stupid trip with his friends," she cried. "Can you believe it?"

"How do you know?" I asked in disbelief, realizing Roy was back in the game.

"He came over begging for forgiveness."

"And..?"

"I sent him away," she claimed and blew her nose into a paper tissue. "What the hell am I supposed to do now? My God, I almost killed myself . . ."

"Sh..," I tried to calm her down. "It'll be all right . . ."

"All right?" she threw at me, "I'm a fucking junky . . . for what . . . for who . . . why?" She held her hand over her open mouth, shocked to find herself in such deep trouble for no reason at all.

She sat on my bed.

"We'll find a way out of this. You'll see." I tried to offer some false consolation.

"Am I so unimportant? Am I not worth a dime for a short phone call?" She asked herself with horror. "What have I done to deserve this?"

I walked to the window and looked out, realizing that I had misjudged the whole situation. It did not take me long to realize that I was left with no other option than to activate my Doom's Day strategy.

"Lisa. You can't let him back into your life!" I stated decisively, collecting as much courage as possible. I turned around to capture her reaction. She stared at me with a harsh facial expression. I walked closer to her, sat beside her on the bed and took her hand in mine. "Honey," I said calmly but unequivocally. "You know I only want what's best for you and as difficult and painful as it may sound, you have no choice now but to disengage from Roy and disengage for good!" She raised her head and looked into my eyes. "It's not smart to have him back in your life. It's not smart for you to be around him anymore. He is dangerous. You won't be able to stand another breakup. We barely managed to save your life *this* time around. Think what would happen if he decides to ditch you for *real*. You can't risk that."

"I . . ." she tried to say but I continued.

"Your life is precious. There is nothing more important than keeping it! You need to let go of Roy no matter how strong your feelings are for him, because he holds your fate in the palms of his hands. Lisa, you must understand that Roy is a constant threat to your life!"

She stared at me with uncertainty. I saw her facial expression turning harsher and darker by the second. There was no going back from what I had just released into the atmosphere. I knew I had to be strong now and defend my stance with all my might. She looked away and heaved a heavy sigh mixed with her quiet weeping.

"What is life without the person you love more than life itself?" she whispered to herself. I remained silent. "Give me my fix please," she said after about a minute of mutual silent contemplation. "I can't handle this right now."

For the next couple of weeks, Roy kept calling and Lisa kept asking for time to think. The anger she held inside intensified. My stance on the matter and the shame she felt for being so weak, sinking back down to a junky status made things more complicated for her and prevented her from doing what she longed for with all her heart—reunite with the man she loved. One day I went too far and pushed her too hard on the matter. She stormed at me like a raging blizzard, accusing me of doing exactly what Roy had warned her about—the termination of their relationship. I just looked at her with a sad face and promised I would never speak my mind again. That led to a minute of silence after which she apologized and asked me always to speak my mind around her.

I'm taking my make up off. My heart suddenly starts beating fast for no reason whatsoever. I feel my blood pressure rising and I get little beads of sweat all over my body. I'm about to faint so I sit down on the toilet bowl. I'm confused so I blame it on my addiction. Deep down I know it isn't true but I'm scared to admit it. My stomach starts to ache and I vomit. I do my best to get a grip on myself but I'm in the midst of the worst panic attack I have ever had. I'm fighting it but it possesses me. I finally give up and only then does my body slowly relax . . . it's obvious . . . I'm terrified of remaining alone.

Although still undecided, Lisa was starting to accept the possibility of living life without Roy. The drug made it easier to cope with her soon-to-be-made colossal decision, although she was still in a constant state of bitter melancholy. She became cynical of everyone and everything and lost her usual liveliness. Waiting was excruciating. She would come over every afternoon; we would have our fix together, talk for a while and then she would leave for home. We would occasionally go out together to a movie or to eat something and talk some more. But as much as I loved her, it was suffocating and depressing to be around sad and lonely Lisa. I turned back to my gang and resumed our late nights out on the town.

Meanwhile, Roy was doing awesomely with Expel. The band's live shows were so exciting that teens packed venues all over LA. Eventually the inevitable happened and Vincent Terranova invited the band to perform at his notorious party. Lisa, who had been dragged by Ralph Dillon to that party once, was horrified when Amanda informed her of the band's decision to accept the offer. She overcame her emotions and called Roy. She asked him to meet her at Venice beach. On the warm sands, walking barefoot beside him, Lisa tried unsuccessfully to convince Roy to let the idea go. Although the Terranova's offer was very generous, the main motive, he explained, was prestige. For the past seven years, bands performing at that party were considered the best LA's rock scene had to offer. She returned home empty-handed.

What Lisa saw as a disturbing fact, I saw as an opportunity. I got a ticket to the party, for which I paid $100, and found myself waiting impatiently for the night to arrive. When it finally did, I sat by the phone, nervous and jumpy, waiting to hear from Terranova's people about the location. I was going to meet Roy and offer him a way back into my life. I got the call about an hour before the official starting time and rushed my Corvette to the East San Fernando Valley—far enough and dark enough not to spot from a distance. It took me some time to find the place—about 45 minutes, actually.

Expel was in the midst of Clapton's 'Cocaine' when I arrived. I pushed my way to the bar through hundreds of people, grabbed a can of beer and stood far enough from the stage for Roy not to spot me. I knew the band was scheduled to perform twice, with a fifteen-minute break between sessions. Meanwhile, people all around me were getting drunk or stoned. Even I felt intimidated by what was going on. If not for the anticipation of meeting Roy, I would have escaped. When the band finally took a break, I followed Roy out. I saw him resting on the hood of a nearby car, smoking a cigarette. He exhaled smoke and wore a somber face.

"Hi." I greeted him as I approached. He turned his head and looked at me. "Can I join you?" I asked as he examined my body from head to toe. I had on a very short and sexy black skirt. It got me the attention I was hoping for.

"Yeah, sure," he said unenthusiastically and turned his gaze away. I stood beside him, trying to sniff the scent of his sweating body deep into my lungs.

"Light me a cigarette," I asked. He did. I grabbed it from his hand. The touch of the hand that used to caress my body sent shivers down my spine. "You were really good tonight," I said, inhaling the smoke deep into my lungs, hoping it would make my breathing difficulties go away.

"I'm not in the mood for conversation thank you!"

It stung and burned. He was still the only creature on the face of the earth with the ability to really hurt my feelings.

"Please don't be like that," I begged him, moving to face him, pushing my body gently against his. He did not resist. The touch of his body turned me on. My lips were drawn to his, but he moved his face the other way. "When will you come to your senses?" I whispered in frustration.

He said nothing and I started rubbing my body against his. He pushed me away. "Leave me be!" He ordered, throwing away what was left of his cigarette. "You've done enough damage already."

"We are just friends. Stop acting this way!" I said to him with ever-growing annoyance. He looked at me for a while. His facial expression turned gradually from harsh to compassionate. He heaved a heavy sigh and caressed my naked shoulder, looking into my eyes. "Sweetheart," he said now with tenderness. "I understand what you are going through. If I were not so in love with Lisa, I would probably be madly in love with you." I had tears in my pathetic eyes as he moved to embrace me. I was not going to get my way with him tonight and it hurt like hell.

I spread my hands around his waist and embraced him tightly. "I love you so much," I whispered. "I'll wait for you even if it takes forever."

"No!" He said decisively and pushed me away, looking again into my eyes. "You have to let go of me. Please, promise me you'll do so."

"I can't! I was never in love before." I placed my head on his strong shoulder. He caressed my hair, heaving yet another profound sigh.

"Roy," Ben called from a distance and ruined a beautiful moment. "We have to go back on stage in a minute."

"I'm coming," he said and turned back to me. "Promise me you won't hurt Lisa," he said. I looked at him with disappointment and then looked away. "Promise me!" He ordered, holding both my shoulders. I nodded reluctantly. He kissed my forehead and rushed back inside.

I ran to my car. I got in and closed the door. I breathed heavily, my body shivering uncontrollably. There was no way I was going to spend the remainder of the night alone. I needed someone to hold me.

It was about 1 am when I got to Buzz's apartment building. I parked the car in the street, ran up the stairs to the third floor and knocked on his door with both my fists. He opened the door sleepily and surprised at my sudden and unexpected visit.

"I need to be with you tonight," I whispered. He nodded and I got in. He shut the door behind us. I stopped and looked at him. "Hold me," I cried as he pulled me into his arms. "Hold me and don't say a word. . . . don't say one fucking word."

Chapter 16

Stone in Love

After I left, the LAPD raided the party.

Roy and his band-mates were detained for questioning along with dozens of others. Lisa's powerful lawyer father had the band released during the early hours of the morning. It was all over the papers the following day.

"I was left alone with him in a dark interrogation room," Lisa informed me somberly the following day. "It was horrible. He looked so ashamed and humiliated. I kissed his lips goodbye. It's officially over."

But I knew better. If not handled wisely time would soon have them back in each other's arms.

When the academic year began, I had to literally push Lisa to attend the courses she took. She was always moody and cynical. She hated her teachers and acted indifferently to her new surroundings. She became impossible to be around—always complaining, moaning and bitching about everyone and everything. The girl had most of the campus hunks standing in a queue longer than Space Mountain but she wouldn't give them the time of day. She wouldn't even consider having coffee with them, let alone a date. She kept comparing everybody to Roy the musician, Roy the athlete, Roy the hunk, Roy the sensitive and super-polite individual, Roy the most intelligent person she ever met, Roy . . . Roy . . . Roy . . . bla . . . bla . . . bla. . . . As annoying as it was, truth be told—I'd been approached by no less amazing guys myself but kept rejecting them for the exact same reason.

Meanwhile, the man of our dreams was calling Lisa less frequently and it influenced her moody behavior even further. With time passing, she stopped eating. It was obvious that her brain was giving her the order to disengage but her heart would not let go.

Get the hell over him already! I remember screaming to myself in the bathroom one day, frustrated and angry. *You had your chance with him. You screwed it up. Now it's my turn!*

We got our daily fix in my room every day after college. Later I would try to study but Lisa would just lie there like a zombie, drowsing on and off, sometimes sobbing quietly. It was a depressing period for both of us.

"I'm dropping out!" she informed me one evening. "I am too tired and too depressed to do anything, let alone go to college."

"No. You are not!" I exclaimed. "It's a difficult period for you. I understand. But you must keep on living your life. Don't give up!"

"Go on with your studies. Give up on me."

"It has nothing to do with me. It's all about you. You're supposed to be at your prime and you're falling apart."

"We are drug addicts . . ." she emphasized with a straight face. ". . . We are not at our prime, Jennifer. We are at our lowest point ever."

She was painfully right.

The gang kept me alive through that period, even if we hardly met once a week. One night I dragged them to the Setting Sunshine to catch an Expel show. At a certain point, the band did Journey's 'Stone in Love', and I thought to myself that it was the perfect title for our lives at that specific period. We were usually stoned and we were crazy in love with Roy, who had spotted me in the crowd as he sang and made me rushed out for some air.

A few minutes later, he joined me. We walked slowly down Sunset Boulevard, smoking in silence.

He broke down first. "How is Lisa doing?"

"Fine, I guess." I replied.

"Could you ask her please to call me?" he asked.

"Okay. But you know her decision."

He nodded somberly. "Yeah, I know. I just hope she is not over me. I hoped she would eventually give me a second chance." I stopped walking. He stopped too. I got closer to him.

"Look. I understand your grief, Roy, but it is over with Lisa and both of us know it had nothing to do with me."

He nodded. "Yeah, this was all me and my stupid pride . . ."

"So, if I'm finally off the hook and if Lisa is not an option anymore, you might as well give me a second chance." He looked at me sadly.

"We explored that opportunity once. It ended with a broken heart. I won't break your heart again."

"I'll take my chances," I said. He shook his head. "Why the hell not?" I asked in frustration. "Am I not beautiful enough for you? Am I not intelligent or good in bed? Why should you deserve a second chance while I don't?

He looked away. I walked away and reclined on a nearby car. He approached me and sat on the car's hood beside me.

"Do you want to know the truth?" he asked. I nodded. "I'm dying to take you home right now, strip you of all your clothes and make passionate love to you," he said and my heart started beating fast. "You're the sexiest creature I have ever laid my eyes on and I love you with all my heart." My eyes filled up uncontrollably.

"So . . . what are waiting for?" I asked with a cracked voice, anticipating his answer.

"Because the immense love I have for you is the kind a person has for a friend, not for a lover. I am not in love with you Jennifer, and as much as I want to get in your pants every time I see you, I will not fail myself again. Values are important to me. Do you understand?"

"No! I don't!" I cried. "You want me, come and get me. We'll deal with the consequences of our actions later. Don't give me this bullshit about friendship and moral values. You were the one who screwed your best friend's girlfriend not me."

"Yeah . . . Jenny . . . exactly . . . and I can't live with the shame."

"Well, then. Fuck you and your shame!" I screamed at him and started running away. Soon, he caught up with me and embraced me. He held me in his arms for a very long time without saying anything. Finally, I disengaged from his embrace and took a deep breath of air. "I have never loved anyone as much as I love you, not my parents, not even Lisa. But that has always been my problem . . . right—never yours," I said and went back to the club, looking for my friends.

If not for my love for her, I would have killed Lisa the next evening. It had crossed my mind numerous times, and it was ridiculously easy. I could just do what Ralph Dillon failed to—kill her with an overdose. Then I found myself trembling all over, amazed to realize I had dared let my mind wander in that direction—images of dead Lisa attacked me from all over.

So I stuck to my original plan.

Throughout that period, Amanda Willis, remained the biggest, most annoying obstacle. Lisa's long-time best friend was attending USC now. Consequently, the relations between her and Lisa suffered a heavy blow. Amanda was very busy doing homework or studying for tests and Lisa was very busy being sorry for herself and being depressed; and so, the two met hardly once every two weeks. It became a ritual. Every time they met, Lisa started questioning her *Roy* decision. Amanda would make her rethink. I had to keep her on the right track—as far away from Roy as possible. It was an excruciating process, which left me exhausted. Going over and over the reasons she shouldn't reconnect with her ex left me worn out, but somehow it always worked. Finally, Amanda beat me at the game again. She sent Roy to Lisa's guesthouse and made him confront her face to face. Lisa told me about his visit that same evening. The guy pleaded and begged at first, and then assaulted her verbally for being dumb and for 'listening to me.' Although she was agitated and enraged, I smelled trouble.

I tried my best to remind her of the danger Roy posed to her life, and, although she heard what I said, this time around she did not listen. Her mind was elsewhere. Roy must have said something, or brought something new to the game for her to be so distracted. When she left that evening, I already knew what to expect. Her love for him, the yearning, the anguish over his loss, his pleading, and Amanda's stance on the matter would steer her in only one direction—straight back into his loving arms.

The next time I saw Lisa, she was a new person—alive, talk-ative, wearing nice clothes, makeup. Although she said nothing about it, I suspected Roy was back in her life. She confirmed it only the next day, over the phone, probably avoiding physical proximity with the person who had advised her for months not to do so. They were back together and I was now reduced to being her drug supplier slash college friend. She saw the frustration and disappointment on my face the next time she came and got angry. At the end of a long and loud argument, we embraced and set everything straight; but I understood that I was now under the double magnifying glass of both her and Roy. I would have to calculate my actions very accurately if I wished to stay in the game.

Chapter 17

Living a Lie

Roy returned to the picture big time.

It was remarkable to witness how the life of one human being is so connected to . . . no: *dependent* on, would be a better word, the life of another. I mean, I too was in love with the man; but despite the longing and the yearning, I never had those feelings of helplessness and unworthiness Lisa had in his absence. Happy as can be, Lisa now started excelling in her studies. She spent most of her time doing what she loved the most—learning. She had a lot of free time from Roy to do it because he had a hectic schedule. Realizing that, Lisa made him sleep over at her place as often as possible so they could at least spend their nights together.

At this point, I would have settled for just cuddling in bed between the two of them.

Although Roy remained ambivalent about our friendship, Lisa knew I genuinely cared for her. In fact, surprisingly so, during that period, Lisa and I reconnected on a different level. She was no longer miserable and lonely and I had become a real friend—a friend she could confide in and trust. Yet, that impossible duality remained agonizing.

By now, it was obvious Buzz was very much in love with me. He was a no-nonsense kind of a guy, and he always treated me right. In a way, I felt obligated to keep him in the picture of my life. After all, we had a complicated history together and he had spent time in prison because of me. Still, I had to level down his expectations. He was not my knight in shining armor and although we had some very long conversations about that, he remained optimistic.

"I'm going to keep hoping you'll grow up some day in the near future," he said to me one night, as we were smoking grass together, after some wild sex. "I'm not giving up on you yet."

By then Buzz and I were all that was left of the gang. Heather and Doug had left for New York. She was studying psychology at Columbia and he was pursuing an architecture degree from City College. They got a small studio apartment on the 2nd Avenue and urged me to come and visit. All that was left of their careless Punk days and Punk-Rock disguises were the tattoos they would bear on their skins for the rest of their lives. Now that they were out to conquer the world, they found them embarrassing and did their best to conceal them.

A constant irritation was the drug factor. I enjoyed a steady supply of the chemical and God knows Lisa and I were never short of money to buy it; yet the physical reactions to it, the continuous concern and the constant state of fatigue took their toll. We were not only drug addicts; we were living a lie and deceiving everyone we loved. We discussed ways of getting rid of the nasty habit but could not find any that didn't involve telling our parents and going through a long and painful rehabilitation process. Lisa was most terrified of telling Roy; for her, telling him was worse than telling her parents. She knew him well and anticipated his reaction. She was certain he'd leave her. I believed she was right.

Desperate to find a way out, an idea popped into her head that would dominate the next few months—marriage. What triggered that idea was the invitation she got to the wedding of Roy's good friends Jean-Paul and Pascal. If successful, this would be the kiss of death to my Grand Design and it scared me. I knew how much Roy loved that woman. If faced with an ultimatum, chances were he would succumb to her wishes.

In essence, Lisa's plan was to marry 18-year-old Roy and thus officially secure their relationship. Then, she would work to stabilize their marriage, and when things settled down, she would disclose her circumstance to him. In the short-term, she anticipated he would get mad as hell and lose trust in her, but by then he would be married and bound to the basic marital obligation of 'in sickness and in health.' "Once I'm clean," she said to me solemnly, "I'll use our love to recover his trust." I looked at her bewildered. "It's a shameful trick, I know, but I have no other choice."

"Would you marry him if you were not on drugs?" I tried to show her the absurdity of her plan.

Roy's initial response was complete rejection but Lisa gave him no way out, acting hurt and upset. Consequently, he promised to consider engagement and then see how it goes. Knowing Roy was most vulnerable where values were concerned, I was now looking for an idea that would show Lisa up as a valueless and dishonest person. I needed to find something, other than the drug problem, in order to shake his trust in her. Ironically, Lisa unintentionally helped me come up with the idea. She was about to trick Roy into marriage; so, I thought, why not tricking him into pregnancy? I know you probably think that I had lost my mind completely. Well . . . maybe I did. It was a long shot but one worth exploring. Let me explain the rationale behind it.

If there was one thing I thought I had learned from my marijuana incident, it was that Roy held no less unyielding position on deception than on the mere use of drugs. Lisa was on the pill. Getting pregnant, now after she was trying relentlessly to get him to agree to marry her, would give him grounds for suspicion that she had done so deliberately. I would be there to whisper in his ear.

Wait, it gets better.

Lisa's pregnancy would bring upon them the wrath of their respective conservative Jewish parents, but especially of her powerful lawyer father, Jacob. The last thing that would come out of the mess, I believed back then, would be marriage.

I anticipated abortion and separation.

Retrieving some of my sketches from that period, examining them thoroughly while spread on the floor, I could not ignore the one central theme running through all of them: Lisa was portrayed as the devil in a wedding gown waiting to steal Roy's soul once he says "I do." I was there too, waiting for my chance to save his soul, and, by that, to keep it for myself as God's reward for outsmarting the devil.

Pregnancy seemed like the perfect solution, and I was ready now to plant the seeds of trouble. The next evening, while studying together in Lisa's guesthouse, I chose to open the matter for discussion.

"He keeps evading me on the matter," she replied to my question with frustration written all over her face.

"You've been complaining about it every day for the last three months. Isn't it time you did something about it?" I challenged her, trying my best to act casually.

"What do you mean?"

"Lock him in. Create the solution with your natural biology."

"What?" she cried out. "You mean get pregnant?" she said shaking her head. "Are you out of your mind? I would never do that!"

"It's the only way to get your way."

"No! Absolutely not! It's out of the question! I love him too much to even think about it."

I had to bring something more shocking into the discussion, so I went sleazy: "Yeah, okay, and what do you think he's doing every night when you sit all by yourself waiting?"

She looked at me surprised. "He is playing." She said with a look that gave her instantly away.

"Playing? Where? On whom?" I giggled, watching Lisa get all red and offended.

"You're out of line!" she barked at me; but at the same time she couldn't hide the doubt digging further into the soil of her drugged up reasoning.

It was working so well that I had to find something to push it even deeper. "Come on, dear, you know I'm just kidding," I said smiling. "But really, don't say it hadn't crossed your mind." She did not answer. "He's good looking, almost a rock star. Both of us know he's a killer in bed . . ."

"Stop it!" She said angrily. "If he were here, he would have said that this is exactly why I shouldn't hang out with you."

"Okay . . . okay . . . calm down," I said, realizing I had gone too far with the infidelity argument. "I'm just teasing you; but I'm dead serious about throwing the net over him. All I'm saying is that sometimes one has to use unconventional methods to get one's man. Believe me, men like him are rare."

"He will despise me for the rest of his life. Our relationship is based on trust," she claimed. *Some trust,* I thought to myself, *you're doing drugs, and on top of that you're scheming to trick him into marriage,* but I allowed her the courtesy and remained silent.

"Think about it. You give up the pill for a day or two and you get pregnant. Your father gets mad as hell; his parents won't talk to him. Everybody will practically push you into it and you get married."

She got to her feet, looking at me furiously. "Jennifer Svensen!" she exclaimed with determination. "This is the last time you'll ever bring up this subject! Is that understood?"

At that exact moment we heard the front door slamming. "Hi," Roy called from the guesthouse's first floor, "It's me."

"I'm here," she replied, surprised and very happy at his unexpected early arrival. She rushed downstairs to greet him like a child expecting candy.

I started collecting my stuff, cursing my luck.

Roy climbed the stairs. I greeted him with a smile when he passed the room on his way to the shower. He stopped for a split second and threw me the meanest, nastiest look I ever got from anybody in my entire life.

I wanted to die.

Chapter 18

Worst Case Scenario

People are different in their reactions to heroin. This I have learned with time. It turned out I was a bit more durable than Lisa. Although experiencing fatigue and other drug-related effects, nobody could tell I was a user. Lisa's body, on the other hand, was a constant threat to our secret. It was showing external signs of deterioration.

The girl lost her appetite completely and consequently started losing weight. I had to squeeze food into her mouth during lunch at the cafeteria so she could continue functioning normally. Her medical doctor mother was very concerned about it. She even asked her if she was using drugs. Lisa blamed college pressure and acted offended about her mother's suspicions. Meanwhile, Dr. Epstein prescribed some pills aimed at strengthening her body. She was now living on those pills.

But her body would not settle for this. From time to time, at the worst possible moment, she would find herself trembling helplessly for an excruciatingly long moment. She also experienced hot and cold waves through her body, sweat attacks and restless sleeping patterns at night. She had nightmares, waking up in the middle of the night trembling, crying and mumbling. If Roy was there, he would try his best to calm her down.

Time was working against us. Someone was bound to figure out eventually what was going on. We both realized that a very dark and heavy cloud was hanging over our heads, and that eventually it would be raining acid rain on our lives. My main concern if Lisa were to break down and admit her addiction was that all fingers would point at me—especially Roy's.

One time, I lost contact with my supplier for a day or so for no feasible reason. I was left with a four-day supply of the drugs. Lisa freaked out and I had to be the responsible grownup, calming her down and promising that everything would be all right. Make no mistake—deep down inside I was in panic. It took me a couple of days to get the name of another supplier and another couple of days to find him and get the stuff. The transaction was supposed to have taken place within 24 hours, but the dealer kept changing our place of rendezvous—probably to make sure I was not trying to set him up. I got the drug at about 9:20 pm. The same evening, UCLA was holding a party for its students. I promised Lisa to meet her at the party and give her the daily portion so she could take it later at home.

I got to the party at about 9:50 pm and was very surprised to discover that Lisa had left for home with her boyfriend. Succumbing to the urge for the drug, I rushed home and took my fix without spending too much time dwelling on it. I woke up in the middle of the night to the sound of loud knocking on the guesthouse's back door. I walked down sleepy and unbalanced and opened the door. Lisa was there wearing her nightgown. She looked terrible.

"Did you get it?" she asked hysterically. I nodded. "Thank God."

She rushed up the stairs and I followed.

"What happened?" I asked as I gave her the stuff.

"I'll tell you later," she replied, grabbing her portion. She spent most of the night sleeping by my side. When I woke up at about 9 am, she was already gone. Later that day she told me how close that call had been. Expel had a gig cancelled and Roy thought to surprise her at the party. Normally, she would have loved the gesture, but facing the kind of circumstances she faced that evening—Roy was the last person she wanted to see. She was so overwhelmed to see him and so scared she wouldn't relieve her need that her body started giving out all the indication of a drug problem. In a moment of weakness, she almost disclosed her addiction to him. That night, she waited anxiously for him to fall asleep and rushed to my house when he finally did. Luckily for her, Roy was still sound-asleep that morning when she finally returned home.

"You have no idea of the acrobatics I performed to steer him off the course of suspicion," she testified.

"You have to keep trying!" I said with frustration. "I have my own addiction to deal with. I'm not taking the fall for yours too." She placed her arm on my shoulder and looked at me with compassion.

"I know, honey. I'm insensitive sometimes. It's turned me into a bitch and I'm sorry. We're in this together. I will not let anyone . . . ever . . . blame you for my addiction. Thank you for being there for me always."

Another incident occurred when the couple travelled to San Diego, not long after. Roy had met one of his Israeli friends and Lisa was alarmed when she overheard them talk about the possibility of enlisting into the Israeli army. Her Israeli boyfriend had just turned 18 and he was obliged to start his mandatory army service that summer. That same evening Expel had a gig in San Diego. Lisa decided to join him for the trip to make sure he was not seriously considering that possibility. They had lunch on the beach and then rented a motel room nearby. There and then, Lisa was struck by her worst trembling attack ever. She lost control over her body completely, crying and mumbling while shaking in Roy's arms. Roy wanted her to seek medical help immediately, but she dismissed it again as college pressure. He did not buy it this time around in what posed the most dangerous challenge to our secret up until then. She promised him she would see a doctor the next day. Feeling the urge, Lisa left Roy sleeping in the motel room and rushed back to LA.

With all of this in mind, the month of July saw my life, as I knew it, coming to a brutal and devastating end.

Just like any other ordinary day, Lisa and I had gotten stoned together, lying on my bed. While drifting away, I envisioned Roy coming into the room. This was not something out of the ordinary. I had envisioned that many times in the past. It was always a wonderful trip to higher places when I envisioned him near me.

It took us some time to recover. Soon, Lisa regained control and went down stairs for a glass of water. The minutes went by and she didn't return. I thought it odd. She never left without saying goodbye. I dragged myself down the stairs to look for her. What I saw half way through was the realization of the worst-case scenario. Roy was standing in the middle of the room looking at me with a sad face. Lisa was sitting on the sofa, all cuddled inside herself sobbing quietly. I now realized that the Roy I envisioned while surfing on the waves of drugs had been real.

I froze, terrified that the man from my marijuana incident will strike violently again.

He didn't. He came towards me and offered me his hand. I took it. He led me gently to the sofa, where I sat beside Lisa. I looked down. I just couldn't look him in the eyes. He sat between us and extended his arms over both our shoulders. Lisa kept crying silently. I placed my head on his shoulder and waited, petrified of what was about to happen. After some time he got up and sat down on the small table in front of me. He got closer as he spoke.

"Look at me!" he commanded. I was too afraid to do so. "Please, Jenny, look at me!" he said in a more tender tone of voice. I raised my gaze and saw his tormented face. "Is this how you get back at me for being honest?" he asked. "Is this my punishment for telling you plain and simple that I loved Lisa?" Tears filled my eyes when I looked into his eyes. "Lisa never did you wrong. You promised me you'd never hurt her." I began crying silently, realizing the damage this would bring to my relations with both of them. To make matters worse, Lisa extended her hand and caressed my shoulder as a show of support. She did not believe I would ever hurt her. "You need to understand that as much as I care for you, I don't love you," Roy said and sent a poison arrow straight into my heart. I looked into his eyes while the tears washed my face like a river.

"I am to blame, not her," Lisa whispered. Roy silenced her immediately with an angry look.

He shifted his gaze back to me. "Why? Jenny, I need you to tell me why," he insisted softly while caressing my shoulder.

"You know why," I whispered.

"Yes, I do," he said, "but I want you to say it anyway."

There was a moment of silence. "I couldn't stand the fact that the only man I ever loved was in love with someone else," I said looking down ashamed.

Lisa cried out astounded. "What? You said you love me," she wailed with pain. "I loved you with all my heart . . ."

"I'm sorry," I cried. "I didn't mean to hurt you. I do love you. I always loved you. Lisa, please don't hate me. Everybody hates me." I exclaimed, breaking down, crying a deep and painful cry.

"Nobody hates you," Roy said softly, still caressing my shoulder, "but you did us wrong."

"I'm sorry. Roy, I thought . . ." Lisa cried, stretching out her hand, placing it on his. In anger, he pulled his hand away from the person who had deceived him the most and got up. He walked a few steps away from us, standing undecided, wearing a sad face—lost for action. A moment later, he came back and sat on the table in front of me again. He kissed my forehead and embraced me warmly. "I will always have strong feelings for you and I will always be your friend." He said softly in what made me burst into tears again. "I'm sorry your love for me caused you so much pain." He pushed me gently away and looked into my tearful eyes. "I want you to promise me you'll take care of yourself." I nodded in confirmation, wiping my tears with my sleeve. "I want you to promise me you'll do your best to overcome this problem and rehabilitate your life." I nodded my head again. "I mean it," he said and kissed my forehead again.

He sat straight, shifting his gaze toward Lisa. "Take your stuff!" he said to her in a commanding, ruthless tone of voice. "You are coming with me!"

She got up and collected her bag from the floor. Just before leaving, she gave me a look of profound disappointment. Then, she followed Roy out.

Chapter 19

Abyss

The door closes behind my loved ones. It darkens my reality. I sit on the sofa alone for an hour or so in utter shock. I don't know what to make of the situation. I am in a state of complete alarm. I'm crying silently while a heavy rock ploughs deeper and deeper into my chest. It makes breathing difficult. My thoughts are running wild and they make no sense. I'm confused and numb. Reality and daydreaming mix to a point where I can't differentiate between the two. I sink into a catatonic state of mind. It takes me a long time to get back to my new and dismal reality.

Tragedy, sin, wickedness, evil, darkness, calamity, catastrophe, transgression—these, and others of the sort, were the titles I gave the sketches I made during those unforgettable days of devastation; the days which followed the disappearance of Roy Cohen and Lisa Anne Epstein from my life.

Still confounded, I tried calling Lisa's private number dozens of times that awful day but to no avail. I even went over to her guesthouse that evening but it was locked and all the lights were out. I waited for hours, sitting on the stairs leading to the back door in hope of getting a chance to beg for forgiveness. Then I moved to my car and waited there for another hour or so. I left for home at about 3 am. I spent the remaining hours of the night lying on my bed helplessly, feeling sorry for myself. Roy showed me up for what I was—guilty for all that had gone wrong in their lives. The burden of guilt was impossible to bear. I wanted to cry it out but couldn't. The words and images of the previous day haunted me and would not let go of my aching consciousness.

I spent most of the next day in bed, calling Lisa every 15 minutes or so, sinking deeper and deeper into a dark and lonely void.

I took my fix earlier that day to detach myself from reality. It was the worst experience of my drug-life. I puked repeatedly and my body temperature hit a record high.

Finally, I was able to cry. I cried like never before, seated on the toilet bowel, naked, shaking and trembling. I fell asleep bent over, still sitting there, exhausted from the pain. At about 5 pm the telephone rang. I woke up in my bed, to where I had apparently dragged myself into at some point.

"Lisa?" I whispered.

"Yes . . ." she responded.

"I'm sorry," I quivered into the phone. "I'm so sorry . . . please. I beg you, Lisa, say you forgive me . . ."

"I don't have time for this now!" she whispered. "Calm down and listen to me! I need your help and I need it fast."

"Please . . ." I cried.

"Calm down already!" she commanded. "I don't have time for this now. We're in San Francisco. Roy is asleep and wouldn't appreciate this call. I need you to contact your supplier and see if he has someone here that can get me the stuff as soon as possible."

"Okay . . ." I sniffled.

"I'll call you in half an hour," she said and hung up.

"Lisa . . . Lisa . . ." I cried out.

I called my supplier. He did know someone in San Francisco. He gave me an address and a password.

"Did you get it?" she asked when I picked up the ringing phone about twenty five minutes later.

"Yes."

"Good. Tell me!"

"His nickname is Kilimanjaro; he's at the Boise bar on Balboa and 47th. The password is Bogota," I said.

"Thanks," she whispered.

"Don't hang up . . . please . . ." I begged her. She didn't. There was silence on the other side of the telephone line. "I love you more than anything! I'm sorry. Please tell me you know that . . . please, honey," I cried. Still silence on the other side . . . "Please forgive me . . ." Still silence. "Lisa . . .?"

"Jennifer . . ." she whispered, "I trusted you with my life . . ."

"I know . . . I'm so sorry . . ."

"We are beyond that. I'm in the deepest shit ever . . . you should have known better . . ." she said and started to cry. "You should have known better . . ." she repeated and hung up.

"Lisa," I cried out, "don't hang up . . . please . . . please . . ."

That evening my father came knocking on my guesthouse door. He was there with Lisa's father, Jacob.

"Mr. Epstein is worried about his daughter. Can we come in?" I nodded and walked inside. They followed me in. "What's wrong?" my father asked when I turned on the light and he saw I was crying.

"Nothing . . ." I said. "I just woke up."

"Do you know where Lisa is?" Jacob interrupted.

"No. I'm looking for her too. The last time I saw her was two days ago," I lied. It was obvious Jacob did not believe me. He looked at me harshly. "Look, Jennifer, I think Lisa is in trouble." He said. "Roy called us today from a motel somewhere but didn't tell us where. I know my daughter is in trouble. I ask you again: do you know their whereabouts?"

"No. I don't," I replied.

"Sweetheart," my father intervened, probably not believing me himself. "I will not be angry at you. Just tell us what you know."

"I don't know anything," I maintained. "I'm looking for Lisa myself. I've called her dozens of times in the last two days but she is not answering the phone. I swear to God . . ." Jacob and my father exchanged looks.

"Jake, I know my daughter. She doesn't know," my father said and stuck by me. Jacob nodded reluctantly.

"Okay . . . Jennifer . . ." Jacob said. "I urge you to call me if you hear from her. Will you do that?" he asked.

"Of course," I replied.

The information concerning what happened next was gathered from different sources over time—none of which were Roy or Lisa. Obsessed with these two people as I had become throughout the years, I researched the facts, speaking eventually with both their parents and friends. Yet, although very close to the truth, this segment in my story is the only segment which I cannot vouch for to be one hundred percent accurate because I was not directly involved in it.

Leaving my house that day, Roy drove to San Francisco where he saw Lisa undergo a very difficult three days. Lisa's father had the police track down one of Roy's phone calls to them, and soon the police broke into the room and freed Lisa from captivity.

Jacob Epstein, the mighty lawyer, did not press charges against Roy Cohen but he did forbid him from ever coming close to Lisa again. Believing he was to blame for Lisa's decline and agreeing with her father as to the solution, Roy disconnected himself from Lisa. Three days later, my beloved Roy flew back home—to Israel.

Lisa kept her promise to me. Seeing that nobody was coming after me, I understood that my name was left out of the mess. Nonetheless, I called Lisa's mom about a week later and begged her to let me visit her daughter in the rehabilitation center. Dr. Epstein politely declined. She apologized and explained that her daughter had to disengage from her old life and friends.

I asked my father to help. He contacted some mutual friends to help him set up a meeting with Jacob Epstein. We met Lisa's father at his office the next day. He looked tired and preoccupied.

"Look, Jennifer," Jacob addressed me with a compassionate, yet gloomy look on his face. "I've just banned Roy from Lisa's life. I see him as the main reason for her decline. I trusted him and he failed me—he failed her. She does not understand it yet, but time will make her understand."

"What does this have to do with me?" I asked, turning emotional, realizing we had come to his office in vain.

"Lisa hates me for doing that," he continued, disregarding my comment, "but I am determined to cut off every relationship she's had for the last year or so. I don't want to offend you, but you were her closest friend. Didn't you know she had a heroin addiction? Where were you all this time?"

"Jake . . ." my father intervene, "what are you suggesting?"

"Angus, my friend, I'm not suggesting anything. I'm trying to . . ."

"Daddy . . ." I cried. "Do something . . ." But instead, Angus helped me up and Jacob accompanied us to the door.

"I wish you and your family all the best," my father said as they shook hands at the door. "If you ever need anything, please don't hesitate to ask." Jacob nodded in appreciation. We left.

As it turned out, I soon grasped, that gloomy situation presented a positive side. Circumstances had eliminated Lisa from Roy's life. Now I had to complete the assignment by reuniting with Roy. An exciting plan surfaced in the ocean of my being. The more I thought about it the more excited I became. I called Roy's mother and asked for his address in Israel. I claimed that I wanted to keep in touch by correspondence. She was quite happy to give me the information, telling me that her son was living with his grandparents in Jerusalem and was getting ready to enlist to the army in November.

Yes . . .!

I was going to Israel and regardless of the consequences—I was going to spend the rest of my life there with the man I loved.

Chapter 20

Holy Ground

Reaching a decision and executing it are very different things, as my decision to travel to Israel taught me.

I was a junky. How could I fly to Israel without a steady supply of drugs? I went berserk searching for a solution. I knew I could go without consumption for 24 hours, maybe 36. Theoretically, this gave me enough time to fly to Israel and get the stuff over there. But I knew no one in the whole country, so in my search for solutions, I presented a challenge to my supplier.

"Find some Israeli who knows the country. You certainly have tons of them here in LA," he advised when we met for my weekly supply.

"Don't you have Israelis on the *demand* side of your equation," I asked him impatiently. He nodded. "Give me a name?"

"I'll have to ask their permission. You would have to make it worth their while though . . ." he said.

"How about a week's supply of that crap you're selling us?"

He nodded again. "Yeah . . . that would probably do the job."

The next day he left a message on my machine with a name and a number. I called. The person on the other side of the line was willing to meet me only if I brought with me "what has been promised." I waited for him in a dark alley in Brentwood at about 10 pm, with the stuff stashed in my backpack. A man wearing a long black coat and a hat approached me. "Matilda?" he asked, using the nickname my supplier gave me.

"Yes . . ."

"Follow me!" he ordered.

I followed him into an underground parking lot. The guy was creepy and it was rather scary—an unexpected dose of adrenaline.

We entered the building's boiler room. He closed the door behind us and took off his hat revealing an impressive looking face. He was a man in his mid or late thirties and, in a way, resembled Richard Ward, my mythological shrink.

"Take off your clothes!" he commanded. I was taken aback, fearing the worst.

"No fucking way!" I answered, ready to defend myself with anything I could get a hold of.

"Then our deal is off," he said and started walking out the door.

"Wait!" I said. "Why the hell do you need me to get undressed?"

"I want to make sure you're not wearing a wire," he said.

"Okay . . . okay . . . don't go," I said, as he got closer. "Stand over there!" I commanded and pointed to the opposite wall. He did as I asked, staring at me indifferently. I got undressed, leaving on only my panties and bra.

"Take it all off!" he demanded.

"Come, on . . . you can see I have nothing on me."

"Take it all off or I'm gone!" I looked at him for a long minute. Images of Roy and me walking hand in hand in the street of Jerusalem convinced me to do as the creep wanted. I took off the final pieces of clothes left on my body.

"Satisfied?" I asked angrily. "Maybe you want to jerk-off while you're watching . . ."

"You're a beautiful woman," he said softly with a sad face. "You can put your clothes on now." I got dressed as I locked my eyes with his. "Did you bring it?" He asked.

"Yes, I did," I said as I buttoned my shirt. I took the brown bag out of my backpack and tossed it to him. He lifted it from the floor and peeked in.

"Okay . . . what do you want to know?"

"I'm traveling to Israel. I need to know how to get some stuff while I'm there," I said as I tied my shoe.

He looked at me, deep in thought. "What's your cover story?" he asked.

"What do you mean?"

"Do you have family or friends in Israel?"

"No," I replied.

"Then don't enter through Ben-Gurion airport! You'll need to cross the border from Egypt."

"Egypt?" I asked surprised.

"Yes. The airport is an edgy place and you're not Jewish. Without a credible story you'll be raising suspicion. If no one who can vouch for you is expecting you outside the terminal, you'll be deported on the next flight out."

"Won't it be the same at the crossings from Egypt?"

"No. If you are an American tourist entering from Sinai into Taba, the border control officers would assume you're one of thousands of tourists entering Israel with the intention of enjoying Eilat."

"What's Eilat?"

"It's a seaside resort in the southern part of Israel with access to the Red Sea."

"Okay, how do I get the stuff in Egypt then?"

"Do you have a pen?" he asked. I took one out of my bag and showed it to him. "Do you have a piece of paper?" I looked inside my bag again and found an empty envelope. "Now start writing!"

"Okay . . ." I said confused.

"You have to fly to Cairo," he said and I wrote it down. "Take another flight from Cairo airport to Sharm-El-Sheikh. It's a small town in the Sinai Peninsula. From there you'll take a bus to Nuweiba. You can get drugs easily there from the Bedouins. Only buy enough for one fix and take it there. This will buy you time and you won't be tempted to do anything stupid. Then take a bus to the Taba crossing. In Israel, take a taxi from Taba to Eilat Central Bus Station and from there to Tel Aviv. When you're at the bus station—it's a huge spread-out place—look for 'Café Til' and ask for Shuki. He will take care of you."

"But I need to get to Jerusalem, not to Tel Aviv." I stated.

"Sorry honey," he said, "I don't know anyone there. It's only an hour away. Have a nice life." He started walking to the door.

"Wait!" I commended. He stopped and turned around. "How come you know so much about Egypt?"

He smiled sadly. "I fought the Egyptians in '67 and '73 and then served most of my army reserve time in Sinai. Friends died and worse . . ." he chuckled. "I guess I belong to the *worse* category," he said bitterly, looking into the brown bag. He looked at me again for a second. "You really are a beautiful woman," he said and left.

The next day I called the Egyptian and Israeli Consulates in Los Angeles and discovered that I wouldn't need a visa to either places. The advantages of being an American citizen . . . I took one of my shoeboxes out of my hiding place and grabbed about $2,000 in cash. An hour later I was making my way back home excited with a plane ticket to Cairo scheduled for the day after tomorrow.

That night, equipped with a flashlight, I searched for my passport. I went into my father's study and rummaged through some of his drawers. I found it inside a small black box, along with the more important family documents. I opened my old passport with a beating heart fearing it was no longer valid. Luckily for me it was—for another year or so. The next day I went shopping for maps and guidebooks. Then, I packed a small backpack, filled it mainly with cash, and wrote a small note to my parents explaining I had gone on a trip with friends for a few days. I asked them not to worry.

I woke up at 4 am and took my last fix before the flight to New York. I had about 24 hours before the craving would start again; by then I would, hopefully, be on Egyptian soil. It was early morning when I landed in Cairo. Although the flight was exhausting, the excitement and concerns would not give my body a break. As a result, I didn't sleep at all. I had six hours left before my usual fix and I was already getting anxious.

The airport in Cairo was old, outdated, hectic and packed. It was hot and the air conditioning system didn't work. I was sweating like a pig as I walked about frantically. I finally found the counter selling tickets to Sharm-El-Shiekh. After buying the ticket, I realized that I still had an hour or so in anticipation and then another hour and a half inside a very old piston plane, in what is considered by me until this very day as the worst and most terrifying flight I ever took. I thanked God when we landed safely in Sharm-El-Sheikh's tiny airport.

The bus to the village of Nuweiba was packed with tourists from all over the world. I got into a conversation with a good-looking Italian college student who went by the nickname, Pepe. It was clear to me that the man had only one thing on his mine. Later that night I would see his wishes fulfilled, but for now, I thought of using him for my own purposes. Pepe said he was looking to buy some local Hashish and I needed a man with me when I went out looking for the harder stuff among the locals. Once off the bus, we walked together into the Bedouin part of the village. We managed to find a dealer rather easily and bought the stuff we wanted rather cheaply. I took my fix that afternoon inside a deserted shack on the outskirts of the village, about 25 hours after my last dose. Pepe looked after me while I dozed off for about an hour.

It was early evening when we crossed into Taba. Back then, it was still under Israeli control. I was exhausted from the rough trip and from being awake for almost two days. I took a room at the Hilton and rewarded Pepe for his companionship before diving into a deep sleep. The following morning I left him sound asleep, paid the hotel bill and took a taxi to Eilat's central bus station. From there I took the bus to my next destination—Tel Aviv.

Some six hour later, making my way through the vendors of Tel-Aviv's dilapidated bus station in search of the Til (that's *missile* in Hebrew) café, I found myself experiencing culture shock. The market was loud and crowded, and dozens of armed soldiers were all around me, making their way there and about as if it was the most natural thing in the world. I found it intriguing but intimidating.

When I finally found the café, I asked for Shuki. The barman directed me to a small moneychanger across the street. The person behind the counter at the money exchange stand cross-examined me until he was sure I was an innocent tourist who was looking for non-commercial quantities of stuff. He asked one of his people to lead me to the dealer. I followed him for about five minutes until we finally got to a rather isolated alley. A man was waiting for us there. He searched my bags and checked my body, touching me everywhere possible to make sure I was not carrying anything incriminating. Then we exchanged the money for a large envelope. The envelope contained a week's supply of drugs and accessories. At last, I felt relieved.

Once the technical details had been settled, the next thing was to find Roy.

I suddenly panicked. I was so excited that I could not think straight. I needed time to prepare for our meeting, so I postponed my trip to Jerusalem and got myself a room in a fancy hotel by the Tel Aviv seashore. I spent the evening walking along the promenade with hundreds of people around me, thinking of ways to convince Roy I was not evil and that I'm all he's got now that Lisa is out of the game. It was pathetic . . . I realize that now . . . but after a very long reflection, I concluded that that was all I had to offer. I remember dining by myself at an Italian restaurant near the beach, trying my best to come up with some convincing arguments and rehearsing texts in preparation for my encounter with the object of my eternal love. I knew Roy would be shattered, blaming me for anything and everything that happened since the crucifixion of Christ; yet I hoped he would also see the benefits of having me around. I counted on the time factor to make him adjust eventually to the new situation. I was willing to do anything for him. I was willing to leave my past behind and stay in Israel for the rest of my life, if he would just agree to let me into his heart again.

The next morning I took a bus to Jerusalem and a taxi to Roy's address—the one given to me by his parents. I walked for about half an hour in search of the apartment building. When I finally found it, I rushed up and knocked on the door with a beating heart. An elderly man with a well-kept mustache opened the door. "Shalom," he said and then continued in Hebrew, saying something I did not understand.

"I'm looking for Roy," I said in English.

"Roy is not home," he answered in English. "Are you a friend of his?"

"Yes." I said. "We went to the same school in Beverly Hills. I have a letter I need to give him. When will he be back?"

"He went on a trip to the north and I have no idea when he'll be back. Would you like to leave the letter with me? I'll give it to him when he returns."

"No thanks. I want to give it to him myself. Do you know where he's staying?"

"He called us yesterday from Kibutz Merom Golan. It's on the Golan Heights."

"Merom Golan, you said?" I asked and took out of my backpack the new notebook I had bought in Tel Aviv. He nodded as I wrote it down. "Thank you sir," I said as I placed it back in my backpack. "Can I get your phone number so I can call Roy when he's back?"

"Of course. It's 02 for Jerusalem and then 439187."

"Thank you kindly. Are you Roy's grandfather?"

"Yes. I am," he said. "My name is Joseph. Nice to meet you," he said and we shook hands. "Would you like to come in and have some tea?"

"No, thank you. Maybe some other time," I said as sweetly as possible. "Goodbye."

"Do you want to leave your name and telephone number?" he asked as I made my way down the stairs.

"No sir. I would like to surprise him. Thanks." I said and rushed down the stairs, making my way back to Jerusalem's Central bus station.

My next destination: Kibutz Merom Golan.

Chapter 21

The Search

It was evening when I got to Kibbutz Merom Golan. I was exhausted and my body craved for a fix.

I went to the Kibbutz's secretariat and asked if they had a room for rent. They had none. I must have looked very tired and troubled because the woman I addressed there called a young woman by the name of Tamara and asked her to help me find some kind of temporary lodgings. This angel of a girl invited me to share her room. Normally she shared it with another woman who by chance was spending that night on duty at her army base. Tamara had kitchen duty that evening. That gave me the opportunity to take my fix with no interruptions. About two hours, a shower and one heroin dose later, I went out to search for my man. I heard some music coming from the Kibbutz's dining room and walked towards, hoping it was a gathering of some kind. As many people as possible gathered in one place was the best thing that could happen to me. It would diminish the time I had to invest going from one house to another, searching for Roy—something I had intended to do.

I walked inside in the midst of a singing performance, so I had to wait until it was over before I could start inquiring. One woman suggested I go to the Feldman house and gave me directions. She said she had seen a young man fitting Roy's description coming to the dining room with their eldest son Yaniv. I practically ran all the way. I was trying to catch my breath as I knocked on the door. A young man, about my age, opened the door for me.

"Wow . . ." he said with a smile on his face and then threw into the air some sentences in Hebrew.

"Hi. I'm Jennifer. Sorry . . . I don't speak Hebrew . . ." I said.

"Oh! I just said, how pleasantly surprising to find such a beautiful thing in this God forsaken place." He said and I smiled in gratitude.

"Thanks . . . I'm looking for Roy Cohen," I said, cutting at once the unimportant small talk.

"Roy . . . how did you know he was here?" he asked surprised.

"So, he's here?" I asked overwhelmed with emotions.

"Was here," he said. "He left this morning."

"Shit . . ." I said disappointed. "Do you know where he's headed?"

"Rosh Hanikra," he replied.

"Where is that?"

"About two hours drive from here—depending on traffic."

"Take me there now!" I commanded. "I'll pay you."

"I would do it for free, you gorgeous thing, if I only had a car," he said smiling a cute smile. I remained unmoved. "You'll have to wait for the morning. There's a bus leaving at about 7:30." I took some steps away from him and sat on the nearby bench, looking angry and gloomy. He stepped out, shut the door behind him, and sat beside me.

"Just my luck," I whispered in frustration.

"Roy is one hell of a lucky guy to have someone like you looking for him." I stared at him for a long second, smiling a sarcastic smile.

"Yeah. . . . sure . . ."

"I'm Yaniv by the way," he said and sent his hand out to me.

"Jennifer," I said and shook it.

"You know, I grew up with Roy in Jerusalem until he left for America and I had to move with my parents to this dump. The Roy that left Israel was always optimistic and happy. I have a feeling you know why the Roy that came back is so depressed and cynical." I looked at him again with a sad face."

"Broken heart," I said and looked forward, trying to plan.

"I guess you're the reason . . . huh..?"

"I wish. . . ." I whispered sadly.

I spent the next four days chasing what I thought were Roy's tracks until I lost them completely. His grandfather Joseph, whom I called almost every day to check if Roy had called, was kind enough to help me, suggesting places he might visit. At a certain point, I not only lost track of Roy but was left with only one dose of heroin. I had to put my search on hold and travel back south to Tel-Aviv. This time I would play it safe and get two weeks supply.

An idea popped into my head, which I was determined to execute. I would hire a professional private investigator. I traveled back to Jerusalem. After a good night's sleep, I opened the English yellow pages I found in my hotel room, searching for one. I found a PI by the name of David Schwartz. The ad said he was a retired police investigator with a lot of experience. I met with him the next day. I expected to find a man in his fifties or sixties but instead found myself sitting across from a man in his mid-thirties. He was friendly, direct and forthcoming. He had a good command of the English language and seemed very knowledgeable professionally. PI Schwartz accepted the job on the spot. I gave him a $2,000 down payment and asked him to begin working on the case.

"It will take a day or two but I can track him down for you," he promised. "What do you want to do with the info?"

"Just find him. I'll do the rest."

He looked at me with a question mark on his face, "Are you sure?" he asked and smiled. "I mean . . . I don't really care about the reason you need to track him down, but you do realize you're paying me a small fortune just to supply you with an address." I nodded. "I hope he's worth it."

He gave me his business card, I gave him my address and phone numbers in case worse came to worse and I had to leave back home empty-handed.

I rushed to the Til Café. Shuki had one of his people accompany me again to the alley. As the transaction was completed and we had exchanged the money for the drug, about a dozen police officers stormed us. They had caught me red handed. I was cuffed and taken to a detention facility named Abu-Kabir, not far from Tel Aviv. I spent the night in a small cell with four other female offenders—an abusing mother and three prostitutes.

I'm sitting on a dirty bed in a dirty cell with four older women. One of them is shouting at the guards in Hebrew, the other one is talking to herself, probably cursing; and the third one refuses to stop sobbing. None of them is speaking to me or looking at me. I don't exist and I don't speak their language. Someone vomits in another cell and doors slam. There are no guards around. I'm terrified. I'm reminded of the fix I missed and the one I'll miss tomorrow. I get stomach cramps just from thinking about it. I start feeling bad, and there is no one around I can bother.

The next day I was interrogated for about three hours and then returned to my stinking cell. It was something I thought could never happen to me. Personal consumption of drugs was a felony all right, but it wasn't as bad as dealing the stuff. If at all, I was supposed to receive some minor punishment in the form and shape of a fine or community service. I wasn't concerned about that. My greatest concern was the possibility that the Israeli judge would decide to deport me.

The craving for the drug started hurting. It had been about 40 hours since I took my last fix and I started puking. I was rushed to a nearby hospital where they eased my pain with an injection of Methadone. Lying on the clean bed in the Emergency Room, I thought of my situation and decided to do anything in my power to stay in this country until I found Roy. I needed a good lawyer, and I was willing to pay whatever I had left in my backpack, some $8,000. That evening a young lawyer visited me. He was probably fresh out of law school and was appointed to me by the State. We had an hour-long conversation, during which I told him my story and he explained to me my options. I was going to see a judge the next morning. This judge was going to decide if to extend the term of my incarceration or deport me from the country.

"I have to stay in Israel!" I exclaimed. "You need to work on a third option."

"In theory, every option is a valid one, but I don't see it happening. The best case scenario for you is deportation," he explained.

Well, I was not going to surrender without a fight. I decided to plead my case in court. The next day, after another dose of

Methadone at a local clinic, I was taken to court. The prosecutor asked the judge to allow the police more time to conclude the investigation. The judge asked me if I had anything to say. I admitted the felony, stating that my only crime was being a junky, a fact that had caused me pain and sorrow more than any punishment by any court would ever cause.

"Why are you here young lady?" he asked.

"Because of love," I admitted truthfully. He nodded. I thought I hit a nerve there so I continued with this line of defense. "He is Israeli. He came back to serve in the army. I've been searching for him the last four or five days but couldn't find him. I had to get drugs to function normally. I'm sorry your honor, but I had no choice. I beg the court to release me and allow me to resume my search."

The judge was sympathetic. Nevertheless, he explained that I had broken the law and had to pay the price. He allowed the police to hold me for three more days, after which they must release me. I hoped this meant release into Israel, but my lawyer told me it meant deportation with a black stamp on my passport limiting my access to the country for an entire five years. Angry and frustrated, I was taken back to my cell. About an hour later, a consular officer from the American embassy came to see me. He was a man in his early forties. Sitting there listening to a lecture about my status and rights, it occurred to me that this government official was probably the only chance I had left to remain in the country.

"I need you to find a way to release me into Israel," I said when he was done talking.

"Sorry. It is not possible!" He exclaimed.

"Nothing is impossible!" I said in defiance.

"You will be deported home in a day or two. That is the best we can hope for; and let me tell you Ms. Svensen, you are lucky not to be sentenced to prison."

"Listen, mister," I said getting angrier by the second. "We give this country billions; we supply them with state-of-the-art weapons and we support their behinds in the international arena. This is a small favor to ask in return." Being a man his look traveled unintentionally to the crack between my boobs and remained there for a second or two, giving me something to use if push came to shove.

"I'm sorry, but this is not a matter of asking favors," he said looking back up to my face again. "You are a felon and a foreigner. We are even tougher back home with cases like yours."

"What would it take to change your mind?" I asked him. "I have to stay here and search for someone and I'm willing to pay in whatever commodity I have that you desire."

"Don't even think of going there!" He commanded, somewhat taken aback.

"Money? Just say how much . . ."

"Who do you think you are?" he said surprised by my directness.

"Sex? Just tell me where and when and I'll give you the best blow job you ever got . . ."

"Young lady! I'm an American diplomatic officer," he barked at me. "How dare you speak to me like that . . ." He got up to his feet. I just looked at his crotch with a belittling smile.

"American diplomatic officer my ass," I said with a disrespectful look. "Any satellite orbiting earth can see your hard-on, you pathetic creature. Leave! I don't need you or your government. I'll handle things on my own"!" I exclaimed. "Guard," I shouted before the man could react. The Israeli prison guard appeared at the door. "Please escort this man out of here . . . He is bothering me."

The next person to show up was my father. He was traveling to London for business when my Mom told him of my whereabouts and arrest. She had been notified by the State Department. He took the first plane to Tel Aviv and came directly from the airport. My well-connected father made sure the American Ambassador placed the right calls to the right people so he could see me face to face and not through a glass pane. The guard escorted me into the room. My father stood there, looking at me with disappointment written all over his face.

"I was afraid of this happening," he said sadly when the guard closed the door behind us. I didn't respond. He came closer and embraced me. We sat in front of each other—the old desk between us. I looked down. "Jennifer . . . drugs? My god . . ." he said with a tormented face. I looked at him with defiance. "Why honey. Why?" I looked away again, trying my best to overcome the desire to start crying like a little girl, having my strong father embrace and comfort me. "I gave you everything you needed, everything you wanted. Why didn't you come to me, sweetheart? I would have given anything to ensure your happiness."

"I'm tired of living . . ." I whispered.

"Don't say that . . . please! Jenny, let me help you . . ."

"You can't! Nobody can!"

"At least let me try."

"I want Roy back in my life. Can you do that?" I asked.

"No," he said.

"You see."

"You've got to let go of him."

"I love him more than anything. . . . Jesus I'm so tired of trying to always search for ways to win him back . . . I just want him to love me . . ." he got to his feet and came closer, bending over to embraced me. I remained seated, indifferent, looking away, while he caressed my hair.

"Roy is history, sweetheart. You must put the past behind you and look to the future."

"I can't give up on him . . ."

"You must! At least for now . . ."

"I will never give up on him. Do you hear?" I whispered. "Never!"

Chapter 22

Picking Up the Pieces

They deported me like a common criminal.

I waited at the airport for my flight to embark, seating in the detention area for hours with some other deportees—cuffed and stinking like a pig. I hadn't even taken a decent shower in the five days I was incarcerated. Looking and smelling the way I did humiliated and degraded me.

The passengers aboard the 747 stared at me with reproof as I was escorted by a police officer into the plane. We went up to the second floor, where the first class section was located. I was seated beside my father. Only then did the Israeli police officer remove my cuffs.

It was a shameful experience all right, but nothing compared to the devastation I felt for the loss of Roy. I spent about an hour in the lavatories after takeoff. I washed myself and then sat on the bowl, crying my heart out. It struck me then and there that life as I knew it was over. Going back to my designated seat, wearing fresh clothes my father had bought for me, I avoided eye contact. He placed his hand on mine. "Everything will be okay now honey. You'll see." I did not respond. "I saw to it that you'll be admitted to an excellent recovery center. We will overcome your addiction and you can open a new page. I'm going to be there for you, Jen, I promise."

We landed in Los Angeles. An ambulance took me to a rehab center in Malibu where my room overlooked the ocean. My mother visited almost every day, and slept in my room every other night. I didn't give a shit.

The loss of the two people who dominated my life thus far combined with the guilt for ruining both their lives tormented my soul on a minute-to-minute basis. I spent the first week or two in bed, not speaking to anyone. I slept a lot and sketched, repeatedly reliving scenes from my life while trying to figure out what to do next. College was out of the question. I found no real interest in going without Lisa keeping me close to Roy. I debated my future internally: What did I want to do with my life? How do I want to live and where? Buzz, Doug and Heather came almost every weekend; but in October Heather and Doug left for New York. Only Buzz remained, waiting for me in LA. It was painful to realize that I had no friends in the world but these three. I felt sorry for myself for being so lonely.

On the physical side, they gave me Methadone. On the psychological side, they had me undergo hours of useless talk. Somehow I managed to defeat my addiction. I was released home in November with a decision to pursue modeling as a temporary solution. It was the easiest way I could think of out of my dismal situation. I mean, I had the looks and I had a mother in the industry.

"Fine," my mother said to me after days of persuasion, "but *you* will be the one telling your father."

"Over my dead body!" he exclaimed when I did.

"I'm almost 20 and I don't need your permission. You need to learn to live with that."

"Did your mother tell you how it was? Did she tell you about all her sleepless nights, about how I had to calm her down after being molested and touched by creeps all over, photographers with an erection, other lowlife worse?" I looked at my mother. She looked sadly away.

"I'm going for it with or without your consent!" I exclaimed.

He took a big gulp of air and calmed himself down. "Listen, Jennifer," he said formally, still very much agitated but in a softer tone of voice, "you're a rebel. Nothing I say would change your mind. I know that. But I urge you to please reconsider. I can open many doors for you. It doesn't have to be the fashion world."

"It's what I want!" I said. "Now please set me up with a photographer so I can produce a professional portfolio."

Two days later, I had a nine-hour session in one of the best studios in town. Two top-notch makeup artists and a dressing specialist—females, mind you—were making it happen for me, and two top executives from my mother's company—males—were there to evaluate my potential, staring at my sometimes-naked body with shining eyes. My mother gave the orders. All in attendance appreciated the results.

Truthfully, at that stage I still didn't give a shit. I wasn't really looking for a career. I just needed a distraction. My conscience was still killing me. I had to do something to shift my thoughts from the ongoing self-hatred. So, soon enough, I adopted a wild and extensive nightlife that included a lot of sex and alcohol. It proved to be the perfect remedy.

Buzz was there, as always, accompanying me, protecting me and sexing me. He was practically running his uncle's business singlehanded; but he was always there. He loved me and I took advantage of it. I did value Buzz's friendship, but I was no friend to him. I dragged him to the most wild and outrageous parties in town and never missed an opportunity to screw around, often while Buzz was looking for me—probably suspecting and eating his heart out. Today I realize that, in a sense, by living this kind of a life back then, I was being vindictive towards myself.

In March 1986 I landed my first campaign. Later, I found out that my mother had gotten me the deal upon orders directly from my father. My agent had to succumb to the limitations my father had imposed; otherwise, he had threatened to leave my mother if she dared throw his immature and reckless daughter straight into the teeth of the sharks. "No runways!" He had commanded, "Only shooting campaigns! If somebody lays a finger on her, I swear I'll kill him—literally!"

Therefore, I promoted sandals with my long, naked, silky white legs. Soon I found my legs everywhere. The brand boosted its sales three-fold and I was chosen to do their next couple of campaigns as well. Yet, my lifestyle was giving me a problematic reputation. I was difficult to work with, nasty and obnoxious to the photographers and campaign staff, always arriving late with a hangover and getting into endless fights with everyone. Luckily, the reputation didn't do a lot of damage: the agency kept getting calls and the gossip columns starred me on a weekly basis.

As time passed and my reputation evolved, I suddenly realized I had a lot to lose if I didn't start taking my career more seriously. I decided to move to New York. Looking back, this decision rescued me from an abyss of self-pity and ruination. I decided to shift my attention from the past to the future. I had Heather by my side, now, helping me to balance my life out and preaching.

Soon enough, the creeps my father had warned me about came out of their holes. I was the new name, the potential, the one with the exceptional beauty, the one with the bad reputation; and they wanted a taste. Some of them were the industry's top rollers, so I had to be careful not to piss them off. I played along, allowing bodily access only to the most important ones. Whether I liked it or not, I suddenly had a successful career to protect.

It was only then that I finally understood what my mother had been doing all those years. She had been protecting our livelihood. I never forgave her but I began to appreciate her motives. I was becoming her. But unlike her difficult circumstances—supporting a husband and struggling in a new and strange place—I did it simply because I could! And because I needed to forget . . .

Then, one day I received an envelope from PI Schwartz. It contained a letter and a photo of Roy Cohen in army uniform.

Chapter 23

A VIP Ticket to Hell

PI Swartz's letter was an example of something that had characterized my mature life. It was the systematic reoccurrence of things that drew me back into a past I was trying to escape—a past replete with my iconic peers. I decided to keep him on a generous retainer. Getting updated news about Roy eased up the loss but kept the yearning burning.

Meanwhile, Lisa had disappeared. Her father's decision to disconnect her from her surroundings was executed immaculately. I eventually heard they had moved to San Diego and thought of driving there. But I suspected that by now Lisa hated my guts for everything that had gone wrong in her life. Even if I tried to reconnect, what would I say to her? How could I ever defend myself? I mean . . . how do I explain Ralph Dillon? or the relentless effort to steal her boyfriend away? or the fact that I supplied her with drugs to maintain leverage?

Campaigns kept pouring in and my father's grip got weaker as I started to understand the rules of the game. I was realizing that my rebellious behavior was giving me the kind of reputation I was now adamant to avoid. So about two years into my professional life, I began pulling myself together. Contrary to me, Heather had been leading a quiet, normal life with Doug at her side. For some mysterious reason, she had never given up on me. We would speak on the phone almost every day and she had me over for dinner about twice a month.

It was Heather, not my parents, who got the call from me one night after the inevitable happened. I had been beaten and brutally raped after pushing my luck beyond any reasonable limit. She found me cuddled up in bed, crying, shaking, bleeding from my nose and mouth, bruises all over my body—in a state of shock.

Steve Flannigan was a top industry executive at the leading fashion house 'Exquisitely Hip', who I thought should get special treatment. He looked good and he was always the coolest guy around. Flannigan held in his hands the decision making process for huge, prestigious and very lucrative campaigns, which I wanted to be a part of. Rumors had it that the winners of those campaigns had to go through his bed. I was willing to pay that small price, so I hunted him down patiently. I followed him to parties and functions. It took some time, much more than I had anticipated, but finally he got the message. He took me to dinner and then we got a room in a fancy hotel nearby. Everything was great until we got undressed. All of a sudden, this gentle and well-mannered man turned into the incredible Hulk. Without warning he pushed me forcefully on to the bed, jumped on me, grabbed my neck with one hand, spread my legs with the other and penetrated me with so much force I literally saw stars. He came in and out of me like a beast, treating me like a whore, cursing and looking nasty.

Now . . . god knows I have been around. I have slept with men who liked to get physical and curse. In some cases, I even played along. But no one came close to being as violent as Flannigan. I asked him to calm down but it just made it worse. I asked him to stop but he would not listen. I started resisting, realizing I was being raped, but it was pointless; the guy was too strong. Then he started beating me. I lay there, underneath his massive body, helpless, unable to resist, unable to speak, unable to cry. I was stunned and astounded. Ultimately, I stopped resisting and waited for the nightmare to end. It seemed like forever.

Eventually he was done with me.

"Complain to anyone and I'll have your career exterminated," he said when he got dressed. I just covered my body with the blanket and cuddled up, protecting myself from the world, unable to grasp what had just happened to me. "You were a lousy fuck!" he said before leaving, "you miserable bitch."

Heather begged me to let her drive me to the hospital and file a complaint against Flannigan with the police. "They'll get a semen sample from you and the son of a bitch is screwed for life . . ." she said.

"I seduced him. I went there freely, of my own will," I whispered. "With my lifestyle and his high standing, who in his right mind would believe me?"

"But he violently raped you!" She exclaimed with pain in her eyes.

"Oh . . . he'll pay a price for that. . . ."

"When?" She asked softly. I did not answer.

She helped me wash up and treated my wounds. "No-one can ever know about this!" I commanded. "Promise me!"

Heather nodded. "Jenny, you have to stop leading this life. This is a message from above—life is more than pursuing a career."

"I have no alternative Ms. Psychology major," I whispered. "I'm useless and untalented. I can't do anything else."

"That's bullshit and you know it! What will you do when your modeling career is over?" she asked and forced me to draw out from my mind something I had been thinking about lately.

"I don't know," I said. "Maybe study fashion design."

"Great. There are some good colleges in New York. Promise me you'll consider enrolling if I find you a suitable program." I nodded. "You can combine modeling with studying, just like your mother did back in her day."

"Yeah . . . why the hell not?" I said sarcastically, "I'm becoming my mother in every other way . . . I guess it's in my genes."

The next morning I called my agent. I had him reschedule a campaign I was supposed to start shooting that week. I claimed I wasn't feeling well, but the truth of the matter was that my body had to recover from the blows and my soul from the humiliation. My parents were out of town so nobody but Heather, Flannigan and I knew what had happened.

Oh . . . sorry . . . I forgot . . . Doug knew. Heather was so upset from my ordeal that she had to tell him. He called me the next day. "I'll dislocate his head . . . I swear to god . . . Jenny . . . let me find that son of a bitch and beat the shit out of him."

"No! Doug, sweetheart, please calm down. I need you guys to stand by my decision now. We will find the time and place for revenge—I promise."

By now, you have a comprehensive idea of the kind of woman I had become—reckless, foolish and mean, but also strong, unyielding and uncompromising. I could take beatings, suffer emotional pain, and come out stronger. Yet, something happened to me that night. I realized how vulnerable I was, and in a way, it humbled me. I finally realized I wasn't invincible. Moreover, the rape had also sent me back to Lisa. Ralph Dillon had raped the poor thing more than once and frequently shared her with his friends. The girl was barely 16 when it happened. *My God, what had I done?*

It took me weeks to recover from the ordeal. Well, *recover* is not the word one can use about a rape. I think a better description would be 'pull through.'

From that moment and for the next four years I combined work and studies. I majored in fashion design and then studied fashion marketing and management. It was during that period that I started dreaming of designing my own clothes and owning my own label. This ambition stabilized my life and helped me push aside all thoughts of my legendary friends, who were still haunting me on a regular basis.

But, I'm running ahead too fast. Things happened during those four years, which are important to mention, some tantalized my world and reminded me of my Lucifer Curse.

Although the industry loved my looks, the fact that I was not doing runways diminished my chances to make it big internationally. I felt okay with that. My studies were too important and the dream to own my own label someday was superior to any aspirations I might have had about my modeling career. My bed encounters were still paying the dividends I expected. I still had campaigns coming my way and I made good money. It allowed me to be picky. I chose the ones I could shoot in New York and refrained from overburdening my schedule with campaigns abroad. Buzz would visit us in New York about once a month for a weekend. I looked forward to his visits. He was a good friend and a good listener. I felt safe around him and loved him for that. He was the only man, apart from iconic Roy, whose arms I could fall asleep in. The only trouble was that Buzz loved me beyond comprehension. Although I slept with him occasionally, I never mislead him . . . or at least so I believed.

About a year into my studies, Buzz did the unthinkable: he proposed. We were having dinner when he opened a small box and showed me a diamond ring.

"Are you out of your mind?" I barked at him impatiently. "I can't marry you, or anyone else for that matter." He looked at me devastated. I calmed myself down, realizing I had hurt his feelings. I took a deep breath and released the air slowly. "Oh . . . Buzzy . . ." I said softly, "we have talked about it endlessly. We are friends not lovers."

"I love you! I'm not just a friend!" he said with ever-growing frustration.

"You are not just a friend. You're my best friend," I emphasized as I placed my hand over his. "Please, honey, try to understand." He pulled his hand from underneath mine, reclining on his backrest, looking the other way.

"Is there any chance you would ever change your mind?" he asked. "I'm willing to wait."

"Jesus . . . Buzz . . ." I threw to the air. He looked at me sadly. There was a moment of silence.

". . . take the ring. Wear it . . . for me," he begged me and handed me the box.

I shook my head, looking at him with compassion. "Buzz, honey. You need to move on, please! It's not going to happen . . . save the ring for the woman you marry."

"It's you or no one else!" he exclaimed.

"Buzz . . . I hate seeing you like this." I moved to the side chair and embraced him. We sat there for about ten minutes without saying a word to each other. He calmed down.

"Okay. I get it," he said finally. "But I bought this ring for you, so at least accept it as a gift." I smiled sadly, realizing it would be the only gesture I could make that would ease his pain. I took the ring out of the box and placed it on my ring finger. "It's beautiful. Thank you."

I drove Buzz to the airport the next evening and saw him off. I kissed his lips a long and loving kiss and then embraced him. "You'll always be my best friend," I whispered to his ear and then looked into his tearful, kind eyes. He pushed me gently away, picked up his handbag and walked to the departure gates. I watched him leaving, hating myself for hurting him. He then turned around and looked at me. I waved.

The look Buzz gave me then haunts me to this very day.

The next evening, as I was studying in my apartment, the doorbell rang. I rushed down the stairs and opened it. Doug and Heather, both with tearful eyes looked at me with profound sadness. Buzz was found dead that morning in his LA apartment after cutting his wrists.

I had finally earned my VIP ticket to hell fair and square.

Chapter 24

Jen-Sven

Buzz's funeral was heartbreaking. We stood in a cemetery in Culver City, Heather, Doug and I crying while the priest outlined Buzz's many qualities. We saw his coffin lowered into the grave and covered with soil.

I could not face his shattered parents. I avoided their looks. I must have looked guilty as hell because they avoided me, too. I remained in front of Buzz's fresh grave for an entire hour, asking my friends to leave me alone with him. I just stood there, unable to say anything, unable to detach myself from a person who had truly loved me. I fell on my knees and cried forever, caressing the fresh soil on his grave.

I'm sitting on the bathroom floor. The hot water is gently caressing my body. My skin turns reddish. I want to cry but nothing comes out. I grasp the implications Buzz's death has on my life and I panic. The world has just become a lonelier place and much more hostile. I no longer have the only person who could offer me shelter and comfort. I look around me. I think I see images—faces of dead people. I close my eyes as hard as I can until it hurts. I open them and the images are gone. The only face looking at me now is Buzz's. He is not smiling his wonderful smile. He just stares at me with ice cold, unforgiving eyes.

Time froze. Everything halted. The world was on hold—my career, my studies, my social life. Life's direction was no longer clear. Guilt turned me numb and helpless. The internal turmoil, the self-hatred and remorse inflicted a pain that was unimaginable.

I wanted to escape my miserable reality but felt locked in a prison cell. I drowned myself in alcohol and, if not for Heather pulling me out just in time, I would have been drawn back to drugs. She moved in with me for about a month, fearing I would harm myself and trying in the process to implement whatever she had learned as a psychology major.

She saw me through the shock/denial/anger/acceptance phase theory mumbo jumbo, only allowing herself to return home after concluding that I was well into the last of them.

Acceptance my fucking white Scandinavian ass . . .

The truth of the matter was that I never fully recovered from Buzz's suicide. I'm burning from pain and guilt as I type these words on a keyboard, using my very own fingers . . . one of which still wears the ring Buzz gave me the day he chose to end his life. An unnecessary death that could have been prevented if I had set him free sooner or handled the situation better. As time passed, I learned to live with the pain just as I learned to manage the loss of Jerry, Lisa and Roy.

I gradually threw myself back into reality, investing all I had in finishing my studies. I graduated with honors but I was not ready yet for the next stage. So, I found myself fully involved in my modeling career, moving from one country to another. I was constantly traveling, moving from one shooting location to the other, from one hotel to the other and from one beach to another. A few months down the line, I became known enough to win the Sports Illustrated cover and center pages. I even got an offer from Playboy, which I declined.

And then one morning, I woke up in some fancy hotel on Brazil's Ipanema Beach with the decision to end my modeling career. I stood on the balcony overlooking the ocean and felt strong and clear enough to take the next step.

Now . . . I'm not indifferent to the fact that finance has never been an issue for me. Although I made good money during my short modeling career, my father's fortune, estimated in the hundreds of millions, made whatever I earned irrelevant to my future monetary capacity. But that day in Rio de Janeiro, for the first time in my entire life, I really believed I could finally achieve something meaningful on my own.

Both my parents were excited to hear of the course I had chosen. My mother got me an internship at 'Body Shade', a small but prestigious New York fashion house, as an assistant to Jill Mason, their chief designer. For the next year or so Jill, not only taught me everything I needed to know, but also dressed me up with whatever she was working on, stating that my body was a work of art. I did not appreciate the fact that she turned me into her in-house model, but it was a small price to pay for the opportunity to get such exposure to her professional skills and experience. Gradually, under her professional supervision, I started designing my own clothes, finally bringing my sketching talent to good use. Shortly after, I got my first dress into the company's summer collection. Looking back, I think this was one of the happiest and most rewarding periods of my life. At last, I had done something worthwhile. I was considered a promising young designer.

All through that time, I worked on my own collection of winter clothes, planning ahead. My mother, experienced and proficient, was truly astonished when I showed her my sketches and explained my concept. She thought it was brilliant.

"We have to do something with these designs of yours!" she exclaimed over the dinner table one evening. "They are unique and marketable. Angus, you've got to see her sketches."

"Show them to me after dinner sweetheart," he asked me and I nodded.

"Did you show them to Jill?"

"Nope," I said, chewing, sticking my fork and knife at the piece of chicken breast lying on my plate. "This is going to be my first collection under my new label."

"So we have reached that stage?" my father asked with a big smile.

"Yes, daddy, it's our time to shine."

"Do you have a name for your brand?" my mother asked curiously.

"Jen-Sven," I emphatically replied.

"Awesome!" my father exclaimed, probably satisfied with the use I did of both the name he had given me and his father's family name.

"I'm glad you like it because you're the investor!" I said conclusively. "Mom," I addressed her; "you're going to be the managing director! As for me, I'm going to design clothes."

"Sounds like a plan to me," my father said compassionately. "I believe in you, sweetheart. I always did. Your amazing work in Body Shade just proves I was right to believe in you all along."

"Thanks dad. I appreciate it."

"I will back you with whatever you need: money, time, effort . . . you name it—it's yours!" I looked at him with a satisfied smile and it was obvious it made him happy.

"Sorry to ruin this wonderful father-daughter moment but what did you say my role in this initiative would be?" my mom asked.

"You . . . mom . . . are going to run the company."

"Well. I'm truly honored but I can't just pack up and leave my job."

I looked into her eyes. "All your life you've been working for others. It's your turn to be in the front seat. It is your time to take all the experience you've earned with so much hard work and run your own show. Be the decision maker! Decide on the path we'll take; recruit your own staff—be your own master."

"Sounds tempting, I must admit. Still, easier said than done," she said amused.

"Mom, I'm dead serious. I'm offering you a chance to influence the fashion world." She looked at me for a short while and then at my father.

"Mariana, you said so yourself," my father interjected. "Jennifer is a talented designer. We have the best tools for the job. Jenny knows the fashion world and she is well known. Together with your experience and professional prestige in the industry, the sky is the limit. We'll need to think of a good business plan and to work on a wise media strategy; but otherwise we are practically good to go."

"I need to sleep on it," she said.

"Dad, while mom is sleeping on it, I'll need you to help me get started." I said.

"When do we start?" he said smiling.

I sat for hours with my father's lawyers and business advisers in order to prepare a workable business plan. We went over the procedures required to create a new company. Angus Svensen didn't miss a meeting, watching me state my case and defend my principles. He backed me up all the way to the final decisions on location, time, budget and strategy. He was the sole investor so we decided to keep him as the sole owner of our new company.

While this was going on, my mother decided to come on-board.

"I will be there for you honey and we will make it work," she said to me when I visited her office one day; "but we need to cement two golden rules and stick to them if we are to work together." I nodded. "Running the company is my turf and I will be the decision maker in everything that has to do with the 'how' side of the equation." I nodded again. "You are welcome to influence my decisions and I will always take them into consideration, but once I decide—you follow!"

"Sure mom, that's the whole idea."

"Good. The second golden rule has to do with your part of the equation. I would be the final decision maker on running the business but you will be the final decision maker on the products we produce. I will always give you my input, but it will always be your final call. Agreed?"

"Agreed!" I stated and we shook hands. I pulled her close to me and embraced her. "Thanks mom. I will never forget you helped me realize my dream." I whispered.

When we parted our embrace, I detected two little pools in her eyes and realized that the woman had never really received a loving hug from me before, not to mention one initiated by me, so I pulled her in and embraced her again.

Interest in our new label was immediate. The famous mother and daughter ex-models initiative was enough to bring a lot of industry attention our way. We also had a Joker down our sleeve in the form and shape of a public relations specialist who went by the name of Courtney Henderson. The woman was amazing. We stole her from one of our rivals by offering to double her salary. Her experience and competence drew so much attention our way that my first collection was headline news before we even showed it on the catwalk.

We held Jen-Sven's first fashion show at the Waldorf Astoria Grand Ball Room. A professional production company we hired gave it a special twist. Hundreds of colored lights, huge video screens, about a dozen cameras capturing and displaying my designs on the screens from every possible angle, and a specially designed stage and catwalk were the perfect background. My designs did the rest. I got a standing ovation when I came up on stage. I was overwhelmed. We were all over the place the following day—TV, newspapers, radio . . . and talk about sales—wow! I had orders from all over retail America; and, soon enough, teenage girls and grownup women were wearing my clothes. Within a few weeks, Jen-Sven logo was showing up on shirts, pants, dresses, skirts, jackets, cardigans and women's ties. Within a year, my father recuperated his investment and started making very good money. But the best thing of all was the respect I got for being innovative and courageous.

Seven years after I met him for the first time in Jerusalem, PI Schwartz was still sending me information about Roy. The object of my eternal love had spent four years in the Israeli Defense Forces and was now studying political science at the Hebrew University. He had a steady girlfriend and led a simple life. I often reflect on what life could have been like if there had been no Lisa Anne Epstein. I would have probably glued myself to Roy, and that wonderful summer of 1983 would have continued forever. I wanted to believe he would have been proud of me in light of Jen-Sven's meteoric success. Among dozens of sketches concentrating on ideas for new clothes, I recently found one showing my mythological lover standing up, clapping his hands in a show of appreciation, looking at radiant me, while I make my way down the catwalk, surrounded by a dozen models wearing my designs.

How I wished it were true.

Chapter 25

Illicit Diamonds

Successful as we were during those marvelous years of breaking ground in the fashion world, 1996 was a very difficult and eye-opening year for us three Svensens.

Some background is in order before we continue:

About a year earlier, a billionaire-shipping tycoon from San Diego by the name of Polly Murphy was arrested for allegedly killing his wife. The media claimed he had thrown her overboard from their yacht. This came after months of extensive media coverage of the couple's separation and property battles. Considering the circumstances and the fact that their children had testified to a loud argument on the upper deck the night of their mother's disappearance, public opinion found him guilty before the trial began. It was obvious to everyone that Murphy was about to spend the rest of his life in prison . . . at best.

Defending Murphy was Richard Shepherd, one of the best criminal lawyers in the country. My father knew the man personally and thought he was "the biggest asshole he had ever met, yet the best at the business . . ." One evening, while I was eating dinner and watching the news, a breaking news item stated that Murphy had fired Shepherd and replaced him with a young lawyer named Anne Sears. The commentator thought it was odd that Murphy had decided to deposit his fate in the hands of an inexperienced young lawyer, even if she was considered a brilliant rising star. The name was not familiar to me but the image on screen almost caused me to choke on a piece of bread I was chewing. The elegant woman shown walking down the courthouse steps was no other than Lisa Anne Epstein.

Getting updated information about Roy's life was something I longed for, something that kept burning inside of me. Not so was the case for Lisa. I wanted to know as little about her life as possible. Thinking about her, remembering all the pain I had caused her always made me feel like shit; so until that point in time, I had simply detached myself from anything that had to do with her. That day, watching her meticulously give a short and intelligent interview to the media, claiming her client was innocent and that this fact would be proven beyond reasonable doubt in court, changed my mind all together. She looked so confident, so strong and charismatic. She had obviously rehabilitated her life and moved on, and this made me feel sheer joy. It meant that my horrendous actions had not ruined her life completely.

Suddenly, I was curious about everything that had to do with her. Long and painful emotions, which I was certain were buried in the cellars of my soul, started surfacing. I had no idea she was married. I did not know why she had chosen such a profession for herself or why she went by her second name instead of her first. I asked my lawyers to collect whatever data they could about Lisa's private and professional life.

A couple of days later I got a written report.

The story, in a nutshell—in 1989, Lisa had graduated Harvard Law School at the top of her class and joined her father's prestigious law firm. She had worked for her father for about five years. She was now married to Michal Sears, a known and a very successful lawyer. They had a three-year-old daughter named Dorothy. Astonishingly for me, her camp of expertise was criminal law. I never imagined that this fragile butterfly would choose such a nasty profession. I mean . . . to defend outlaws and felons you had to deal with them directly.

Lisa's star started shining bright very early in her career; and at 28, she had already established her own private practice.

To make a long story short, Lisa got immense national exposure thanks to the Polly Murphy case. Eventually, she managed to get him off the hook. By the end of 1995, she had become a national figure and her photos and interviews were all over the

place. She even got into some very respectable fashion magazines like Vogue, Glamour and Elle. At 29 Lisa was prettier and
sexier than ever—tall, well shaped with amazing blond hair and
a face shaped in heaven. And she could really dress. She was
always strict about her appearance, wearing dresses and skirts
to complement her perfect figure. The fashion world loved writing about the combination of beauty and of an exquisite taste in
clothes with astounding intellectual capacity.

Now back to the sequence of events.

It was about 2 am on June 11, 1996 when the police stormed
our house in Beverly Hills, arrested my father and led him out
cuffed like a common criminal into a police car. A few of them
stayed behind to search the house, taking with them some com-
puters and files, leaving our home in complete disarray. The
mighty Angus Svensen got himself arrested for allegedly smuggling hundreds of millions of dollars worth of diamonds from
Asia into the US over the past decade or so.

I was in New York at the time of the arrest. My mother called
me hysterically, informing of the arrest. She asked me to fly home
and help her seek the best legal defense possible. As I packed my
suitcase at early dawn, I knew exactly who to turn to. I knew Lisa
would bring to the case, not only expertise but also a personal
touch. For a very long period in both our lives, Lisa had practically lived with me in our guesthouse. She had joined our family
for lunch and dinner, and we considered her part of the family.
I remembered how much she liked my parents and how she respected their achievements. My father respected her no less. He
loved the idea that I hung out with such an intelligent person, not
to mention her breathtaking beauty.

So it had to be Lisa. With such grave accusations, losing the
case meant financial devastation for all of us and a long prison
term for my father. Losing was not an option!

I flew to San Diego that morning. I was a nervous wreck
when I got to Lisa's office building and had to calm down in a
coffee shop nearby before taking the elevator up. I was trembling
when I stood in front of her secretary, asking to see her. I had a
lump in my throat and a tear in the corner of my eye when she

came out. She was looking no less pale and overwhelmed with emotions.

"Lisa. . . ." I said and the nagging tear finally left my eye and streamed down my cheek. She came over with a sad smile hung on her perfect lips and embraced me.

"Let's go into my office," she suggested and led me into the fancy room. The woman sure had style. Her office was beautiful. We sat on a leather sofa, holding hands, looking at each other with disbelief, not able to speak.

"Jenny," she whispered. "It's been so long. How are you doing?"

"I'm doing fine, but I'm here today because my father is not doing well at all. I need your help desperately."

"What's wrong?" she inquired concerned.

"He's been arrested for smuggling diamonds," I informed her with a cracked voice. "Lisa, please help us."

She heaved a sigh, looking away for few seconds, contemplating the situation then she looked back at me. "Where is Angus now?"

"He is being held at California State Prison, in Lancaster."

She scratched her forehead thinking, just as I remembered her doing back when we were in our teens. "I have to be in court in about an hour. Then I have meetings until about six thirty. Let's meet in the café across the street at about seven. By then I'll know if I'll be able to visit your father in prison tomorrow. I'll decide if to take the case after speaking with him."

"Thank you, Lisa . . . Anne . . . Why Anne?"

"I'd rather not talk about it!" she said matter of fact.

"I missed you . . ." I said candidly. She placed her hand on mine and looked into my eyes, but otherwise said nothing.

I checked into a nearby hotel and sat in the lobby for about two hours, while conducting dozens of telephone conversations with my mother and my father's lawyers. All thought my decision to hire Lisa was problematic. Even if they admitted she was a meteor in the criminal world, they also claimed she did not have the expertise necessary to defend a suspect on customs and international duties charges.

I stuck to my decision.

"Mom," I told her during our sixth or seventh phone call. "I don't trust anyone with dad's freedom. Everyone around us has hidden agendas—even *our* lawyers. Lisa would bring her heart and soul into defending him. She is very intelligent and she's a quick learner. I just hope she takes the case."

"I'm a wreck right now," she said with impatience, "I can't think straight and our lawyers are driving me crazy with doomsday scenarios. Trust your instincts. But if Lisa decides to take the case, she will have to take on board tax and customs specialists."

Sitting in the bar, waiting for Lisa to arrive, my body gave me signs it was displeased with my treatment of it. I had not slept the night before and I could not eat. I was worried sick about my father's condition in detention and loaded with guilt about all the abuse Lisa had been through because of me. I was shivering when she came in. She saw me pale and emotional when she sat at my table. "Are you all right?" she asked concerned, holding my arm and looking into my eyes. I shook my head, overwhelmed with emotions.

"No. I'm not," I whispered, feeling drained from energy—all my defenses down. "I feel like shit. I'm helpless and incapable of doing anything."

"You're dealing with a major personal crisis. It's natural."

"Yeah . . . but my dad . . . we felt invincible when he was around. Shit . . ." I nearly started sobbing. "All my life I gave him such a hard time . . ." She looked at me with sympathy but said nothing for a while, allowing me to get a grip on myself. "I'm a strong woman. I almost never cry. I'm sorry you have to see me like this. I hate being this way."

She nodded, smiling a sad smile, "Yeah . . . I know the feeling . . ."

"I never stopped thinking about you," I confessed after about a minute of silence. I was playing with my cup as I said that. I couldn't look her in the eye. "I loved you with all my heart and I was shattered when you left, thinking I was out there to hurt you."

"It's in the past now," she whispered, looking away. Seeing me after all these years must have sent her back to some mutual memories. Seeing the look she had on her face that moment, it was evident that these memories did not agree with her at all.

"Lisa, what happened?" I asked.

"I'd rather not talk about it," she replied. "Let's concentrate on the case."

"Okay," I said, gulping air into my lungs, releasing it slowly back to the atmosphere. "I came to you because you are the best and the only one I trust. I followed the Murphy case and I've been following your career ever since. I need your skill and your reputation. Please take the case."

"We'll see tomorrow," she said. There was another minute of silence. I remember thinking to myself that she must have found the situation even more painful than I imagined; otherwise, I could not explain the difficulty she found in doing something she was an expert at—speaking. "What are you doing these days?" she finally asked.

I got up to my feet and held in my hand the small label tagged to my dress. She looked at me with a question mark on her pretty face and I was disappointed to realize that she had never made the connection. "Doesn't the label Jen-Sven ring a bell?" She smiled, realizing for the first time that the famous fashion label was named after me. "My dad owns the fashion house and I design the clothes."

"Wow . . . good for you . . ." she said and I saw the sincerity in her eyes. It gave me courage to try again.

I sat down and looked at her with a serious face. "Please talk to me," I whispered. "Don't treat me like a stranger." She looked away. "Lisa, please."

"It's Anne. I'm not Lisa anymore," she said. Again—a long moment of silence. "Look, Jenny," she said finally, "I won't lie to you. I'm fighting here to stay correct. I don't know whether to hug and kiss you or to send you the hell away."

I nodded. "I don't blame you . . . Lisa. . . . Anne . . . I deserve it. But I did love you. You were the best friend I ever had." She looked at me with a troubled face. "Anne . . . you have no idea of the pain I carried in my heart for so long. The longing for Roy was unbearable. Remember, he was my boyfriend long before he was yours and I never loved another." Her facial expression turned harsher by the minute. "The guy had the capacity to dive into the depth of your soul and plant a seed of love that grew every single second ever bigger, ever stronger. Like a Sequoia."

"Tell me about it," she whispered, looking away, her eyes getting moist.

"It took me years to get over him," I lied to her face.

She heaved a sigh. "You're lucky," she whispered, "I never did."

If you only knew, I thought to myself but decided to let it go. I needed Lisa's good will now and did not want to antagonize her. *There will come a day*, I promised myself, *when I will tell you everything.*

"Do you have a place to stay?" she asked me before we parted. "If you don't, you are welcome to sleep over at our place."

I was moved by the gesture. It meant that she did not consider me a stranger. "Thank you so much Lis . . . Anne. I'm staying at the Marriott."

We flew to Lancaster together the next day. We didn't say much because Lisa spent the flight reading my father's police file and some legal precedents her assistant had gathered for her. I spent the flight sleeping, after another sleepless night.

A limo picked us up from the airport. Lisa spent the ride reading the Los Angeles Times. She avoided me ruthlessly; and, although it burned me from the inside, I understood. She was going through the same emotional turmoil I was and she was no less confused. I decided not to burden her with my emotions. I was a distraction now and I needed her focused.

Once at the prison, a guard led us to the lawyer's room. We waited there for about twenty minutes before my father was brought in. He was wearing a prisoner's uniforms. I wanted to die. Seeing him like that, treated with disrespect, humiliated and degraded was an awful experience. For the next hour or so, Lisa did her job, getting the information she needed from her client. Just before we left I embraced my father, whispering in his ear that I would do my best to get him out as soon as possible. Then, in the limo, on our way back, I burst into tears. The stress and the sight of my powerful father in prisoner's garb caused me to collapse emotionally.

Chapter 26

The Void

Go figure my father.

The man was as rich as can be without going the extra un-lawful mile. I thought I knew him better. I'd never detected any unlawful tendencies and he was far from being corrupt. The opposite was true. His heart always seemed to be in the right place. Growing up, I hated his guts for not being there for me or for leading the kind of life he lead, but I never doubted his other values.

Since then, my father and I had held dozens of conversations about his debacle. My conclusion from these talks was that Angus Svensen was just a brilliant businessman who found loopholes in the system and wasn't strong enough to battle the temptation. Answering Lisa's questions that day in Lancaster prison, Angus was short and correct. He did not admit the guilt, but everybody in the room understood too well the gravity of the situation. I watched Lisa's face carefully as she interviewed him. Her face was one of an experienced expert who had recognized her client's guilt. She did not push him too hard or too far. I could see from the start that she was concentrating on seeking a legal solution—not on judgment.

During the process of helping us understand our circumstances better, she did her best to convince my parents and I that she wasn't the right lawyer for the job. She claimed she had no experience defending customs offenders. "It's a world as wide as the ocean and as deep as the sea," she said, "and I would be just a broken raft fighting the waves in the midst of a storm." But we would not have it. We asked her to take the case nonetheless because, apart from her phenomenal professional skills, there was no one in the legal world who cared for us as much. She hesitated.

It took her a week to make up her mind. Meanwhile, our lawyers got my father out on $1.2 million bail. At the second encounter with my father, at our estate in Beverly Hills, she informed him she was taking the case. She declared she would be doing it pro bono because she really did care. Whether I liked her motive for coming on board or not, it made sure she was committed not only professionally but also emotionally—exactly what I had been aiming for in the first place.

As for the motive, as my father informed me, Lisa was doing it for Roy. Yeah . . . mythological Roy . . . the man she was forever in love with. When he asked for an explanation, she described to him how much her high school sweetheart had adored him. She told him how he felt forever thankful to him for making two of his dreams come true: the summer job that allowed him the means to buy a car and that black Fender Stratocaster he had bought for him during that unforgettable weekend in Palm Springs.

Lisa's first step was to seek a legal way to allow my father's company to continue with its business activity. She had my father sign dozens of documents, transferring to my mother, temporarily, all authority to run the company. Going on with its' usual activity saved my father's company hundreds of thousands of dollars. As for the charges, my father's business partner in Hong Kong, the one responsible for sending him the consignments of diamonds and other valuable stones, was arrested for allegedly smuggling illegal diamonds to the US. During his interrogation, he not only admitted the crimes but also had implicated a few US based companies—among them my father's. He had testified that my father knew, approved and had played along for years with the scheme.

These kinds of cases, Lisa explained to me one day, were complicated because they impinged upon the jurisdictions of different countries with different revenue laws and customs duties. Smuggling was IRS turf and messing with the Taxman was always counter-productive. To our dismay, my father was facing a long period of incarceration if convicted, because diamond smuggling had become an epidemic and the law enforcement apparatus was demanding tough punishment as deterrence.

I took some time off work and Lisa was kind enough to let me hang around her team for the first two weeks. I even flew with her twice to Hong Kong in order to gather information. I used the time in Hong Kong to try to reconnect with her on a personal level. The longer I hung around her, the more I understood how I missed her in my life. But she was distant and refused to open up.

"I admire you," I told her candidly one evening, while we were having dinner together.

"There is nothing to admire. I'm a fake and I hate my line of profession."

"So why did you choose it?" I asked curiously.

"Because it takes my mind off my dismal life," she said and wiped her mouth with the napkin. "And because being around my clients makes me feel like I'm not the worse person in the world after all."

I smiled. "Come on . . . why are you so hard on yourself?" She said nothing. "Why are you so sad sweetheart?" I asked. "I've been hanging around you for the past two weeks and all I see in you is profound sadness."

She put her fork down and reached for her water. "You wouldn't understand," she stated as she drank from it.

"Try me," I challenged her. "I'm pretty well equipped to understand whatever you'll throw my way."

"Are you?" she asked with cynicism in her tone of voice.

"Yeah . . . you have no idea . . ."

"Okay . . . how about dying inside . . . have you ever felt that feeling?" she asked with a cold and nasty look that took me off balance completely.

"No shit . . . I've died inside so many times that there's a huge cemetery in my head dedicated only to myself . . ." I said, looking into her eyes. She looked at me undecided for a long minute and then looked into her cup. I felt that the intensity of the moment and my honest reply moved something inside of her.

"Life offers no second chances for people like me," she whispered rhetorically.

"You are married to a successful lawyer, you are a mother and you're a national acclaimed criminal lawyer. You got your second chance . . ."

"The hell I did," she said angrily, "I would trade it all in a swift second if I could only have Roy back in my life," she said, fighting her emotions. I nodded. I knew exactly what she meant.

"It's been eleven years since he left . . ." I said, trying to look surprised.

"I told you, you wouldn't understand. . . ."

"I'm just stating a fact. You know what they say about time as a healer . . ."

"Yeah . . . like I haven't heard that dumb cliché so many times in my life."

"It worked for me." I lied again.

"Well, good for you," she said calmly. "For me it has done the opposite. There is not a day that goes by when I don't think of how my life could have been if my loving father would not have deported Roy from my life. I think of the children I might have had with him. I think of enjoying happiness. I think of being content with what I have. I think of the profession I would have chosen for myself instead of keeping the scum of the earth out of prison . . . no offence intended."

"L . . . You should let go. You're obsessing . . ."

"Yes, Jennifer, I am, and there is nothing I can do about it. You can ask my shrink . . . she's made a fortune treating this obsession of mine." She took a gulp from her water and looked at me with a harsh face. "Why am I telling you all of this?"

"Because you know that I'm the only person in the whole world who understands how you feel," I whispered sadly.

"No. Jenny. You are not able to fully grasp how I feel. Nobody can. In this respect, I'm the loneliest person on the planet."

"You loved him very much. It was obvious back when we were teenagers," I said. "He was your high school sweetheart and he was a wonderful young man. We always hold a special place in our hearts for our high school sweethearts."

"Loved him . . . high school sweetheart . . . I told you that you wouldn't understand," she chuckled in pain.

"Then please explain to me. I'm no stranger and I can keep a secret." I said. She looked away and took another gulp of air. I was pushing her to places she did not want to go.

"Does the name Ralph Dillon sound familiar to you?" she asked in a surprisingly calm tone of voice. My heart went bungee jumping. I nodded, terrified. "I was only fifteen . . ." she said and her voice cracked, "I did drugs. I had sex . . . with total strangers . . . only fifteen. I was dying inside every single time the guy injected me the stuff and used me as his human inflatable sex doll. I lived inside a void. I burned each and every time that happened in the ovens of hell. . . ." Tears were falling down her beautiful face like waterfalls but her face was stone sealed. "You see, Jennifer. You never understood what Roy really meant to me. Roy wasn't just the man I loved or my high school sweetheart. He was my savior." She stopped talking, looking away, drying her tears with a paper tissue. Then she looked at me. "I was digging my own grave when this perfect teenager came into my life. For some reason I never understood, he wanted to be with screwed-up-me and only me. This was at a time when everybody else wanted nothing to do with Lisa the Junky . . . and he loved me! My god . . ." her tears intensified. "He truly loved me."

Witnessing her pain, my eyes filled with tears too. "Yes . . . honey . . . he loved you . . ." I whispered putting my hands on hers.

She slowly pulled her hand from underneath mine. "Roy loved me without reservations," she continued. "He helped me rehabilitate my life. Time made me realize that Roy Cohen is just a memory now and he will never come back; but I love him today no less than I loved him the day he left and I'm doomed to love him for the rest of my life . . ."

As the days passed, Lisa was getting more and more pessimistic as to the outcome of the trial. Her new approach was to search for technicalities in the process. When this was also found to be a dead-end, she began looking for ways to reach a settlement with the IRS that would maybe impinge upon my father's financial situation but would keep him out of prison.

She took me out for dinner one night in order to explain the circumstances. The case against my father was solid. He had negotiated his deals discretely and with no one present but the highest decision makers on the other side. There were no written protocols or witnesses to the deals, save for the words and handshakes of the parties involved. As much as this fact was unfavorable to us, she added, it was unfavorable also to the prosecution. They too lacked a solid basis of evidence. Yet, for them the case was strong enough because they could prove the discrepancies between the tax reports my father's accountants had filed over the last few years and the quantities of merchandise sold vs. that which was in his current possession. The rational conclusion was that he had smuggled the balance in illegally. Every rational judge in the country would rule against him.

The next evening, in our estate in Beverly Hills, Lisa scolded my father for not giving her the whole picture. "Look, you hired me for my brains, didn't you?" she asked.

"I sure did," he answered carefully.

"So why are you treating me like a fool? Don't you think I would be able to perform better if you entrusted me with the facts?"

He smiled, wearing a fatherly look—a look I knew too well. "Lisa, being young and extremely intelligent is not necessarily always being wise. Sometimes, the facts should not be discussed and I think you're wise enough to know when." She shook her head and smiled.

"Okay, Angus . . . fine. You insist on making my life complicated. I'll try to keep you out of prison nonetheless . . ."

I had to fly back to New York. My company needed me. Apart from my own duties, my mother was in a very shaky situation and needed my help. The prospect of having my father convicted had made her edgy and very emotional. It was clear she was unable to perform her job the way she was expected. I gave her some time off so she could fly back to LA to be close to her husband.

Distracted and preoccupied as I was, I had no choice but to take upon myself the ongoing management of Jen-Sven.

Lisa asked me to be patient and to refrain from calling her. She promised to call every other day or so for a short briefing and she kept her promise. These phone conversations didn't give us much hope and my father was starting to come to terms with the fact that he would have to spend time in prison. Lisa, on the other hand, kept on asking us not to lose faith. "I will find a way to win this case," she promised me during one of our conversations. "You all have to be strong and keep your cool."

Then, one night, staying at my parents' estate in Beverly Hills, I got a telephone call from Lisa. She was calling me from her hotel room in Washington D.C. "Jennifer. It's over," she said. "Your father is free to continue his life undisturbed. The IRS is dropping the case. The bail will be cancelled in a couple of hours. Send your lawyers to collect the money tomorrow morning."

"What? . . . Why? . . . How?" I muttered while doing my best to get a grip on my rising excitement.

"Sorry. It's confidential. It's part of a deal I made with the IRS. I keep my mouth shut and your father gets his freedom. We'll talk tomorrow. Congratulations."

"Oh . . . Anne . . . thank you . . . I'm so relieved . . . thank you. . . . thank you . . ." I managed to mumble, but she had already hung up.

My father's bail was indeed cancelled that same night. He was free to continue his life without further interruptions and without any criminal or financial repercussions.

I spent the early hours of that specific morning talking to my father. Excited, unable to sleep, we sat outside in our garden by the pool, in complete euphoria. We were curious to know how Lisa was able to pull off such a miracle. My father thought it had to do with the inquiries Lisa made into his tax reports for the past ten years. He believed there might have been something unconstitutional in IRS practices. He knew for a fact that his company was not the only company to be overcharged for years by the taxman. The problem was that no one dared mess with such a powerful governmental agency. Like him, everybody chose to pay than to expose their businesses to the Taxman's wrath.

The next morning we drove to Lisa's office in San Diego. My father held inside the inner pocket of his Jacket a check for $2.5 million that he intended to pay his lawyer, regardless of her intention to do it pro bono. He said it was a small price to pay for his freedom and for the safeguarding of his fortune. Lisa deserved a respectable compensation for all the time and effort she had invested in keeping him out of prison.

"How did you do it?" he asked his lawyer curiously, trying to solve the mystery. "I started getting used to the idea I was going to spend time in prison."

"Well, you almost did," she said.

"So, why am I free?"

"Well, sometimes the facts should not be discussed," she echoed his shrewd remark, smiling wide, her mouth full of white and perfect teeth. "I believe you are wise enough to know when."

My father laughed, realizing he had been beaten at his own game. "I guess I can live with that," he said. Then he drew the envelope out of his jacket and handed it to Lisa. "Here, this is yours."

"Thank you," she said, taking the envelope and placing it on her desk.

"Don't you want to open it?" I asked excited.

"No," she said. He nodded, respecting her wish. Then he embraced her and left the room.

"Can we be friends?" I asked her. "Like we used to be?"

She placed her hand on my cheek and shook her head. "No, Jenny, we can't."

"Why?" I asked somberly.

"You would be a constant reminder of calamity and of Roy and I just can't handle that." I looked at her for a moment, then nodded and left her office.

On the way back to Los Angeles, sitting in my father's Benz, I thought of Roy. There is a Jewish saying he had once recited to me: "the good things you do will come back to reward you."

When I convinced my father to hire Roy as his temporary driver, back in the eighties, and when my father bought that beautiful black Stratocaster from that mall in Palm Springs, we never imagined that these wonderful deeds would make a brilliant lawyer somewhere in the future take my father's legal case and save our family from ruin.

Chapter 27

For Old Times Sakes

It was not the world. It was me. That catch that reappeared frequently in my life, that abnormality, that curve, the twisted angle in the picture—I was now mature enough to accept the fact that it was my gravitational force which propelled whatever came my way, and it had a price.

My father's debacle demonstrated that his wide web of connections and wealth did not make us untouchables. The belief that nothing dire could ever happen to the Svensens as long as Angus was around blew up in our faces and left us confused. The magnitude of the realization that the real world was a hostile environment, punched a huge hole in our rubber boat, just as it was making its way through the middle of the ocean, rushing into the perfect storm.

It made me re-think my life and led me to the conclusion that it was time for me to grow up and stabilize it. I stopped drinking and I stopped sleeping around.

"I'm feeling suffocated, jailed in my narrow reality. I need some time off from it." I explained to my friends over dinner at their little Manhattan apartment.

"You are missing out on the world," Heather said while refilling my wine cup. "You are too busy with your everyday life to see that six billion other people are walking the earth. They are speaking other languages, cultivating other cultures, living in different countries on different continents."

"We had a blast in Guatemala last summer, Jen. Go traveling. It will clear your head," Doug added.

It made sense, so I took their advice.

About a month down the line, I found myself climbing the Annapurna Mountain in Nepal with a group of American hikers. A week later, I was rafting Laos' Luang Prabang. By the end of my 37-day trip to South-East Asia, I even managed to see some of Thailand and Cambodia.

Doug and Heather were right. It helped me clear my head. Every single day was a brand new experience. I met fascinating people, experienced first-hand new cultures, and encountered other codes of behaviors and unique sets of beliefs.

The whole experience was refreshing, purifying and empowering. The simplicity and authenticity moved me. It was humbling to see how ordinary people, lacking all the material advantages and fame I had so plenty of, were actually much happier than I could ever be. At nights, whether in a cabin up the mountains of Nepal, in a small guesthouse in Southern Laos or in a luxurious hotel in Bangkok, I struggled with my thoughts and recollections. I found it hard to believe that I have been swimming in such shallow waters for so many years.

All my life's axioms and beliefs went under painful scrutiny; and the answers to the questions I posed to myself slashed back at me ruthlessly. It was difficult to admit that, spiritually, I was in the dark and that I was empty. Excepting that awful truth was refining. In a way, it freed me from my old self and cleared the way for a humble learning process, which I still conduct until this very day. Haunting my days and nights was my lack of direction. It drove me crazy. I knew exactly what I wanted for Jen-Sven but I knew nothing whatsoever as for what I wanted for Jennifer Svensen. It was clear that I would not be able to continue my meaningless existence. I needed more than just a career—I needed a life.

The time I took off gave me time to myself, all alone, with no distractions. It allowed me finally to think proportionally about material things and financial success. I won't lie, I was still eager to conquer the world where my vocation where concerned; but this had to complement a constant search for meaning and finding a sense of direction. It was obvious to me that I needed to settle down and ease up on the rhythm of things. It was also clear to me that it was time to be monogamous.

The trip was a turning point after which my life changed dramatically. I came back a different person and saw the world in different colors. I had a new set of goals and none of them were material.

I got back to work with some new ideas. The most exciting popped into my head and started an avalanche of concepts to revolutionize a niche I never thought would ever interest me—men's clothes. Consequently, I became part of the nineties revolution in men's fashion. Goodbye Levi's, farewell Polo shirts and T-shirts—hello Jen-Sven skinny jeans, tight shirts and cardigans for men. Not long after I returned to the states, I had some samples made out that I wanted to display to my professional team. We held a small in-house fashion show. The catwalk was followed by a discussion on each and every item in the collection.

It was there that I met my companion for the next three years—a breathtaking 22 year old hunk by the name of Bryan Taylor.

Bryan was a small child imprisoned in an impeccable man's body. He was innocent, timid and naïve. He was modest, gentle and well-mannered. He had come to the big city from a small town in Arizona looking for a break, finding everything in the metropolis new and exciting, wearing sometimes a childish grin on his statue-like face that both amused and impressed me.

The day I first met him, I took him straight to my bed. When we were done, he hugged me, caressed my hair and told me I was beautiful. That was enough for me to decide I wanted him near. A week later, he moved in with me. For years, I had been a loner. I liked living on my own and doing as I pleased. Well . . . I had had enough of that. I thought I needed someone nearby who really cared for me and Bryan was too innocent to fake the emotion. So, without thinking, I had gotten myself into something that was about to complicate my complicated life even further.

But there was more to my Bryan adventure. My new man was nine years younger than I was, and he drew me back into the lives of twenty year olds who were searching to jump-start their lives. It was refreshing. Not that his immaturity didn't drive me crazy at times, but the overall package was worth giving up my privacy for.

I did not fall in love with my new man. That emotion never showed up again since Roy Cohen, but I did care for Bryan. I went out of my way to help his career. Soon, he became my in-house-male-model, staring in most of the shooting campaigns of my new men's designs, which by the way paid off big time. My mother liked Bryan but did not appreciate the fact that we were too dependent on him business-wise.

As always with the life of Jennifer Svensen, something had to happen to rock the boat.

I got a call from PI Schwartz, who by now enjoyed solid connections with a few members of Roy's close social circle. He informed me that Roy had just returned from a six-day trip to the US, during which he had met Lisa in San Diego. It seems that he too had never recovered from our teenage ordeal. He returned home empty-handed. Worse for him, returning to Israel, he learned that his Israeli girlfriend—sick of fighting phantoms—had left him.

Within a swift second, Bryan was nonexistent. I had been waiting for this chance for so long. All I could think about now was Roy Cohen. Lisa was married with child and his long-time girlfriend was out of the picture—a once in a lifetime window of opportunity. Without any hesitations, I cancelled all plans, bought a ticket to Israel and started packing.

To my relief, nobody asked me about my troubled past when I landed in Ben-Gurion's airport. I spent my first night in a fancy hotel by the city coastline. It was an entirely different city than the one I was deported from about 13 years ago—more welcoming, more modern and vibrant.

The next morning, jogging along the city's promenade in the early hours of the morning, I used the time to formulate my case—the one I was going to present to Roy shortly. A few hours later, I parked the rented car at the Hebrew University, where I soon lost my way, trying to find Roy's room. When I finally arrived, I could hardly bring myself to knock on the door. To my dismay, or maybe relief, Roy was not there. A quick inquiry revealed that Roy was on campus and supposed to meet students shortly. I waited outside his room. Soon the benches filled up with young students who had come to seek his guidance. At 31, so PI Swartz had told me, Roy was about a year away from his Ph.D. He was working at the University full time.

When I heard his voice from the other end of the hall, I freaked out and took off like a rocket ship. He was accompanied by a bunch of students, too involved in conversation to notice me.

I spent the next fifteen minutes trying to recuperate in the nearby cafeteria. I hadn't seen him for thirteen years and the mere sight of him threw me back to the marijuana incident. I was terrified he would send me away.

I went back and waited impatiently on the bench outside his office until the very last student came out. The hallway was desolate and quiet. Now it was my turn. I knocked on the door, sweating in the palms of my hands, my heart beating fast and my lips shivering with exhilaration.

"Ken . . ." he called in Hebrew from inside, *"efshar lehikanes."* I opened the door and stepped inside. Roy was sitting by his desk in a tiny room. A pile of books lay on the left side of his desk and a large computer screen on the right. He looked at me astounded, his mouth wide open in amazement. I smiled a weak and weary smile. My voice cracked when I said, "Hi Roy . . . remember me?"

He got up slowly, still unable to say anything, starting to digest what was going on, understanding that the girl from his teens, the one responsible for so much trouble was standing right in front of him. Gradually, his features began to soften and a wonderful, compassionate smile conquered his strong face. It gave me courage and I came closer to him. I stopped but a step from him, still smiling my fragile smile, my lips still trembling— a tear in the corner of my eye.

"Jenny . . ." he said and I burst into tears. He opened his arms and I cuddled into them, embracing him tightly, crying on his firm shoulder a happy, enjoyable kind of cry. We stood there embracing until he disengaged and looked at me with his charismatic face. I examined it. Not the face of a teenage boy anymore but one of a mature man—still very striking, strong and impressive. His dark green eyes were as beautiful and as penetrating as I remembered them, his brown hair meticulously combed, and his lips so sensual that I wanted to kiss them instantly.

"What are you doing here?" he asked softly.

"I came to see you?" I answered candidly.

"It's been a long time . . ." he whispered.

"Give or take thirteen years, but who's counting?" I tried to break the ice. He smiled again, this time a weak and unnatural smile.

"You're still so beautiful," he whispered compassionately and I just stood there smiling bashfully, remembering how as a boy he succeeded in making me feel like a normal teenager. There was a moment of silence that Roy broke first. "You came to see me . . . how incredible. . . ."

"Incredible but true."

"Wow . . ." he whispered, still bewildered. "I mean . . . I just came back from the States. I went there for the exact same reason."

"You did?" I asked, faking a surprised facial expression.

"Yeah . . ." he said and his face became dark, "I played with the notion of reuniting with Lisa." I lost my smile and he noticed. There was another moment of silence.

"And . . .?" I asked.

He heaved a sigh. "She is married and she has a beautiful daughter. Her name is Dorothy." Pain reflected from his eyes. Again—a long minute of silence. "Wow . . . Jenny . . . I can't believe this is happening." He said smiling, as if he had just woken up from a daydream. "It's amazing . . . what are the odds of you appearing only ten days after I met Lisa for the first time in thirteen years?"

If you only knew . . . I thought to myself. "It's Karma," I replied looking at him longingly. Roy's face started turning serious and I feared he was connecting the dots.

"Are you here on vacation or is it a business trip?" he said when he was done reflecting on both improbable possibilities.

"Neither. I came to see you. I'm dead serious."

"I'm glad you did," he said after a long second. "Let's get out of this stifling room. It's a nice day outside."

We walked through the cobblestone walkways of the university, enjoying the green gardens and the fresh air of Jerusalem's mountaintops, saying nothing. He looked sad.

"It's nice seeing you again," he said as if just to make conversation.

"Is it? Really?" I asked, challenging him to tell me the truth. He stopped and looked at me.

"Yes. Jenny. I am glad. I really am," he said and I could feel his sincerity. "It's just that you catch me at a difficult period and I'm not the best person to be around right now."

"I'm sorry to hear that," I said with sympathy. We walked for a while without saying anything until we bumped into a small cafeteria.

"Let me buy you a cup of coffee," Roy offered.

I sat at a small table while Roy stood in line. I watched his body language. It was obvious he was very nervous.

"I didn't just reappear in your life for small talk." I said after he sat down. "We need to talk seriously and I ask that you dedicate some of your time to hear me out. Would you allow me this courtesy? For old time sakes . . ."

"Of course . . . what did you want to talk to me about?"

"I don't want to do it here. I need your full attention and I need you to be relaxed. It's too important," I stressed. He nodded. "Let me take you out to dinner this evening," I suggested, "I'm not local so you'll have to choose the place."

"Sure, that would be wonderful," he said and looked at me with a look that seemed to signal appreciation. I blushed all over. He smiled. "You are so beautiful," he mentioned again. "No wonder you found your way to Sports Illustrated."

I was overwhelmed. "You saw that . . .?"

"Of course I did . . . and I was very proud."

"I feel like a teenager around you," I said embarrassed as I blushed again. He just smiled modestly. There was a moment of silence. "Do you remember our marijuana incident?" I asked him and started laughing out of sheer awkwardness.

He nodded, still smiling. "I'm so sorry for that," he said. "I acted violently and hated myself for it . . . I was a very hot-headed teenager."

"You are sorry?" I asked surprised. "What you did back then was to show me for the first time in my life that someone truly cared for pathetic me . . ." Roy lost his smile as I started feeling the lump in my throat. "That day, when you splashed that cold water over my body, you showed me what love really means."

"Yes, Jenny. I did love you . . . very much . . ." He said and I fought my emotions.

"You see, Roy. What you failed to understand back then was that I didn't just fall in love with the impressive teenager you were . . . I wanted to hold on to the only human being on the face of the earth who I believed truly cared for me."

He picked me up from my hotel that evening and drove us to a beautiful restaurant overlooking the Mount of Olives and the Old City walls. After about an hour of small talk, during which we drank two bottles of excellent Israeli Cabernet Sauvignon, I finally got to the point.

"I want you to consider moving with me to New York." I stated. He was completely and utterly surprised, slicing me to small pieces with his piercing look. "You can continue your Ph.D. research at Columbia or at NYU. You don't have to work. Just conduct your research."

"Move with you to New York?" he asked and I detected sarcasm in his tone of voice. "As what? Your lover?"

"Yes Roy, as my lover, but not in the cheap kind of way you're implying." He looked away. "There is nothing I want more than to someday be your wife."

"You don't know me at all. You haven't seen me in ages. How can you suggest such a thing?"

"I've loved you all my life. I yearned for you. I missed you. I know enough."

"I'm not the boy you remember," he said, changing his tone of voice. "Believe me, Jennifer; you don't want me in your life. I've done . . . I've seen . . . *stuff*! I'm empty, I'm shallow. I'm worthless."

"I don't believe that." I said. "Look . . . you're my only chance for true love and for normalcy. I am a pathetic creature who has been stuck for years loving a teenager."

"That was a very long time ago!" he exclaimed.

"It seems like yesterday to me," I said softly, trying to get a grip on myself, fighting a tide of emotions. He saw that and placed his hand over mine for a few second. Then, he reclined backward on his seat and looked out the big window.

"How time flies," he whispered.

"Please consider my request," I begged him. He looked at me with compassion. It was obvious I had touched a nerve.

"Let me tell you something about contemporary me—it might make you change your mind," he said quietly. He sat straight and looked into my eyes. "I deserted the person I loved the most in her toughest moment. Then, I had a wonderful woman at my side for the last six years. She loved me and wanted to be my wife. I never loved her, and yet I stuck to the relationship as a fallback position. She left me about a week ago, while I was searching the streets and cities of California for my high school sweetheart, trying to realize a pathetic dream. I broke the heart of two women who truly loved me. I'm not going to break the heart of another."

We looked at each other for a long time, sipping from our wine glasses, saying nothing. I broke the silence first. "I'll take my chances with you if you'll let me." I said. He signaled the waiter. When he came, Roy asked for another bottle of wine. "Roy . . . honey . . . you've had enough," I said. He looked at me with bitter eyes.

"I need to get drunk tonight!" he stated. "Do you have a pen?" I reached for my bag and gave him one. He took a clean paper napkin and wrote something in English. "This is my address. Tell the taxi driver to take us there."

Any hopes of seduction I may have entertained had been swept clearly away by a tidal wave of alcohol. Roy was completely drunk as I supported his body up the stairs and into his small apartment. There we emptied what remained of a bottle of Johnny Walker.

I woke up the next day, suffering from the worst hangover ever.

I looked around groggy. Roy was in the living room sitting on the sofa in his shorts, holding his head in both his hands. I went up to him and embraced him. We stayed in that position for a few minutes without talking. He gradually got a hold of himself.

"You have to leave now, Jen," he whispered. "Please."

"Don't send me away," I pleaded. "I want to stay with you for a few days."

"Don't waste your life on a loser like me," he said emotional.

"Roy . . . please . . . I love you. Give me a chance."

"It'll never work. I just screw whatever I come across."

"Come on. Don't be so harsh on yourself." I whispered. He turned around and embraced me.

"Please, go home sweetheart," he said tenderly. "My answer is no! Live your life. I love another. I always loved her. I'm cursed for life."

"Roy . . . Please . . ." I begged him with eyes filled with salty tears. "We can have a wonderful life together . . . just give it a chance."

"We can have a life together, but it won't be wonderful. I'll be bitter and you'll realize eventually that I was just another huge mistake." He tightened his embrace and allowed me to cry on his shoulder.

"Please . . ." I begged him.

"Jennifer," he said, "I'm just a reminder from a different era, a shadow. You are hanging on to a thread—on a silhouette. As much as it hurts me to see you in pain, my decision is final."

He got up, got dressed and left the apartment.

Chapter 28

What the . . .

I returned home empty-handed. I felt sorry for myself because Roy would not give me a chance even now, when he was single again and Lisa was not an option anymore. Adult Roy Cohen had shown me a soft and fragile side you seldom see in men and it just made me love him more. The most difficult part was the reminder that I was the main reason for his life-long grief. There was no escape from the repercussions of my teenage actions. It anguished me to realize that my actions had ended or ruined other people's lives.

It was February when I came back from Israel. Bryan was waiting for me, ready to serve as my backrest and make love to me. He made sure I would not fall apart. He was used to my frequent work-related trips and I told him nothing about Roy or about my voyage to Israel. I just explained the moods and frequent sobbing as stress-related. He was not the kind to ask too many questions anyway. He just understood I needed his support so he gave it.

Luckily for me, we were about to launch my men's clothing campaign and we had a deadline to meet. My annual summer fashion show was about to take place in New York in April 1998. Soon enough the frantic schedule, the pressures and the long working hours pushed aside the remorse. We worked like crazy, knowing we were probably gambling on the future of my new brand. If my men's collection failed, the competition would make me the laughing stock of the industry.

Brilliant Courtney Henderson managed to start a rumor that something new and exciting was happening at Jen-Sven. The fashion media started speculating. Some offered the possibility of a growing rift between my mother and me over policy; others argued we had financial problems. The nasty ones went further to discuss my notorious bed habits as the cause. I despised those fashion reporters who knew nothing about fashion and used their papers for spreading cheap and sleazy gossip, but I well appreciated the commotion the media produced around Jen-Sven. There was anticipation in the air and it created interest. I could not tell anyone outside the company what was really going on. I knew a leak would probably cost me the credit and the prestige associated with being the first to introduce a new concept. If this were to happen, millions of my father's hard-earned dollars would go down the drain.

It was frustrating to be the object of so much disinformation and it created immense pressure that soon enough translated itself to physical anxiety and pain. I started feeling sick on a daily basis; I was weak and I suffered from headaches and dizziness. My mother begged me to see someone, but I had no time for doctors. Then, one morning, as we were about to finalize our budget, I started vomiting in front of everybody. Then I simply fainted. I was rushed to the hospital, where the overall impression was that I must have eaten something rotten because everything else seemed normal.

We waited for about four hours in my hospital room, getting impatient by the minute, demanding to get the proper release. I had no time to waste on unnecessary medical examinations. When the doctor finally came in, I was so impatient that I claimed rudely that they were keeping me in my private room just to make money. He just looked at me in a fatherly manner.

"Can I speak to your daughter in private?" he asked my mother.

"What is this secrecy all about? I don't keep secretes from my mother," I barked at the poor thing.

"It's called doctor-patient confidentiality," he explained patiently, "but if you want your mother around while I disclose private information, than it's fine by me."

"Is it serious?" my mother asked almost hysterically. The truth was that by now even I was becoming concerned.

"Well madam, it depends on how you look at it," he said with a serious face.

"For the love of God," she said looking at him with disproof. "Could you just tell us what's wrong with my daughter instead of putting us through this hideous game of trivia?"

"Mom, calm down," I said. "The guy is only doing his job." I looked at him. "Now, doctor, please tell me what's wrong with me."

"Nothing!" he said. "You are healthy and strong."

"Thank God," my mother said with great relief.

"So what was it all about?" I asked curious.

"It's a rather common ailment we in the money-making industry call pregnancy," he stated matter of fact. My jaw almost fell to the ground.

"What the fuck . . ." I found myself uncontrollably storming him with angry eyes. This was an impossible situation. "I had a tubal ligation done during my early twenties and ever since I've fucked like crazy . . ."

"Jenny . . . Please . . ." my mom intervened.

"I can't be pregnant. It's not possible. What kind of a doctor are you?" I attacked on all fronts. "What kind of hospital are you bozos running here?"

"Well, as much as I'd like to stick around and hear all about your sex history, I have other, more educated patients to serve," he said calmly.

I heaved a sigh. "I'm sorry," I apologized, "but what you're suggesting is not possible."

"It's rare, I admit," he said. "But we have seen cases like yours in the past. I personally saw one in a woman who underwent a procedure of tubal ligation a few months ago."

"No fucking way! I can't be pregnant. You're mistaken!" I exclaimed, refusing to even consider the possibility.

"Ms. Svensen," he said without blinking. "Whether you like it or not—you are pregnant! Now excuse me, I have to see other patients."

I looked at my mother with amazement as he made his way out. "No. No. No!" I said to myself. "There must be some kind of mistake. I want a second opinion!"

It took me a sleepless night to get used to the idea. I suddenly understood all kind of signals my body had been throwing my way: the morning sickness, the sudden swelling and sensitivity, my edgy temper. I was too busy so I had simply dismissed it.

Bryan was a stud all right. Our super-active sex-life must have contributed to this rare phenomenon. *My God, what was I to do now?*

I became numb for the next two days. I found myself walking in Central Park for hours thinking about my situation, examining all the scenarios and possibilities. It was premature to grasp and it took several days; but in a sense, this new mind-blowing situation filled a huge emptiness I had felt for years. It gave me a satisfaction I had never felt before—maybe the fact that I had never planned to be a mother, or the fact that I had never lived a normal life contributed to the mystery.

Another incredible notion I examined thoroughly while walking in the park, was that unfit and unworthy Jennifer Svensen, the one who caused pain and sorrow everywhere and to everyone, was capable of creating a life. My god . . . there was a fetus developing inside of *me* . . . inside my womb . . . A *womb*? I had never thought that that particular organ in my body would ever come in handy during my lifetime.

What a fantastic route of decision-making I underwent back then. It made me think suddenly about the positive aspects of life, things like values and morals and the responsibility of bringing a child into such an imperfect world—a child I could mold as I wished, like a sketch or a new piece of fashion. The dilemma suddenly became a wonderful process of self-examination.

Shockingly surprising, I came rather quickly to the most important decision of my life: I was going to keep the child. Now I needed to inform Bryan. If I was to go for it, I decided unequivocally, then I should do it right. My child would have a father and I would do everything in my power to keep Bryan around for the sake of the innocent soul of my unborn baby.

Bryan Taylor freaked-out! Like a small child—he simply vanished. I couldn't find him for three whole days. When he finally returned, he cried like a baby in my arms. "I'm a kid myself. I can't be a father."

"I'm keeping the child!" I said to him softly, trying to stay calm while wanting to punch him in the face. "It's your decision if to be a part of it or not. I'm not pressing you to do anything you don't want to; but I'm asking you to consider it nonetheless. I want this child to grow up knowing and loving his father."

"Fuck . . .," he whined, "I can't . . . I can't. . . ."

"You can and you will!" I exploded with rage. "Stop howling and take responsibility for your actions!"

"What responsibility? You said we were safe."

"You know what . . . fine . . ., fuck it. . . . I'll raise him on my own . . . you're done. Go get a job . . ." I said and rushed to my room, slamming the door.

It was just acting. I knew Bryan well enough to anticipate he'd come running after me. He was a child to the end. It took him ten whole minutes to arrive and stand outside my door, begging me to open it and let him in. When I finally did, he promised he'd think about it and then took care of my earthly desires, which, by the way, had not diminished due to my pregnancy.

I let the news sink in to his immature brain. I bought him a very expensive new sports car and helped him win a huge campaign for men's underwear, all in an effort to bribe the egghead to be a father to his soon to be born child. He finally cracked and agreed to marry me, but with preconditions: he would not have to change diapers or get up in the middle of the night, and if the marriage turned sour, he walks out without any obligations whatsoever and with a million dollars.

I despised Bryan for his preconditions but I agreed to them nonetheless. The mother in me, the one who had a built-in mechanism to safeguard her child's best interests sensed that they had to do with growing up with a father figure—even if this figure was juvenile Bryan Taylor.

We had a prenuptial agreement drafted by my lawyers, and about a month later, Bryan and I got married at my parents' estate in Beverly Hills. My grandmother Charlotte came especially from Norway. She made my bride's gown and it was the most beautiful thing I had ever seen. In fact, it was the harbinger of Jen-Sven's line of bridal gowns, which I named 'Charlotte Brides'. The line generated more than 6 million dollars in net revenues annually— of which I directed 10% directly to my grandmother's bank account in Norway.

My mother's side of the family and Bryan's family and friends were not in attendance. The former were not invited; as for the latter, well, Bryan did not think it was necessary to inform anyone about his marriage. It was a sign, which I chose to ignore, that my husband was not going to stick around for long.

I never saw my father so happy like he was during my pregnancy. The prospects of a grandchild excited him and sometimes made him ridiculously emotional. It also made him impatient and overprotective. He started inquiring about me on a daily basis, asking if I was feeling well, if I had eaten, drunk, rested enough. He scolded me for not dressing warmly or for not eating three meals a day. It was suffocating for a free bird like me, but I let it go.

My father accompanied me to all my doctor's appointments. He took Bryan's place, who, by the way, acted as though my pregnancy had nothing to do with him. I watched my father's happy face as he stared hypnotized at his grandchild on the ultrasound screen. The day we were told of the fetus's sex was the day he completely lost his composure. It was when the doctor showed us a little tiny penis. My father burst into tears and looked at me overjoyed. It was the first time I had ever seen my father cry. The Svensen dynasty was going to continue. He had been a lonely child and I had been a lonely child too. Coping all these years with Jennifer had finally paid off—the Svensens would linger on.

If my father became overprotective, my mother became over-everything. She started renovating rooms in our Beverly Hills, New York and Miami estates, making them fit for a crown prince. Artists drew beautiful pictures of cartoon heroes on the walls, rooms were stuffed with baby furniture and with toys. They were also filled to overflow with baby accessories and clothes. At work, Mariana scolded my staff for smoking around me, for putting too much pressure on me, for leaving windows open or just for talking too loud whenever I was around. I begged her to stop and she promised she would but she never did.

I'm standing naked in front of a mirror at my parents' estate in Miami, looking at my belly with joy, caressing it. I talk to my fetus lovingly, promising that life on the other side of my womb will be fine and that I'll do my best to love and protect him. Then, without warning, emotions flood me and I start crying uncontrollably—a loud cry. The hormones slash at me like there's no tomorrow. I ask myself if I'm capable of raising a child and giving him the emotional and moral infrastructure to lead his life normally, or if I'm even worthy of such a huge responsibility. My mother hears my cry and rushes into the room. She embraces me and assures me that I'm definitely worthy. She says I'll be a good mother and it seems to really work. I feel better.

Worthiness was a sensation that was new to me; things finally began to make sense. Don't get me wrong, all of you feminists out there. It is not that being a mother is what defined my life; it simply helped me appreciate life better—much better.

Oh . . . yes . . . the men's collection . . . well . . . it was a blast.

Chapter 29

The Perfect Father Figure

Thor Angus Taylor was born on the 11th day of November 1998, about a month prior to his mother's scheduled date. He rushed into the world to save her from herself. And that he certainly did. My life as I had known it had been truly disposed of. Now I had a responsibility and a challenge supreme to any I had ever faced—a challenge I was planning to face head on.

Thor's birth drained me of cynicism, washed me of hatred and antagonism, refined my body from all the toxic waste it had accumulated throughout the years and did wonders for my aching conscience. The new me took a year off and invested herself in her newly born child. We lived at my parents' estate in Beverly Hills. Bryan came over for a short weekend barely once a month, so Thor could have a father figure of sorts. My mother took charge of Jen-Sven and continued sailing the company in the direction I chose.

It was remarkable for me to realize how quickly I adapted to being a mother—how swiftly I turned from reckless and unrestrained Jennifer to a compassionate and easy-going mother. Thor made me feel normal and happy for doing normal things . . . like being his mother. He was a beautiful baby, inheriting his father's brown hair and my father's ocean blue eyes. He was smart, friendly and happy, smiling to everyone, turning heads wherever we went. As I stared at him often at nights, asleep, I could not help but ask myself repeatedly if this incredible creation was really mine.

No matter what they did, where they were or how busy their schedules were, my parents would come home to Beverly Hills every weekend to be with their grandchild. It was a wonderful period and I hated the fact that it had to end eventually. I contemplated staying home with him even longer than the long maternity leave I had given myself, but Jen-Sven needed me. I had a new collection to design. It was long overdue.

About a week before we returned to New York, I decided to do something I should have done long ago but had always been terrified of doing. I went to visit the graves of Jerry and Buzz. I took Thor with me. Somehow, his presence gave me the strength I had never found to face my actions—as if his innocence was a shield from the punishment I deserved.

It was a beautiful morning when I bent over and placed a bunch of red roses on Jerry's gravestone. I caressed the black granite for a long minute and then got up from my knees.

"Hi Jerry," I cried as I addressed him. Thor was sitting in his stroller, looking up at the sky as a flock of seagulls were making their way loudly northwards. "I'm sorry for not coming to visit you sooner . . . I'm a coward—please forgive me." I took a long draught of air, trying to calm myself down. Images of smiling Jerry came to mind and made the effort impossible. I was choking on my own breath. "If you had lived, you would be 32 now. What a wonderful life you could have had if not for my stupid sense of adventure . . ." I burst into a painful cry. Thor looked at me concerned. I went to him, kneeled over and embraced the infant. "Jerry. This is Thor, my son." I whispered. "I want you to know that not a day goes by during which I don't think of you and Buzz . . . not a single day . . ."

I drove to Culver City where I placed a bunch of red roses on Buzz's grave and introduced him to Thor. "Honey," I cried, "what a fine man you were, loving me and protecting me. Please forgive me . . . I was young and stupid. I didn't see the writing on the wall. I could have saved your life." I breathed deeply, trying unsuccessfully to get a grip over myself. "Oh . . . Buzzy . . . I'll never forget you and I will never forgive myself for not being there like you were for me."

Returning to New York, I had to leave Thor unwillingly in the hands of a nanny. I remembered my childhood traumas and made sure I was always home before 5 p.m. My mother did her best to free me from the everyday running of the company so I could spend as much time as possible with my son, and there were mornings when I simply woke up and decided to stay home, regardless of schedule. The sight of my son standing, smiling at me from his baby's bed, looking forward for me to pick him up and play with him would always get the best of me.

Bryan was not a father, or a husband for that matter. The child in him became an adolescent, rebelling against his new set of circumstances. Consequently, we hardly saw him. Sex became as bad as his behavior but I kept sleeping with him to make sure he would stick around. By Thor's second birthday, it was evident that the man wanted nothing to do with me or with his son. By then, I really hated his guts. One evening, after Thor had fallen asleep, I made my father a cup of his favorite tea and we sat by the kitchen table.

"I think we need to talk," he said to me softly, his wise eyes, looking at me with tons of compassion."

"What's on your mind dad?"

"A lot," he confessed. "It's time to let go of Bryan!" he exclaimed. I nodded, looking sadly into my cup. "He is a good kid, but he's not mature enough to handle the responsibility." I nodded again. "But he's just an excuse, isn't he?"

"Excuse? For what?"

"You deserve a husband you love and respect—a man who would be your friend and love you back, someone to take care of you."

"I got what I deserved," I whispered.

"No, sweetheart, you deserve much better."

"Thor makes everything all right . . ."

"No!" he exclaimed. "You need to stop living your life in pieces. Thor is a gift from heaven but you still have your own life to think about. You need to find happiness. You need a worthy companion. You are beautiful, smart, successful and rich and your heart is pure gold," I struggled with my emotions. "Take your time and search for the man of your dreams."

"I gave up on that a long time ago . . ." I whispered and wiped the moisture from my eyes.

He looked at me for about a minute without saying anything. "Well, it's time to resume hope. It's time to change attitude and think positively."

"What about Thor? He needs a father." I said and he smiled. Retrospectively, I led the conversation to exactly where he wanted it to go.

"Would you consider my candidacy?"

"It's not the same." I said.

"Please, honey, let me make up for being such a lousy father to you. Give me the opportunity to clear up some of my aching conscious."

"Oh . . . dad," I said feeling suffocated by the lump in my throat. "You would be the perfect father figure for Thor, but he'll be confused. You're his grandfather . . ."

"Please." He begged me. "Thor is a smart boy. He'll figure out the situation as he grows up. Divorce Bryan! He isn't around anyway. Get a life. Find a lover. Live your life."

"I don't know what to say."

"Yes you do. You just have to be courageous enough to say it." I nodded in agreement.

I looked into his eyes as I took a big gulp of air into my lungs. "Yes dad, I do know what to say: Bryan Taylor is out. From now on, my son's name will be Thor Angus Svensen."

I divorced Bryan the following month. He got his million dollars, drove off in the Ferrari I had bought for him and completely disappeared from our lives. Before he left, I tried to convince him to stay in touch and visit his son from time to time. He promised he would but never did. Clearly, Bryan would have left us at some point anyway, so I just made my life less complicated by sending him away when I did.

My father bought a huge estate in Newark and we all moved in together. Thor had a beautiful private playground where he and his grandfather spent their time together. Angus built a shallow-water swimming pool alongside the big one, just for Thor. My parents seemed happier than ever with us around. Their love for each other intensified as they watched their lives finally on track. Seeing them together always threw me back to the beautiful images of them making love in the dark old days. I started getting used to loving my parents and being proud of them for being wonderful grandparents. And, as Thor grew up, my father spent more and more time with him, taking him hiking and on fishing trips, enjoying time with him in amusement parks, helping him with his homework, buying him everything he needed—spoiling the child to a ridiculous extent.

As time passed by, I realized that my father needed Thor more than Thor needed a father figure. When he started taking six and seven year old Thor to the Knicks or the Yankees, I finally understood how lonely he had been all those years. He had never had a real friend, never had someone he could share his thoughts with and never had a person with whom he felt comfortable enough to go to these games with. In this sense, Thor was no less the perfect companion to my father than the perfect grandson. As for me, I did try to give myself the opportunity to find what my father called "a worthy companion." I dated for a while and even liked some of the men, but none of them succeeded in capturing my heart. At a certain point, I gave up on the notion.

Then Thor turned seven and I struck oil.

We had a birthday party for Thor at our Newark estate and invited all of his school friends to see a show and a clown. When the party was over the parents came to pick up their kids. One father in particular caught my Eye. He was a tall, brown eyed, silver hair, forty-something hunk who had come to pick up his daughter. He was very nice and friendly; and the look he gave me confirmed the message I sent with my smile. He was interested and he was divorced. The only embarrassing detail was that I knew the girl's mother from previous class gatherings.

He called the next day and we went out for dinner. Several dinners and rewarding sex encounters later, I had enough information to decide that this was no ordinary man—he was worth the trouble. My parents liked him and it seemed that Thor didn't mind my seeing the father of one of his classmates . . .

Andrew Van Buren was a successful businessman who owned a small pharmaceutical company specializing in skin-care products. It was always interesting to be around him because of his intelligence and his outlook. He respected what I did and truly appreciated my achievements. He was a man of values and strong character. He was also gentle, compassion and kind. I fell in love with him. Consequently, we got married.

Now, I don't want to get too-philosophical about it, but the process of falling in love with Andy brought me to the conclusion that love comes in quantities. Andy is only the third person outside of my nuclear family I had ever loved. The other two were Roy and Lisa. My love for him, profound and true as it is, never matched the magnitude and impact of the emotion I had for my teenage counterparts. It is a different kind of love—mature, correct and measured. It resides within the frontiers of rationality.

Perhaps what freed me to fall in love at all was the news I received from PI Swartz that Roy and Lisa—both now divorced—were finally back together. It relieved a set of interlocked feelings combining love, guilt and shame that had held me back. I had undergone a period of mourning for the death of my wish to reunite someday with Roy, after which I became stronger, ready to face a new set of circumstances, ready to fall in love; and the appearance of Andy in my life came at just the right moment.

I sent a very generous check to Mr. Schwartz, informing him that his services were no longer required. I no longer needed information about Roy Cohen.

Relieved and somewhat happy, I had closed the gate on my previous life.

Or so I thought . . .

Chapter 30

Unpredictable Predicament

I turned 40 in 2006, believing that all of my emotional circles had firmly been completed. I felt that things were almost perfect. I say almost . . .

As I excavated into the inner layers of my soul, I discovered a deep scar so painful and humiliating that had to be resolved finally, and that scar's name was Steve Flannigan.

As if the rape itself had not been excruciating enough, I had to deal ever since with nightmares. In them, Flannigan repeated his act over and over again. I would wake up in a cold sweat, trembling, sometimes screaming. It got worse when I was pregnant. Not yet aware of my baby's sex, I saw vividly into the future Flannigan raping my soon to be born daughter. After Thor was born, the nightmares eased up a little but they would resume full force each time I would run into Flannigan at some fashion-related event. Living in the fashion world, I would run into him all too often—at fashion shows, parties and other events. To my annoyance, the creep was successful. A year earlier, he had become the CEO of 'Exquisitely Hip'—making him even more cocky and shameless.

I bumped into him at a reception honoring one of the industry's leading designers.

"Jennifer Svensen . . . what a wonderful sight . . . almost forty and still a knockout," he said as he sat in the stool beside me. He managed to take me off balance. I turned pale as a sheet of paper and did my best to evade his look. "You've been avoiding me for years. Was I that bad in bed to be punished that harshly?" he asked and laughed a vulgar kind of a laugh.

"Fuck you Flannigan," I barked at him and turned away.

"My thoughts exactly. I have a room on the 17th floor. We could re-capture some of our greatest moments together," he said. I turned my gaze towards him. His face generated contempt.

"You are a sorry excuse for a human being," I said as I escaped to the toilets, where I threw up, promising to avenge his ever-lasting contamination of my body.

Then, as I turned 40, the time for that had arrived. I had the power and the maturity to fight back. And . . . yes . . . I had a plan.

Back in the nineties, just a few months after my horrible experience, I had been chosen along with four other models for an advertisement campaign of a New York based fashion house. At one stage of the shoot, as we were taking a break, I overheard one of the models mentioning Flannigan. Patricia Douglas, was telling her friend about a terrible sexual experience she had had with him. I chose to disregard it; it was too painful for me to share my experience.

About a decade later, I tracked her down in Philadelphia and asked if she would be willing to help me find more of Flannigan victims and send him to jail. She was reluctant because she didn't want her husband, her kids or her parents to ever know of her ordeal.

"This is my card," I said to her just before I was about to leave, "call me if you decide to join the battle."

"I think you are very courageous to do what you're doing," she said to me.

I stopped, turned around, walked to her and took her hand in mine. "Pat. This has nothing to do with courage. It has to do with justice. I was just a young model when this creep threw me on a bed, chocked me, humiliated me and inflicted pain like I never knew before, physically and emotionally. I almost fainted. He came in and out of me like a beast, hurting me, punching my face." I turned and started walking away.

"Wait, Jenny . . . please . . . wait a minute . . . let me breathe," she whispered. I turned to face her. She nodded. "I need some time to tell my husband and my parents about it . . ." She sat down on the sofa again and I sat beside her. "He did the same to me . . ." she said and started sobbing. "He had me do stuff that was so sick, Jesus . . . I'm so ashamed. Then he brutally raped me and beat the shit out of me too . . . I asked him to stop but he wouldn't . . . it lasted so long I thought it would never end . . . I still have nightmares. He broke two of my teeth . . ."

I looked at her as she dubbed her eyes with a paper tissue.

"Look, Pat." I said with sympathy, "There are moments in life when we have to decide who we are. I never liked who I was. Recently, I decided who I wanted to be and it changed my life. It means disengaging from yourself and becoming someone you wish you could be. You are much stronger than you think and you can decide to be that person. As for your family, after you give them the time, they will admire you for doing this. It's a powerful message to your kids. We need to send this asshole to prison for life."

She nodded. "Let's do it!"

Pat gave me the name and number of another woman who had been a victim of Flannigan, and that ex-model gave me the names of two others. I had them send me depositions, which I filed with an official complaint at the NYPD.

Flannigan was arrested that same day. By now, he was very famous, so the media extensively reported his trial. We ex-models—all five of us—took the stand and testified courageously, describing in detail the small and appalling components of rape, shocking the jury, the audience and the general public with an in-depth account of brutality.

Flannigan was found guilty and sentenced to the maximum penalty—25 years in prison.

Pat and I guest-starred in some Television and radio talk shows. We gave interviews to newspapers and magazines, stressing the need for women to come forward if ever sexually harassed or raped. We addressed some other ills of the fashion world as well.

"Our justice system works," I stated during one of my interviews. "You just have to come forward, present your case and let it do its' job."

Now that Flannigan was behind bars for the rest of his life, a wonderful routine took over our lives. I was finally at peace with myself, Andy by my side, Thor growing up perfectly and my parents close by.

This was the background to a new and exciting adventure I was about to take Jen-Sven—Jewelry. I had decided to utilize my father's company infrastructure, knowledge and vast web of connections so that manufacturers all over the world would manufacture items I had designed. Contrary to garments, jewelry was an extremely costly field. If it failed, especially with the dire state of the US economy at that period, it could take Jen-Sven's new spring collection down with it. I decided to take the risk because I wanted to expand my field and to be considered an artist—something I could never achieve designing clothes.

To my full satisfaction, the first line made a wonderful profit—although it received a lukewarm reception by professional jewelers. I had come from the fashion industry and 'what the hell did I know' about jewelry design? With the next line, a year down the line however, I was credited for my originality and courage by those same people.

And then, as I was making a fortune, something occurred that once again turned my life upside down.

Ever since Thor was a small child, he loved wearing his hair very long. Being so close to my father, loving and adoring him, Thor wanted to imitate his grandfather's Ugly Vikings Sixties rock star look. I had never objected; and as long as he was happy, so was I. Just about when Thor turned 12, something in his look made me lose a heartbeat each time I saw him. I could not put my finger on it, but as he matured, an uneasy feeling grew inside of me. With time, I had pushed it aside, but it was always there in the back of my mind, reminding me that I was deliberately disregarding something important about my son.

At 14, my son was a tall and striking young man who still wore his brown hair very long. My mother said his look was a beautiful combination of my father and of his hunk father Bryan. I thanked God every single day for exempting my child from his mother's complicated character and psychological complexity. Thor was a good boy, disciplined and well mannered. He had respect for his family, for people in general and for life. He did well in school and was very successful socially.

All of that crushed down upon me one day when my mother finally managed to convince Thor to cut his hair.

"You need to look at your handsome son," my mother said to me, "I finally convinced him to have a decent haircut. Now we can see his wonderful blue eyes." I raised my gaze and froze; for suddenly, I saw not Thor Angus Svensen, but Roy Cohen . . .

All of what I have managed to push aside for the last two years blew up in my face with the magnitude of an atomic mega-blast. All of Thor's personal characteristics, all of my past mis-takes and my present achievements, all of my fears and hopes for the future, all of my wishes, all of my dreams—all of that came back to rock my world and sent me running into the bathroom, crying hysterically.

All I could remember of that drunken night in Roy's bed was the haze. I had certainly *wanted* it to include sex, but I was sure that, had there been any, I would have remembered. Could it be that the one most important sexual caper of my entire life had been forgotten, and lost forever in an alcoholic haze?

So, there I was in the bathroom crying myself to exhaustion. I cried joyfully for that Thor had received the father he deserved. He got a worthy father like my iconic lover, not a coward that cracked, fled and never return. Alongside it, there was also the painful cry for the realization that this discovery would most likely inflict yet another blow on my teenage friends, who were married happily now and might even have joint children of their own. *Was this my one function in life? Ruining their lives?*

My mother and Thor, concerned that after about twenty min-utes I was still crying in the bathroom, unable to calm down, called the fire department. The door was opened by a firefighter and I was taken to the hospital and treated with tranquilizers. I slept for about two hours.

"What's wrong?" my mother asked concerned when I re-gained the capacity to speak.

"Is there anything in Thor that reminds you of someone we once knew?" I whispered trembling. She looked at me with a very big question mark all over her face. "Thor was not born prematurely. He was born in the ninth month of my pregnancy," I tried to explain, getting emotional again.

"So . . ." she asked confused. I started to cry uncontrollably again.

"Mom, Thor is not Bryan's son . . ." I cried.

"He's not?" she asked astonished.

I shook my head, taking a deep breath, calming myself up to the point of regaining my capacity to speak. "I never told you about it, but about 14 years ago I flew to Israel. I had this dream of reuniting with Roy Cohen." My mom's face turned darker. "I met him and we went out for dinner. We got drunk and the next morning I woke up in his bed. Today . . . as you came into the house, I saw Thor with short hair, a spitting image of Roy, I knew . . . I just knew . . ."

She sat down on the chair, realizing I was making sense. "Dear god!" was all she uttered.

Chapter 31

Predestination

We told my father and Andy about the discovery but decided to keep Thor out of the picture for the time being. I needed conclusive evidence first.

It took us about a week to track Bryan down. Now in his late thirties, the man was living in Miami, still single, working as a sales clerk for an appliance store. I flew to Florida and asked him to take a paternity test. I had to pay the jerk 50,000 dollars to agree to take it and to sign full disclosure on the results. I even accompanied him to the clinic to make sure he took the test. I hated being around him.

I had a long conversation with Andy the night before. I told him about my suspicion and gave him some background information about Roy. He asked to see a photo of the man. I handed him the 1984 Beverly High yearbook from our private library.

He looked at me with sympathy. "You don't need a DNA test, honey. This guy is definitely Thor's father."

"Are you okay with that?" I asked.

He nodded. "Do what you have to do. Thor must know his father isn't that useless Bryan."

"What about Roy? Should I tell him?" I asked with a cracked voice. Andy came close and embraced me tight.

"If I was him," he whispered and kissed my forehead, "I would want to know."

Thor took the test the same day we got Bryan's results. I asked my son to be patient and promised to tell him once the results came in. Three days later, no one in the family was remotely surprised to learn that Bryan was not Thor's Father. The next step had to be asking Roy to take the test.

I was terrified of Roy's reaction to the news. It involved a trip to Israel to face him. . . . and Lisa; and it scared me.

Ever since Andy had come into my life, I no longer found it necessary to be the tough and rigid woman I pretended to be. At times, I allowed myself to be fragile and weak, and it was all right. Now I was fragile and weak as never before and my husband was a rock—supporting and helping me make the right decisions.

"Thor must know," he said to me one night, "there is no other way."

The following evening I went into my son's room. It was just after his girlfriend Julia had left. He was sitting on the carpet; reclining against the wall, busy playing his Xbox. I sat on the carpet beside him and placed my head on his shoulder. It took me a while before I could say anything. He saw I was going through something but just kept playing his game.

"Just spit it out mom," he said to me when the game was over. He placed the joystick aside and looked at me. "I read about the test I took. Either you're trying to find in me some kind of a genetic disease or you want to establish if I'm your child." I looked at my super-smart son and smiled sadly. For a moment, he was pleased with his little joke. "Which of the two options should I prepare myself for?"

"The second," I whispered. He nodded, realizing that my motherhood had little that needed establishing. "I'm your mother, you can't escape that, kiddo," I said, doing my best to keep my composure, ". . . but . . . Bryan . . . I thought all these years . . . I didn't know, believe me sweetheart, I didn't know . . ."

I took a deep breath in order to calm myself down. I was doing a lousy job of conveying the information in a mature way. He saw me struggling and embraced me.

"Mom . . . what are you trying to tell me? Is Bryan my father or not?"

I shook my head. "No, honey, he's not."

"Okay . . ." he said, looking indifferent, "I can't say I'm saddened by it."

I smiled. "Yeah . . . I can't say that I am too . . ."

"So . . ." he said after a long anticipation, "who is the poor slob?"

"We still need to run another test . . . but I'm pretty confident of his identity and he is a wonderful man. I've always loved him with all my heart and in a way, I still do."

"Does he know I'm his son?"

"No. Not yet. But I'm going to tell him soon."

"What's his name?" I looked at my son. He projected strength and by that gave me courage to continue.

"Roy . . . Roy Cohen."

We talked for about an hour. Thor was curious and somewhat excited. He wanted to know everything about his father and the circumstances that had brought us together. I tried my best to give him as much information as I could, especially about the role Roy played in my teenage years. I told him about Roy's strong character and the importance of values to him.

"Mom! You're cool?" he said smiling surprised at the realization that not *his* generation had invented rebellion. I told him of Roy's reaction to my marijuana smoking. "What a fool. He should have smoked with you . . .," he said and we laughed.

I tried to explain to Thor the impact Roy had over my life. I also told him about my friendship with Lisa, and how fate had split the three of us apart back in 1985. The hardest thing was to tell my 14-year-old son he wasn't planned.

"You are the fruit of my enormous love for Roy," I said with moisture in my eyes, "and don't you ever forget that!"

"Do you think he'll be happy to learn of my existence?" he asked me and sent my emotions on a trip to the end of the universe.

I just looked at him with weary eyes. "It could take some time, but I'm sure he will . . . eventually . . ."

That week PI Swartz managed to get me Roy's cell phone number. Excited, I gathered the courage needed to call him. The voice on the other side seemed truly happy to speak to me after all these years. I informed him of my pending arrival in Israel and asked if he would be kind enough to spare me an hour of his time. He asked if he could bring Lisa along. He was sure she would be happy to meet me. I replied with a cracked voice that I wanted to meet her too, more than he could ever know; but that it can only happen after I meet him alone.

"Are you okay?" he asked concerned.

"Yes . . . No, no, I'm fine," I replied, "I just need to talk to you privately about something important."

I had been promising myself for years to find the opportunity to come clean with Lisa about our teenage years. When I hung up the phone after ending my conversation with Roy that day, I decided to finally do so. Although I suspected she would probably despise me for the rest of her life, there was no escaping it now. She deserved to know and I deserved a chance to relieve myself of the years-long heavy burden.

I flew to Israel the following week, carrying with me Thor's test results and a photo album containing his most recent photos. I met Roy at a Jerusalem hotel. I was tired and emotional, jet-lagged and in a state of complete disarray.

"Let me look at you," I said and screened him head to toe. Still the striking man he always was, tall and handsome. "You've hardly changed."

We sat in the hotel coffee shop overlooking the old city wall.

"So, Jenny, what's up?" he asked after about half an hour of filling some of the gaps in our lives. He was married to Lisa now, and they had a joint 4-year-old son named Tom. I told him about my career and my own 14 year old. "Our last conversation left me wondering if everything was okay," he said. I looked at him seriously, feeling the blood rising up to my face. Then I looked at my coffee cup, breathing heavily. "Jenny . . ." he said. I looked up and saw his concern.

"I always loved you . . ." I said, on the verge of losing it. He smiled compassionately but said nothing. "You were the man of my dreams . . ."

He looked at me with apathy and anticipation. "Jenny. Just say what you came here to say . . ."

Suddenly I became numb, deadhead—a zombie. I couldn't say anything for a very long moment. The blood raced through every vein of my body, my heart was working overtime to supply the demand. It became hard to breathe. Suffocated by emotions, I inserted my hand into my bag and pulled out Thor's photo album. I handed it to him. He took it, placed it on the table, gazed at me for a second or two with a strange expression. Then, hesitantly, he looked at the album.

Thor's first photo did the job. There was no need to see the others. Roy turned pale. Small dots of sweat covered his forehead. He looked at me with confusion written all over his face. ". . . This is Thor . . ." I stammered, feeling the tears running uncontrollably down my cheeks. "He is a good boy . . ." I cried. "He is in the track team . . ." I said sobbing, trying to sell the boy to his father and stopping when I realized I could never really do justice by that—neither to Thor nor to his biological father.

Roy stood up, looking helpless. His face left no room for misinterpretation—it showed distress. After about a minute, he sat slowly back in his chair, staring at Thor's photo again. Then, gradually, he turned the pages. Soon he had looked at them all. It took him forever to raise his eyes from the last photo and look at me.

"How could this be Jennifer? How could this be?" He whispered with what I thought was pain.

"Our last encounter . . . we were drunk . . . I didn't know . . . I don't even *remember!*" I said apologetically.

He looked away, heaving a heavy sigh. I took a breath of air, getting ready for the second part of our conversation, in which I begged him to take the test, just for the record. ". . . I know you're confused and probably angry; but I want you to know that Thor is the light of my life, my reason to live . . . my sense of purpose. He changed my life for the better and rescued me from the awful Jennifer you remember." He looked at me with a sad face, still trying to digest the enormity of the situation. "Even if unintentionally," I continued, "you gave me the greatest gift of all . . . knowing he is yours makes me the happiest person on the planet." I dried my face with a paper tissue I had in my bag.

"How could you keep this from me all these years?" He asked with frustration and maybe even some guilt.

"I didn't know he was yours . . . I swear on our son's life. That morning, when I saw you on the sofa, I was sure you'd slept there. I couldn't remember. You have to believe me. It only occurred to me about two weeks ago, and I needed Thor and the man we'd thought was his father to take the tests. Once the results came in I called you immediately."

"My god . . . he is a spitting image of me . . ." he said, looking at Thor's photo again, still with a very troubled facial expression. "You must have suspected he was mine."

"I guess . . . in the back of my mind. . . . yes . . . maybe I did. But it was so far-fetched . . ." he placed his hand over his face and took another heavy sigh. "Roy, please believe me. I came to Israel back in 1998 to see if we could have a future together, not to trick you into anything. Please, say you believe me."

He looked at me with a sad face and then opened the album again, turning the pages. The silence was killing me as I documented in my brain every single expression his face made while he was looking at his son's photos.

"Okay," he said finally, closing the album. "I don't know what to say or how to react . . . I'm overwhelmed . . . what's next Jenny . . . what's next?"

"I need you to take a blood test, just to make sure . . ."

He nodded. "Of course . . . although I've just been looking at myself at 14." I got to my feet and moved my chair, sitting closer to him. I placed my hand on his arm and looked at his beautiful, tormented, face.

"Roy . . . fate tied the three of us together from the beginning," I whispered. "I had a tubal legation done in my twenties. This was not supposed to happen; in a way it's not even possible . . ." He remained quiet, staring ahead. I caressed his hair. "Until I found out I was pregnant, I was sharing a bed with everything and everyone that came my way. What were the odds that of all these people, you and a one night stand for that matter . . . what are the odds for that? It's bigger than us; it's almost divine intervention."

He turned his head and looked at me sadly." How do I tell Lisa?"

I pulled back my hand, realizing we were now on different frequencies. "I guess she won't exactly be happy to see me anymore, would she?" I asked rhetorically. "She'll think it's my pre-destination to fuck up your lives . . ."

Roy took a deep breath of air and then looked at me. His face suddenly changed. The dark and tormented guise left his face and I could see clearly that something else had conquered it. I think it may have marked a kind of acceptance. "Jennifer," he addressed me with compassion. "Tell me about Thor." I got so emotional I couldn't speak. My eyes filled with tears and my heart almost exploded from excitement. "Tell me about my son . . . is he a good person?"

Chapter 32

Coming Clean

As it turned out, Israel's law did not permit taking the kind of paternity test we needed without a court decree. This meant going through about a month-long legal process. When he called to inform me of this upsetting information, Roy asked me to join him for a cup of coffee. I was anxious to hear what he had to say, fearing this new development had caused him a change of heart.

"I know Lisa well. She is trying her best to act cool about it, but she is hurting like hell." He said when we finally got our coffee. There was a moment of silence. I didn't know what to say. "Nevertheless, she supports my decision." He continued, nervously playing with his cup.

"What decision?" I asked with suspense.

"To be a father to my son," he said. I smiled with great relief. He looked out to the street. "My god . . . to think Thor had to grow up without a father, to think I didn't get the chance to be a father to him for 14 whole years. It's killing me . . ."

"So the sooner you come to see him the better," I said. "You can use the opportunity to take the test in New York."

He nodded. "Yes . . . I was about to suggest that. It has to be done as soon as possible . . . for everybody's sake."

That same evening I got a call from Lisa. She wanted to meet me . . . "in order to create a more comfortable emotional environment for Roy," was how she put it. "Don't be fooled by his looks," she said, "inside this tall and muscular man hides a delicate soul. I ask that you help me make sure this will be done in a way that doesn't leave another scar on it." What made the situation so excruciating was the realization that the inevitable conversation I was about to have tomorrow with Lisa would probably scar *her* soul to an unimaginable degree.

Sometimes withholding information can prevent grief. With that in mind, I always asked myself a simple question: 'if it was me—would I want to know?' The answer in most cases was positive. I thought I knew Lisa enough to establish that about her too. Roy had lost Lisa because of me and Lisa had gone through life thinking she was an idiot to fall into the abyss of drugs—twice . . . because of me! Even if our conversation caused her grief, in the end, it would free her from the ongoing and agonizing self-blame—of this, I was certain.

Again, the morning I met Lisa, I was jetlagged, fatigued and excited . . . an emotional wreck. Fifteen years had passed since I had last seen her in her San Diego office under much happier circumstances. At 45, walking into the café, she was still the most beautiful human being I had ever seen.

I got immediately to my feet. She gave me an expressionless nod and sat down in front of me. I sat while looking at her longingly. The waiter approached us. She asked for a glass of water. Her face was pale and showed anxiety. "Lisa, you look great."

She looked at me with a sad, undecided face. "Thank you," she whispered.

"Look . . . I know it's tough . . . it's difficult for me no less . . . believe me . . ." she looked away, struggling with her rising emotions. I looked into my cup.

"You have a beautiful boy," she whispered, "he looks just like Roy."

"Thanks." The level of tension in the air was sufficient for lightning to strike. I was anticipating an outburst of emotions but Lisa kept her cool. "I was hoping we could do the test in Israel. We need to put an end to the guessing game. Unfortunately, we can't."

She shook her head. "There is no need for any tests, as far as I'm concerned. Thor is Roy's son. The photo you gave Roy is more than enough to establish that," she said. I let out a sigh of relief. She was making it easy on both of us.

"Yes . . . he resembles his father in every way." I said. There was a moment of silence.

"Jennifer . . . Roy is everything to me." She said with a sad face. "In this respect nothing has changed since our teenage years." I nodded. "It took me twenty whole years to win him back and we are happy together."

"And I'm happy for you both, believe me . . ."

"This could ruin our lives," she whispered. I looked down to my cup. "Where do you want to go with this?"

"I just thought Roy had a right to know . . ."

"You did the right thing!" she established.

"Thank you."

"I'm just scared this new turn might set me and Roy off course."

"It doesn't have to. I'm here just for the sake of Thor and for the sake of the decency I never had. I love you and Roy with all my heart. God knows I inflicted enough pain on both of you back when we were kids."

"We were young and foolish and we made mistakes." She said, opening by that the gates to my heart's darkest alleys, where I had to take her by the hand now for a guided tour to the abyss of my soul.

I took a deep breath of air and released it slowly. "Mistakes. . . ." I chuckled bitterly, "you have no idea." She looked at me puzzled. "We were only twelve when I fell in love with you." I whispered, afraid to look into her eyes. "I used to dream about you. I thought of you night and day and I longed for you." I raised my eyes and looked at her face. It was obvious she found our conversation uneasy. "The emotion was real, Lisa . . . and don't think it was just infatuation. It was strong and painful." I stopped and blew my nose. "We became good friends for a while and I was the happiest person alive. I remember kissing you one day and enjoying the memory of that wonderful kiss for years to come."

"Jennifer . . . what does this have to do with our current circumstances?" she asked impatiently.

". . . just bear with me . . . please . . ." I asked. She gave me a nod. "The love I had for you was so uncontrollable that when you chose Amanda over me, I was devastated for months. I know it sounds silly today, but we were kids and I promised myself to make you pay big time . . ."

"Look, Jennifer, I'm not in the mood for nostalgia . . ." she said nervously and got to her feet. "I have to go now . . ." she said, turned away and started walking.

"Ralph Dillon . . ." I said and she stopped right away. She turned slowly to face me. Her facial expression transmitted anguish. "Lisa. If you go now, you'll never know why I mentioned that name."

She walked back to the table with a harsh look. "What the hell are you talking about?"

"Please . . . Lisa. Please . . . sit down. Give me a chance to come clean . . . please," I begged her. She did as I asked, embracing her bag, looking at me with piercing eyes, waiting to hear why I had chosen to take her back to the worst period of her life. "About three years after you decided to dump me for Amanda, the emotion was still very much alive and deep."

"What about Ralph Dillon. Get to the point!" she ordered with a cold and angry tone of voice.

"You remember me in my teens . . . bad, sexual, looking for trouble, searching for the adrenaline . . . well . . . at a certain point I wanted to try drugs. I got the phone number of a supplier . . . he was very handsome . . . a college student. I slept with him and then offered him a lot of money to let you taste a bit of the heartache you gave me . . ." She placed her hand on her open mouth, starting only now to comprehend the gravity of the information I was kindly bestowing on her. "Ralph Dillon didn't accidently bump into you in the Beverly Hills Public Library—I sent him there."

She was in shock and could not react. Her hands and lips were shaking. Seeing her so hurt was killing me but there was no turning back now. "It won't help now, and you will probably never believe it anyway, but he was never supposed to drug you or to get into your pants. I soon realized the monster I created, but by then it was too late and I had lost control over the situation . . ."

She shook her head, still in shock, shaking all over—totally astounded. "For years I considered myself filth, scum . . .," I cried now, looking down, ashamed. There was a long minute of silence, which I interrupted. "Lisa, I'm telling you this, not because I wish to cause you pain. You could probably walk straight out of here and have me put away or sue my pants off with this information. I swear—if you do, I won't even hire a defense attorney. I tell you this so you can make peace with yourself: You were not to blame for your decline! I was!"

Lisa sent a shaking hand to her water and took a sip, her tears flowing like waterfalls. She suddenly got up. "I . . . I . . .," she tried to mumble.

"You need to sit down, my love . . ." I whispered. "There is more." She helplessly did as I asked. "I fell for Roy completely by accident. Somebody told me he was interested in you and I was terrified he might steal you away from me. I went after him to steer him off course but fell in love with him instead. We became lovers when you refused to let him into your heart. Roy was honest enough to remind me of his love for you. Eventually, he dumped me for you and I just couldn't take it. From that moment on, I did my best to separate you from Roy. I used one of your crises to reconnect you with drugs. I thought it would give me leverage and help me win Roy, but all it did was to separate the three of us eventually." There was, again, a very long silence, during which we both tried to calm ourselves down. "I wish I could go back in time and undo what I did but I can't." I continued. "All is left for me to do is to apologize and beg for your forgiveness. I know it's hard for you to even consider it right now; but know that there is nothing I want more than your forgiveness. We are now connected in ways nobody planned or thought possible." Lisa got to her feet, looking exhausted, shaken, confused. She looked at me not with anger but with torment in her beautiful, tearful eyes. Then she grabbed her bag and fled.

Later that evening Roy called to inquire about Lisa. It was about 9:45 pm and she hadn't returned home.

"It isn't like her," he established. "What happened between you two today?" he asked, logically assuming Lisa's absence had something to do with our meeting.

"I came clean. It was difficult for her. I'm sorry. Can I help in any way?"

"No." He replied abruptly. "Have a safe trip home. We'll talk in a couple of days."

A set of knocks at the door felt like an earthquake . . . *what the hell* . . . It was 4:15 am . . . another set of knocks, this time a much louder one. My veins pounded against my brain like a very heavy hammer as I struggled to get my eyelids open. The last thing I wanted was to get out of bed but I got up nonetheless, groggy, bumping into everything standing in my way.

"Who is it?" I asked when I finally got to the door.

"Jennifer . . . it's me . . . we need to talk."

I opened the door. Lisa stood there with a harsh guise, wearing the same clothes she wore when she met me that afternoon, looking a mess.

"Were you at home today? Did you talk to Roy?" I asked as she got in and sat at the table. "He is worried sick."

She gazed ahead with an angry expression on her tired face, breathing heavily.

"Sit down!" she commanded without looking at me. I sat in front of her, terrified. "What am I supposed to do with the information you gave me?" she whispered. "Why couldn't you just keep it to yourself?"

"I thought you had a right to know." I replied. She raised her gaze and looked at me with what I thought was sheer and refined hatred. Her eyes got moist and her facial expression projected distress.

"I have a right to be happy, do you hear me?" she said with anger.

I nodded. "Yes. . . ." I started.

"Shut up!" she screamed at me. "Don't you dare say one fucking word until I finish!" I lowered my head, ready to take whatever she chose to send my way. "Who gave you the right to play God with my life?" She got to her feet. I stayed seated, still directing my gaze down. "All I ever wanted was to live life with the man I loved. That was all, Jennifer. That was all I ever wanted." She sat down again. "What am I to do now? I can't think straight. I'm scared to death from the implication this will have on Roy. I was the happiest person on the face of the earth. Facing the news about Thor was hard enough . . . Ralph Dillon . . . my god . . . what have you done Jennifer? What have you done?"

"I can't defend my actions," I said, fighting my emotions. "I was evil and mean."

"Look at me!" she commanded. I did. "What do you want now? What more do you want from me? My husband? My happiness? My fate?"

I shook my head and looked down again. "I wish you and your family only the best."

"Then what do you want?" she asked with a cracked voice, her eyes moist, her spirit broken. "For God's sake, Jennifer, tell me . . . what the hell do you want from me?"

"Forgiveness," I whispered.

"Forgiveness? Do you really think I am capable of that now? I'm contemplating storming at your life full force to make sure you rot in prison; and you talk about forgiveness." I said nothing, still staring at the floor. There was silence for a while which I dared not break. I raised my gaze and looked at her with a sad smile, trying to convey with it my deepest apology. She just looked at me with anger. "Say something."

"I don't know what to say," I whispered.

"You realize what you did to me, don't you?" She asked rhetorically. "You put me in an impossible situation. You are the mother of Roy's son for crying out loud. Living with this fact alone is impossible to bear and you had to pull all those details from the past to make me hate you more."

"Please don't hate me," I whispered with tears in my eyes. "Please . . ."

"Give me a reason not to hate you. Help me out here. Give me a reason to forgive you." She begged me. Her eyes were getting moist again. "I really need some assistance here."

"Do it for Tom," I said; and as I said that Lisa slapped my face as hard as she could. I was shocked.

"Don't bring my son into this," she yelled at me. I started crying uncontrollably, shattered at the magnitude of the hatred projected at me from a person I loved with all my heart. Lisa came close and embraced me, crying her heart out with me. "I'm sorry Jenny . . . I'm so sorry . . ." We were in each other's arms for some time until both of us got a grip over ourselves. We parted our embrace and I looked up to see her face. She was still sobbing quietly as she took my face in her hands and gently caressed them.

"Thor and Tom," I whispered, "do it for them. They are innocent souls and they are brothers. They have the same blood running through their veins. Forgive me for the sake of our sons."

"I'm not the person you think I am," she said as she got to her feet, wiping her tears with her fingers, taking a large quantity of air into her lungs. "I am no better than you. I don't think I could ever find the greatness you attribute to me, the one you think makes me capable of ever forgiving you." She said as she walked to the door. She opened it and looked at me with devastation written all over her face. Then she left.

Chapter 33

Biological Stamp

Angus Svensen could not wait to meet the true father of his beloved grandson. When I first broke the news to him about Roy being Thor's father, he became emotional and declared "Thor Angus Svensen is the son of a university professor . . . an intellectual!" His voice cracked when he said that and his lips trembled. "My grandson is the son of a man of values . . . not of a Bryan Taylor!" When Roy's plane landed in JFK, I was waiting for him at the arrival terminal with Angus by my side, thrilled for the chance to embrace him warmly. The teenage boy I loved adored my father for giving him a chance to realize his dream—even if it had been to merely buy a decent car.

"Who ever thought . . ." my father said, making our way to Roy's hotel in his black Bentley, "thirty years later I'm the one driving you . . ." We laughed.

I met Roy for dinner that night. I promised myself to come clean with him too—no matter the consequences.

"How is Lisa doing?" I asked after the host sat us down in front of a table.

"Still digesting . . .," he said.

I nodded. "I thought she was entitled to know the truth . . ." I said in an apologetic tone of voice. He didn't respond. He just looked at me sadly for a short moment and then looked away. "There is no escape from the truth . . . now I want to come clean with you too."

"What about?"

"Our mutual past . . .," I replied.

"I'm not sure I want to know . . .," he said.

"I think you need to, honey . . . I'm no longer some ex. I'm your son's mother and we have to do this; otherwise I'll go crazy."

He nodded. "Go for it."

"There are still two important pieces in the overall puzzle that I kept from Lisa because I thought you needed to hear it from me first." His facial expression remained overtly calm, although I could sense his anticipation.

"Go on . . ." he said.

"My father's hiring you that summer was a carefully planned scheme and both my parents knew they had to go along with it or hell would break loose." Roy moved in his seat with what I thought was sheer annoyance. "And I had an Israeli private investigator send me information about you for many years . . ."

He looked away astounded, shaking his head in disbelief, "Unbelievable . . ."

"I'll understand if you despise me for the rest of your life," I said, looking away, fighting my emotions.

It seemed forever for Roy to respond. He looked away, directing his gaze at the people around us, at the ceiling and at the outside traffic—at anything but me. He was contemplating, trying to digest and absorb the information I had just given him, probably adding it to whatever information Lisa had told him.

"I don't hate or despise you," he said to me finally.

"You don't?" I asked.

"No, Jenny . . . far from that . . ." he said. "If we're in the business of coming clean," he continued, "then I want you to know that I'm ashamed of some of my actions from the time we were together. I had to live all my life hating myself for using you so shamefully."

"Using me?" I asked surprised.

"Yeah . . . I was sixteen when you offered me an open door to your bed. I was no different than any other teenager boy."

"I was a slut, wasn't I?" I said smiling in embarrassment.

"No. you weren't! You were less reserved than most of the other girls I knew back then. This I admit," he said smiling, "but you were not a slut."

"Yeah . . . thanks for putting it so mildly."

"Jennifer," he said, his facial expression turning serious. "I had strong feelings for you . . . but I didn't love you . . . I used you for sex and for my bruised ego." He looked at me without saying anything and then sighed. "If there is one scene that's haunted me for years it's the one where you blamed me for wanting you only for sex." He looked away smiling a sad smile. "You took your clothes off and yelled at me! My god . . . Jenny . . . you were so special. That was one of the most intense moments of my entire life; and let me tell you, I've had more than enough of those . . ." I looked at him with sympathy. "I didn't plan for you to fall in love with me but once you did—there was no going back. I hated myself for years for inflicting pain on your delicate soul."

"Delicate soul? I? You must be kidding," I said.

"Yeah . . . nice try. You never fooled me with this 'fuck the world' image you tried so hard to sell us all . . . strong . . . reckless . . . tough . . . Inside, you were always tender and fragile . . ." The moist was building again in my eyes but I fought the urge to cry. The guy read me like an open book. "You are not a bad person . . . you never were!"

"I'm responsible for the price we all paid throughout the years. My past is filled with shameful events . . ." I lost the battle to my tears.

He placed his hand on mine and looked into my eyes. "Jenny . . . the past is a source of embarrassment, guilt and regrets for most people. The important thing is to learn and give ourselves a break . . . and to forgive . . ."

The biological stamp came forty-eight hours after Roy took the test. It was a clear-cut 100 percent confirmation. Roy Cohen was Thor's father and nothing in the world . . . nothing . . . could ever change that—ever!

Thor took the news maturely. He wanted to meet his father.

Emotionally speaking, it was a unique moment in time for us Svensens. Thor was our hope for a normal future after such an abnormal past; and Roy had come just in time to make it all possible.

To Roy's request, the meeting took place at our estate in Newark, where Thor felt most protected. He asked that my parents and I be there to support Thor. Like the university professor he was, Roy consulted some of his colleagues from the psychology department, and came to New York armed with professional advice. He came to meet his son dressed in jeans and a cool white and orange AC Roma T-shirt. My father quickly rushed to his room, losing the suit in favor of a pair of jeans and his old New York Knicks T-shirt. It broke the ice instantly. Still, nothing prepared us for what happened next. When my teenage son saw his real father, theory became reality in the most moving way. His reaction was so unpredictable and so uncharacteristic that the collective tears shed almost washed us to the ocean.

Thor entered the room, stared at Roy and burst into tears. He strode towards his father and embraced him as though he would never let go. Roy responded with tearful eyes, embracing Thor and caressing his hair. I sat down, trembling, emotional, and unable stay on my feet.

Then we all went out for a walk. We drove to Manhattan and strolled in Central Park.

"I never had a real father," Thor informed Roy. His father acknowledged with a nod. I slowed down and tailed them. "The one I thought I had dumped us when I was two years old. Are you going to be a real father to me?" Roy stopped cold. Everybody did the same. My mythological lover looked at me and saw the mighty battle I had with my emotions. He placed his hand on my shoulder and smiled a compassionate smile. Then, he looked at Thor with the same compassion.

"Well . . . Thor . . ." he said, staring courageously into his son's blue eyes. "I'm certainly going to try."

"Ever since mom told me there's a good chance you're my father, I started reading about the Jewish people. Am I a Jew?" he asked when we resumed our stroll together, making me realize that I had not given that question any thought at all.

Roy smiled, shaking his head. "No. Thor. You're not. You need to be born to a Jewish mother."

"So I'm a Catholic who has a Jewish father." Thor established.

Roy smiles again. "Yeah . . . I guess you are."

Thor and I spent the next day with Roy. We took a tour to the Statue of Liberty and then ate lunch together in a little Italian restaurant in little Italy. Roy was relaxed and made us laugh. He told us some fascinating stories about Israel and Israelis. It was apparent that he wanted his son to understand his background.

"I only hear about Israel when there's shooting . . ." Thor stated.

"Yeah . . . I know," Roy said and nodded his head. "Unfortunately, that's how you sell news. The darker the pictures the more people are interested."

"So why are you silent about it?"

Roy laughed. "We aren't. Actually, we are very vocal. But nobody wants to listen."

I knew my son well enough to realize that he found his father fascinating. Being a curious kid, Thor stormed Roy with questions about the world and about Israel. Roy never failed to deliver intelligent and factual explanations. It was as if Thor was testing his father. But what he found most exciting was Roy's rock band years and his love for music. He told Roy that it was his dream too, to sometime play in a rock band—something I shamefully had to admit I never knew.

"Why didn't you tell me about it?" I asked him surprised.

"It wasn't important. I have no talent whatsoever. It's just a stupid dream." He replied.

"There is no such thing as a stupid dream!" Roy exclaimed. I saw my son nod his head, accepting the first fatherly advice he ever got from his real father, inspired by the show of confidence. "As to your musical talent . . . well . . . you're my son, aren't you?"

On our way back home, we bumped into a guitar store. Roy insisted we enter. He chose a beautiful black electric guitar out of the dozens that hung on the wall, connected it to an amplifier and started playing for us. He could still sing . . . and Thor . . . well . . . it was a sight to see: those beautiful blue eyes were focused on everything his father did with adoration and excitement.

"I dedicate the next song to you Jenny," Roy stated with a wide smile and then played for us Johnny Tutone's song about

Jenny 867-5309. I sang the chorus with him and then laughed so hard I almost peed in my pants.

"I wish I could play like you," Thor said to his father.

Roy gazed at him with affection. "Do you want to learn how to play the guitar?" he asked. Thor gave him a nod. Roy looked at me with happy eyes. "Did your grandpa ever tell you about the guitar he bought for me?" He asked. Thor shook his head. "It's actually the same model as this one. I have three of them at home and the one Angus gave me back in 1983 is still my favorite."

"Awesome," Thor responded with excitement.

"Here . . . take it. . . . hold it . . . feel it," Roy said as he handed his son the guitar. Thor held it in his hands. "It's one of humanities greatest achievements, where musical instruments are concerned. It's a Fender Stratocaster American Standard," Roy explained. Thor started running his fingers on the strings. "Like it?"

"Yeah. It feels awesome." Thor replied with glowing eyes.

"Playing music helped me through some very difficult periods in my life. It's a gift far greater than everything the almighty ever granted me," he said looking at me again, smiling a sad smile. He then returned his gaze to his excited son. "Thor, this guitar is my present to you . . . the one I didn't have a chance to give you for your Bar-Mitzvah." Thor looked at me, seeking confirmation. I nodded, speechlessly. "Now go . . . take the guitar and wait for us near the cashier!" Roy commended. "I'll bring the amp with me." Thor got up and walked toward the counter. We followed him slowly. Roy stopped and looked at me with compassion. I smiled back nervously. "You did good Jenny. . . ." he whispered and placed his hand on my shoulder. "You did great . . ."

Roy was supposed to leave for Israel the next day and I wanted to have one last, private conversation with him before he did.

"I know my record with you and Lisa sucks," I said as we sat down that evening around the table; "but I swear that I did not fly to Israel back in 98 to trick you into anything. I beg you to believe me. Thor is not the result of some cheap scheme . . ." Roy took a gulp from his beer, heaving a sigh. "I'm happy for you and Lisa." I continued, "I really am."

"Thanks," he said and looked into my eyes as if to verify my sincerity.

"Life taught me to believe in fate. It's your fate to be together." Roy smiled a sad smile. "I never stopped loving both of you." I continued, "I love you today no less. Fate made me pay the ultimate price."

"No. Jenny," he disagreed, shaking his head. "Fate had nothing to do with it. We are responsible for our own actions, and in that respect, we hold our own fate. I never blamed you for anything that happened and neither did Lisa. We made our fair share of mistakes and we are solely responsible for them—not you."

"Do you consider Thor a mistake?" I asked, terrified of the answer.

He smiled with empathy. "If he is, Jennifer Svensen, then he is the most wonderful mistake I have ever made."

Epilogue

Fate's Grand Design

It was a hectic August 2012.

We were getting ready for my winter collection show, this time in the good old Grand Ballroom at New York's Waldorf Astoria, the same place where I had held my first fashion show.

I was briefing the models when my assistant approached me with some mail that had arrived at the office. As the briefing ended, I went up to my room, filled myself a hot bath, took my clothes off and got in. Closing my eyes, I dozed off until the water's changing temperature woke me up. I turned on the hot water and took a hefty sip of my wine. I looked around and saw the mail. I stretched out my arm and picked it up from the floor. An envelope from Israel immediately had my heart racing. I recognized the handwriting.

I tore it open. It contained an old colored photo from 1984, displaying a young Lisa and a young me in our bikinis, smiling happily to the camera. Emotionally, I shook the envelope to see if there was a note inside but there was none.

I flipped the photo over and saw the writing on the back:

I forgive.
Lisa

The End

CPSIA information can be obtained at www.ICGtesting.com
Printed in the USA
LVOW12s1807080913

351404LV00002B/68/P